"If you ever wondered what it is like to teach high school, read this book. It's all here—kids, parents, administrators, colleagues and more. In Jenna Bianchi, readers are treated to a true teacher with all her heart, dedication, aspirations, disappointments, frustrations, and pains. She captivated me from page one. Minniti has created not only a great read with engaging characters but a self-help book for any parent with an ADHD child. Like her main character, Minniti has the heart of a teacher and the wit of a Jersey girl."

—**Carol Ringold, Psy.D.**, licensed psychologist

"Project June Bug is a great story about the differences in our behavior patterns. It also provides wonderful insight into Attention Deficit Hyperactivity Disorder. A must-read for parents and students."

—**Cody Fowler Davis**, author of *Green 61*

"With focus and characters as mainstream as Main Street, this fine novel is far more a great read than message tale."

—**Tom Corcoran**, author of *Air Dance Iguana*, *Jimmy Buffett-The Key West Years*, and *Key West in Black and White*

"This story is not only well-written, it is engaging and heartfelt. Minniti's professional background as a teacher provides the experiential background that is so well-suited to her story."

—**Connie Langhorst**, author of *Finding Happy*

"Project June Bug goes to the head of the class. Smart, funny, poignant, and relevant, it captures the best and the worst of a system where no child should be left behind."

—**George Anastasia**, reporter for the *Philadelphia Inquirer* and author of *The Last Gangster*

Project June Bug

Project June Bug

A Novel

Jackie Minniti

iUniverse, Inc.

New York Lincoln Shanghai

Project June Bug

iUniverse books may be ordered through booksellers or by contacting:

iUniverse
2021 Pine Lake Road, Suite 100
Lincoln, NE 68512
www.iuniverse.com
1-800-Authors (1-800-288-4677)

Because of the dynamic nature of the Internet, any Web addresses or links contained in this book may have changed since publication and may no longer be valid.

This is a work of fiction. All of the characters, names, incidents, organizations, and dialogue in this novel are either the products of the author's imagination or are used fictitiously.

ISBN: 978-0-595-45528-7 (pbk)
ISBN: 978-0-595-70105-6 (cloth)
ISBN: 978-0-595-89838-1 (ebk)

Printed in the United States of America

To John—
Still the one

"The dream begins with a teacher who believes in you, who tugs and pushes and leads you to the next plateau, sometimes poking you with a sharp stick called truth."

—Dan Rather

Acknowledgements

My heartfelt thanks—

To John Minniti, a wonderful husband and chef, for sharing his knowledge of all things culinary;

To Anna Doganiero, Joanne Doganiero, Shannon Minniti, Jeanne Hornbaker, and Faith Steinfort for slogging through the early drafts;

To the Anarchist Writers Group@Eckerd College for the invaluable critiques and unflagging support;

To Marian Morton, for her pharmaceutical expertise.

And to all the June Bugs who have passed through my life—thanks for inspiring this book.

Chapter One

Who was snickering?

The hairs on the back of my neck prickled as if a spider had skittered over them. I frowned and glanced over my shoulder. The front row of students was red-faced with suppressed giggles. This was getting seriously weird. I turned to face the class, and the room erupted with laughter. Perspiration dampened my forehead. My cheeks burned.

Putting my hands on my hips in what I hoped was an intimidating pose, I summoned up my sternest teacher-voice. "Would anyone like to tell me what's so funny?"

The well-mannered girl sitting by the door bit back a smile and pointed at me. That's when I caught my reflection in the classroom window. I was standing in front of a roomful of tenth graders, as naked as the loser in a strip poker marathon. I bolted for the door. My legs weren't working, and I lost my balance.

As the laughter rose to an unbearable shriek, my eyes snapped open. I was clutching my pillow, my legs entangled in bed sheets. I groaned and rolled over, waiting for my heart to stop thudding. The shrieking started again, and I pulled the pillow over my head. Not that it would do any good.

"Brutus, be quiet," I shouted, squinting at the glow of the digital clock on the bedside table. The green blur clarified into 6:51.

No—that can't be right. I grabbed the clock and shook it, willing it to correct its mistake. When it refused, I flipped it over and saw that I hadn't set the alarm.

"Dammit!" I slammed the clock down and ran for the living room to preempt another outburst from my hungry parrot. As I rounded the corner, I stubbed my toe on the sofa.

Pain knifed up to my knee. Spouting obscenities no macaw should ever hear, I hopped toward the big picture window where the birdcage stood, hoping none of my neighbors was out for an early morning walk. When I threw the cage cover onto the floor, Brutus cocked his blue-green head and fixed a beady eye on me.

"Dammit," he said. *Note to self: Watch your language around the bird.*

"No time for small talk this morning. I'm late. Good thing you woke me." I limped over to the refrigerator and pulled out some grapes. Brutus's impatient screech made my dental fillings vibrate.

"Give me a break, buddy," I said. "I'm moving as fast as I can."

He ruffled his feathers and gave a shake. When I poked a grape through the bars of his cage, he grasped it with his enormous black beak, transferred it to his claw, and took a bite.

"Mmmmmmmmm," he crooned.

"Enjoy." I tossed two more grapes into his food dish, stuffed the rest into my mouth, and rushed off to shower and dress for work. It was the first day of school, and I'd planned to get there early. Time for Plan B.

I was struggling with the zipper on the back of my dress when Brutus started screeching again. I rushed out of the bedroom, my hair still damp, and darted over to his cage to unlatch the big double locks that kept him from escaping. Macaws can reduce wooden furniture to toothpicks. I'd learned that the hard way.

I inherited Brutus from my Nana Bianchi, along with her house—a package deal. Nana had acquired Brutus shortly after my grandfather died. Grandpop Bianchi was a real talker, and the silence was driving my grandmother crazy. She figured a parrot would be a good substitute. As it turned out, Brutus was a small, feathered version of Grandpop—lovable, boisterous, messy, and an incurably early riser. And, like Grandpop, he fell in love with Nana the moment he laid his little round eyes on her. For some strange reason, Brutus developed an affinity for me. Maybe it was because of my resemblance to Nana. She always said that I looked like a younger version of her. Anyway, I was one of the few people Brutus didn't try to bite. Whenever I came to visit, he would whistle and squawk until I took him out of the cage and let him ride on my shoulder. He loved to play with my hair, pulling the dark curls out straight and letting them spring back. He also learned to mimic the sound of my voice. Nana used to joke that it was like having me with her all the time.

When Nana died of a stroke shortly after my college graduation, I learned that she had left me her house—with the provision that I adopt Brutus and care for him there until he joined her in that great parrot jungle in the sky. Which, given the life span of macaws, could be another fifty years. I moved in soon afterward and became Brutus's housemate.

My first night alone in the house was strange on so many levels. I tiptoed through the rooms, feeling like a visitor in my grandparents' home. It was weirdly empty without them. Memories materialized from the walls, so strong they were almost palpable. Grandpop bursting through the front door, the decibel level sky-rocketing off the chart with his arrival. Nana in the cozy little kitchen, holding a tray of chocolate biscotti or pignoli cookies she'd made just for me. My younger brother, Anthony, playing fort with sofa cushions in the living room. Me, age five, snuggling on my grandmother's lap while she read aloud from Dr. Seuss. The whole family gathered around the table on Sunday afternoons, stuffing ourselves with Nana's homemade pasta. Christmases, Thanksgivings, Easters, birthdays—too many to count.

Sleep didn't come easily, even though my familiar sleigh bed had been moved into the room where my grandparents slept for over fifty years. After a fitful night, I was startled awake by a loud whistle. I staggered into the living room to discover that Brutus had broken out of his cage. He was perched on the back of Nana's Boston rocker and had chewed through four of the maple spindles. Later that morning, I visited Home Depot and returned with two large combination locks.

As I fumbled with the locks, trying to keep my half-zipped dress from slipping off my shoulders, something moved in the bushes under the window. Picturing burglars in black ski masks, I glanced at the front door to confirm that the deadbolt was in place and reached for the baseball bat I kept for protection. I inched closer to the window, holding my breath. With the suddenness of a ninja, Yin-Yang, my neighbor's Siamese and Brutus's arch-nemesis, exploded from the azaleas and landed on the window ledge. Brutus and I let out identical, surprised screams, and I dropped the baseball bat on my sore toe. Ignoring my string of invectives, the cat sat down on her haunches and began washing her face with one paw.

"Scat, you little pest!" I pounded on the glass. Yin-Yang looked at me and blinked. Then she went back to her face-washing, flicking her tail in the cat equivalent of flipping me the bird.

As much as it bothered me to lose a cat fight to an actual cat, I had to finish getting dressed or I'd be late for sure. After nearly dislocating a shoulder trying to reach my zipper, I peeled off my dress and searched the closet for something zipper-free. Back zippers are one of the major disadvantages of living alone.

I pulled out a cotton wrap-around with splashy yellow flowers. It needed ironing, but since I was already way behind schedule, that wasn't happening.

"Too bad you can't learn to work a zipper," I told Brutus, as I rushed past his cage.

He gave me a pitiful look and held up one claw. "Step up," he pleaded.

"Oh, sure. Pour on the guilt. Why should you care if I make it to school on time?" I opened the cage, and Brutus stepped onto my arm, digging in as I dashed to the kitchen. I set him on his perch, poured myself a glass of iced tea, and dropped two slices of cinnamon-raisin bread into the toaster. According to Nana's Felix the Cat clock, it was almost seven-forty. My stomach knotted. I had twenty-five minutes to eat breakfast, get myself out the door, and drive the three miles to Morrison High. Doable, but not by much.

Felix's watchful eyes shifted from side to side as his tail ticked away the seconds. That Nana would have a ticking cat within plain view of her beloved parrot was testament to her perverse sense of humor. But Brutus didn't seem to mind. He watched silently as I smeared peanut butter on the toast. I lopped the crusts off one slice and handed it to him.

"Here you go, just the way you like it. But you'll have to hurry."

"Cracker," Brutus responded. Cracker is his word for anything edible.

I set my glass and toast on the edge of the small kitchen table where class lists and seating charts were spread out in a colorless patchwork. As I wolfed down my breakfast, I wondered which of these faceless names would make me wish for June and which would make me sorry to see the year end. I said a silent prayer for more of the latter as I stuffed the papers into my "#1 Teacher" tote bag.

"CRACKER."

Brutus was licking peanut butter from his claw. All that remained of his toast was a small pile of crumbs, and he regarded me with suspicion when I held out my arm. I looked at the clock. Seven-fifty.

"Come on, Big Guy. Step up. Mommy's gotta go." Brutus was unmoved. He only decided to cooperate when I threw a walnut into his food dish. Brutus never met a walnut he could resist. I whisked him onto the swing in his cage and snapped both locks shut.

"See you later. Be a good boy, and guard the house. Now, where are my damn keys?"

Brutus watched me ransack the living room until I found the keys under a pile of magazines. I heard a sad "Bye-bye" as I locked the front door. Then I raced to my car, praying to the traffic gods for green lights and no speed traps.

Chapter Two

The parking lot was almost full when my blue Dodge Neon screeched into the empty space labeled *J. Bianchi*. The custodian was raising the flag in front of the two-story, red brick building that housed the ninth through twelfth grades of Morrison High School. The flag drooped in the muggy morning air.

"Hi, Tom," I called, as I sprinted up the concrete walk. "All set to go?"

"Hey, Jenna. Your new bookcase came in yesterday. I put it next to your desk. That okay with you?"

"Perfect. Hope the lockers don't drive you too crazy today."

Tom grinned and shook his head. The lockers at Morrison were a standing joke. They were long overdue for replacement, but the tight school budget never included enough funding for new ones. Although Tom was a locker wizard, the first day of school challenged even his legendary skills as locker doors jammed and locks refused to open.

The main office was buzzing with activity as I shouldered my way to the long, maple sign-in desk that separated the outer office from the inner sanctums of the principal and vice-principal. I scribbled my initials on the sign-in sheet. *Made it, with less than a minute to spare!*

Teachers were exchanging greetings and retrieving papers from the honeycomb of mail slots that covered the wall. Shannon Martin, the school secretary, was trying her best to answer two ringing phones and countless questions. The aquarium screensaver on her computer burbled, and lazy tropical fish glided across the screen. But from the look of things, this tranquil scene wasn't making a dent in Shannon's stress level.

The principal, Anna O'Connor, cradled a large jar of chocolate kisses as she greeted everyone from her station behind the sign-in desk. A wiry, forty-something blonde with the metabolism of a mongoose, she spoke in rapid bursts, like machine gun fire. Anna firmly believed in the healing powers of chocolate and always kept an ample supply in her office. She insisted this was the reason for her staff's low absentee rate, but we secretly believed we were too busy to get sick. Anna was the only person I'd ever met who could lose weight eating fudge and Snickers bars. Maybe it was all the caffeine.

"Hi. Good summer?" She thrust the jar at me.

"Pretty good. Just too short." I helped myself to a chocolate kiss.

Anna's alert brown eyes locked on me as I peeled away the foil and poked the chocolate into my mouth. "Better have another," she said.

"Uh-oh. What's up?"

"A new student. Transferred from Elgin Academy. Just registered yesterday. You've got him eighth period. Homeroom, too. Might want to check his records." She handed me a manila folder labeled *Michael Tayler*. It seemed unnaturally thick. I tucked it into my tote and grabbed two more chocolate kisses.

The last of the chocolate's creamy sweetness had melted away by the time I unlocked my classroom. The air was hot and stuffy, scented with chalk dust and old books. I crossed the room to open the windows, my sandals squeaking on the freshly-polished terrazzo. A fat, black fly buzzed in and lazily circled the fluorescent ceiling fixture. There was a pencil embedded point-first in the acoustic ceiling tile, a souvenir from June's year-end festivities. It had somehow been overlooked by the summer custodial crew, and it hung over my head like the sword of Damocles. I turned on the oscillating fan, hoping to circulate some fresh air before the kids came in and started throwing off waves of teenage body heat. Sweat began wicking into my cotton dress. Talk about cruel and unusual punishment. Even prisons have central air.

Standing in front of the fan, I surveyed my classroom. Over the summer, the concrete block walls had been painted a nondescript yellow. Probably some close-out color. An American flag on a wooden stick fluttered listlessly in one corner. The New Jersey state flag hung just below it. My old chalkboard had been replaced with a modern, dry-erase model. A new box of colored markers and a large felt eraser sat on the chalk tray. The bulletin board on the back wall displayed posters with punctuation rules. My new bookcase waited to hold the dictionaries and thesauruses stacked in the closet.

Five rows of desks spanned the room from front to back. I walked up and down the aisles, checking desktops for obscene graffiti. The cleaning crew had done an adequate job, but there were still ghosts of last year's scribblings. *Heather is a skanky bitch. Screw-U. Crissy and Pete 4-ever. Tony M. is HOT. Go, Phillies! Good girls SUCK. Eagles Rule! Who sits here?*

I squeaked over to my standard-issue teacher's desk, its faded blotter littered with memos and notices. In one corner, a stoneware jar labeled *Ashes of Problem Students* held a dozen freshly-sharpened pencils. Next to it was a photo of Brutus in a brass frame. A *Far Side* page-a-day desk calendar indicated that today was September fourth. The cursor on my computer blinked a reminder that I hadn't logged on. I typed *brutusbird* in the password box and hit ENTER. An attendance list appeared on the screen.

I unpacked my tote, tossing Michael Tayler's file onto the growing paper mound. Then I opened a fresh box of Bic gel pens and put them in my "Teachers

Touch the Future" mug. I was searching for my locker list when I heard a knock on the door and turned to see an arm waving an apple.

"Could this be a math teacher bearing gifts?" I asked.

"I thought this would help you say no to O'Connor's chocolates. Am I too late?"

The arm belonged to Christopher Holloway. Chris taught geometry and algebra on the other side of the building. He grinned when he saw me up to my elbows in paper.

"Looks like I'm just in time. Don't tell me you've lost something already." He pushed some papers aside and set the apple on my desk. "The day hasn't even officially started. This is a new record for you."

Chris had been teaching at Morrison for four years when I was hired. We were drawn to each other from the start. Maybe it was because we're so different. He's a tall, handsome blond with a perfect body mass index and blue eyes that make you want to dive in and swim around. I'm a full six inches shorter, with dark curly hair, hazel eyes, and a tendency to blimp up if I let myself go. Which I do more often than I care to admit. Chris is analytical and controlled. I, on the other hand, have never been accused of being organized, and my emotions bubble close to the surface. Cooking is Chris's passion. Eating is mine. If opposites attract, we should be joined at the stomach. We started out as friends, but the chemistry became impossible to ignore. Even though we're dating, we try to be discreet. Workplace romances can be tricky, especially in a small-town high school.

I smacked the desk. "Where the hell's my locker list? I have to assign lockers as soon as the kids come in." I continued shuffling papers. "It's got to be in here somewhere."

"Just calm down and gather these loose papers together." Chris grabbed a stack of papers and tapped them into a tidy pile. "Now we'll go through them one at a time." Sure enough, a few seconds later he held up the list.

"Don't look so smug." I grabbed for the paper, but he waved it beyond my reach and snaked his free arm around my waist. Teasing me is one of his great joys in life. "Come on," I said. "Give it back."

"What's the magic word?" Even his smirk was cute.

"Several words come to mind, but they're all the four-letter variety."

He pulled me against him, and I could smell the clean scent of his Polo Blue aftershave. "I love it when you talk dirty," he whispered into my ear.

A sizzle shot from my earlobe to the base of my spine. I pushed him away before my hormones took over.

"I don't have time for this," I said, trying to sound annoyed.

"Later, then." He winked. "Enjoy the apple. It's good for you—a natural stress reducer."

"I don't need an apple. I need a private secretary."

"Sounds intriguing. I might be interested, depending on the fringe benefits." When he handed me the locker list, he ran his index finger across my palm, causing a pleasurable tickle. "Gotta go now."

I placed the list on the neat stack of papers.

"Wait," I called to him. "Where's the apple?" But he'd already turned down the corridor toward the math department.

Fifteen minutes later, a bell signaled the beginning of a new school year at Morrison High. While names and faces changed each September, there were certain constants. The freshmen always looked uneasy. The sophomores and juniors were more relaxed, getting reacquainted with old friends and speculating about teachers. The seniors exhibited the practiced self-assurance that came from being at the top of the food chain.

Before long, most of the empty desks were filled, and the late bell herded stragglers in from the hall. It was show time.

"Welcome back, everyone. I hope you had a nice summer. My name is Ms. Bianchi. I teach sophomore English, and I'm the advisor for the school newspaper." I turned to write my name on the board, ignoring a flashback of the dream that began my day. "This is Homeroom 204. Please check your schedules to make sure you're in the right place." When no one made a move to leave, I took attendance. The only absentee was Michael Tayler.

"Now I'll give locker assignments. Your lockers are in the hall to the right of our classroom. If your combination doesn't work, see me immediately so that I can call the custodian. After you've opened your—"

"Is this Room 204? Are you Mrs. Blinky? God, what a dump."

I wheeled around to see a sneering face framed by a shaggy mop of red hair. The face belonged to a tall, lanky boy wearing a black Bart Simpson t-shirt that hung to the knees of his baggy jeans. One of his ratty sneakers was untied, its laces jittering as he tapped his foot. I took a second to regain my composure.

"Excuse me, but would you mind telling me who you are?" I nailed him with my best glass-cracking stare, but he didn't flinch.

"I'm Mike Tayler. They told me I was in Homeroom 204 with Mrs. Bunchy or Banshee or something like that."

Why, you little wiseass! I could feel my face beginning to flush. "I'm Ms. Bianchi, and I suggest you take a seat. There's an empty desk at the end of the row by the window. You're late, but since this is your first day with us I'll admit you without a pass. Next time, you'll need to go to the office and—"

"Hey, lady, get off my case. It's not my fault nobody gave me directions."

I gritted my teeth. "That's enough, Mr. Tayler. Please sit down."

He stood there for a moment, his arrogant green eyes boring into me. When I didn't blink, he stomped over to the window, dropping two pencils from his unzipped backpack and knocking a few books onto the floor as he pushed his way to the back of the room. Every eye was on him as, with a loud huff, he dropped into his seat. The uncomfortable silence was broken by a girl's sneeze.

It took every ounce of self-control to keep my voice steady. I started working alphabetically down the locker list, stopping every so often to page Tom for some locker magic. I was almost halfway through when I noticed Michael's empty desk. A quick survey of the room confirmed that he was gone. My first reaction was relief. This was followed by a burst of panic as I pictured myself trying to explain to Anna why my class was one student short.

"Has anyone seen Michael Tayler?" I tried to sound casual.

A dark-eyed boy named Damien raised his hand. "Yeah," he said, a smile twitching at the corners of his mouth. "He went out into the hall."

Before I could go after him, Michael strolled back in, looking as if he'd just dropped by for tea and crumpets. I stared at him, resisting the urge to grab him by his straggly red hair.

"Where have you been?" I asked.

"I had to go to the john. Why? Got a problem with that?"

Not as big as the problem you're gonna have, Carrot Top. A few stifled giggles skipped across the room. My hand tightened around the locker list.

"The problem is that there are rules you need to follow. In the future, please ask permission to use the bathroom, and remember to sign out."

"Yeah, whatever. How about I give you a urine sample, too?" He sat down, took a chewed-up pencil stub out of his pocket, and began tapping on his desk.

Keep this up, and you'll be peeing through your elbow. I ignored him and continued assigning lockers. A high school teacher learns early on to choose battles wisely, but this cease-fire was a short one. After a few minutes, a familiar voice rose from the back of the room.

"This blows. How long's it gonna take? I need to unload my stuff."

I dug my nails into my palms. "Sorry, Michael, but you'll have to wait your turn." *God help me—I sound like a kindergarten teacher.*

"Can't you give me my locker now?" His wheedling tone set my teeth on edge as he began inching up the aisle. "Come on. It'll only take a second."

"You'll get your locker when I get to your name." It wasn't my fault his last name began with T. "Now please go back to your seat—unless you'd rather wait in Mrs. O'Connor's office."

After glaring at me with undisguised hostility, he returned to his desk. He muttered something unintelligible, but I let it pass.

I somehow got all the lockers assigned before the bell put a merciful end to homeroom. I was finished with Michael Tayler, at least until the end of the day.

At lunchtime, I headed straight for the guidance office. The secretary looked surprised as I blew through the door.

"Where's Nancy?" I asked. "I need to see her. Now."

"Jen, is that you? Come on in." Nancy Miller, the school's only guidance counselor, peeked around the corner. When I first met Nancy, I was struck by her resemblance to a middle-aged Mrs. Claus. Her strawberry blond hair framed a round, rosy face, and twinkly blue eyes peered through her rimless glasses. Despite the difference in our ages, Nancy and I became close friends. She was probably the world's most sympathetic listener, but I was one of the few people who knew about her wicked sense of humor. When I was hired at Morrison, Nancy became my mentor and taught me all the stuff I didn't learn in college. Above all, she helped me understand that if I couldn't laugh at myself, I'd never make it to June.

At the moment, though, I didn't feel a bit like laughing.

One look at my face told Nancy the whole story. "Judging from your expression, I'll bet you've had the singular pleasure of meeting Michael Tayler."

"What was your first clue? The steam shooting from my ears?"

"That, and the fact that you're the fourth teacher who's come in here looking this way. The thing you all have in common is young Mr. Tayler."

"That's because he's a nightmare. What's his problem?"

"Good question. Have you read his file?"

I pictured the unopened manila folder buried under the mess on my desk. "Who had time to read? I was too busy dealing with a skinny, redheaded monster who needs a major attitude adjustment."

Nancy chuckled. "Michael Tayler versus Jenna Bianchi. We could sell tickets to that match." Then her eyes narrowed. "Seriously, Jen, take a look. There's something hinky about this kid. Come see me after you've gone through his file, and we'll talk." She looked at her watch. "Now get to lunch. You'll feel better after you've eaten a little something. At least that's what my mother used to say, and I always listened to Mama." She patted her ample hips, and I gave up trying to hold back my smile. It was impossible to stay angry after talking to Nancy—an invaluable trait in a guidance counselor.

"Okay, Nance. Sorry I unloaded on you."

"That's why I'm here. How about a few animal crackers for the road? I just opened a new box."

"No, thanks. Between your animal crackers and Anna's chocolate kisses, this place is the ninth circle of Dieter's Hell. Anyway, I have an apple somewhere on my desk."

"Good luck trying to find it." My friend knew me well.

I decided to skip lunch and get things in order for the afternoon. Two more periods before this long day would finally end. I took a box of paper clips from my desk drawer and began sorting Mount Paper into separate piles. At the bottom was Michael Tayler's folder. Next to it was my apple.

Chapter Three

I took a bite of the apple, opened the folder, and removed the top sheet. It was Michael's last report card from Elgin Academy. His final grades were mostly Ds, an F in American History, and a C minus in English. The teacher comments were depressingly similar. "Fails to complete assignments." "Disorganized." "Disruptive behavior." "Inattentive." "Lacks motivation." "Easily distracted." "Quality of work inconsistent." But one comment surprised me. Michael's English teacher had written "Achievement below ability." *Hmmmm.*

Maybe his elementary records would be more helpful. Elgin Academy was a kindergarten through twelfth grade private school with a reputation for being highly selective. The tuition was obscene, and the waiting list was long. Why had he transferred out?

The records showed that Michael had only spent his freshman year at Elgin. Prior to that, he had attended a string of schools, mostly private and pricey. His report cards were almost identical: low grades, negative teacher comments, disciplinary problems. As I examined the records, a pattern emerged. Michael would attend one school for a year or two. Then he would transfer to another. Yet his home address never changed. He lived in an area of town known as The Hill, an exclusive section on the north side.

I bit off another piece of apple and riffled through the folder until I found the standardized test scores. What I saw made me stop in mid-chew. The scores were consistently well above average, in the eighty-five to ninety percentile range, and Michael's IQ registered a whopping 138. With numbers like these, he should be getting As and Bs without breaking a sweat. There had to be some mistake.

Before I could go any further, the bell ended my lunch period. I tossed the rest of the apple into the trash can and jammed Michael's records back into his folder.

My seventh period class was the advanced placement group—the class from heaven. All the kids were in their seats before the late bell, notebooks open and pens ready, waiting for me to begin dispensing wisdom. You could almost see the halos shimmering over their studious little heads. As they eagerly asked questions and volunteered answers, my nerves began to unjangle. I was startled when the bell rang. Where had the time gone?

A few kids lingered behind to talk to me, so I wasn't watching when the eighth period class came in. As I searched my desk for the class list, I heard a strange, hollow sound coming from the back of the room. My teacher radar locked on the noise—Michael Tayler, drumming on the edge of his desk with his index fingers.

Good grief, he's acting up already. And we've still got forty minutes to go. I decided to get the class started right away. Maybe the drumming would stop when Michael's hands were busy doing something else.

"We're going to begin the year with an activity that will help me get to know all of you. It will also give you a chance to show off your creativity." A loud groan rose from Michael Tayler's vicinity, but I didn't give any indication that I'd heard. "You'll need a sheet of notebook paper, colored pencils, and a pen." A hand shot up. I ignored it. The hand began an exaggerated waving.

"Do you have a question, Michael?" My voice was icy.

"I can't find my pen. Guess I won't be able to write. My bad."

Someone in the back of the room tried to disguise a snort of laughter with a cough. Jessica Corcoran, the cute little brunette sitting next to Michael, rolled her eyes and handed him a Bic. He took it from her, looking surprised.

I tried to re-board my train of thought. "I'd like each of you to compose a syllable cinquain. It's a type of poem that uses this formula." I turned to write the directions on the board as I spoke.

> "Line 1: Two syllables—Name something that's important to you.
> Line 2: Four syllables—Use adjectives describing Line 1.
> Line 3: Six syllables—Use '-ing' verbs relating to Line 1.
> Line 4: Eight syllables—Write a sentence about Line 1.
> Line 5: Two syllables—Give a synonym for Line 1.

When you finish your cinquain, use colored pencils to create a border that expresses the poem's theme. Does anyone have a question?" I steeled myself for Michael's waving. Although there was the usual flurry of questions, not one, surprisingly, came from him. He was either mesmerized by something outside the window or fantasizing about pushing me through it.

The students settled down to work, and I circulated among them offering suggestions or answering questions. When I passed Michael, he was so engrossed in his work that he didn't even notice when I stopped to pick up one of the colored pencils he'd dropped. Not wanting to disturb him, I placed it on the corner of his desk and continued up the row.

When the bell rang, the kids crowded around my desk to hand in their papers. It wasn't until the room had cleared that I noticed a lone student still bent over his work.

"Michael, the period's over. It's time to go. You don't want to miss your bus."

His eyes widened when he realized he was the only kid in the room. He scooped up his pencils and papers and stuffed them into his backpack. He was almost out the door when I reminded him to hand in his cinquain.

"Oh, yeah—here." He pressed the paper into my hand and hurried out to his locker. I shook my head and plopped into my chair. One day down—one hundred eighty-five to go.

I was erasing the board when Chris appeared in the doorway, not a single hair out of place. "So, Teach," he said, his eyes scanning my body. "Still in one piece?"

"Don't ask. Do you have a boy named Michael Tayler in any of your classes?"

"Michael Tayler? No, the name doesn't ring a bell."

"No wonder you're so mellow."

"He's probably in one of the low level classes. Charlie Donner's teaching those."

"Poor Charlie."

Chris grinned. "Got yourself a June Bug, huh?" He'd coined the term "June Bug" to describe a student who bugs a teacher so much, the teacher prays for June.

"Yeah. Picture a male version of the kid in *The Exorcist*. Before the exorcism."

"Oh, come on. He can't be that bad. Maybe you're just cranky from hunger. I missed you in the faculty room at lunch. What happened—lose your lunch money?"

I was not amused. "For your information, I spent my lunch period at my desk reading through Michael Tayler's permanent record. It's a good thing you gave me that apple."

"Want to stop at Burger King on the way home? My treat. There's nothing like greasy fast food to neutralize those stress hormones. I'll even spring for super-size fries."

"Thanks anyway, Donald Trump, but I have to get home and grade these papers." I motioned to the pile of cinquains on my desk. "And poor Brutus has been alone all day. He must be frantic by now."

"Suit yourself, but it doesn't do much for my ego to know you'd rather have dinner with a parrot."

"I'm sure your ego will survive. You're just upset with Brutus because he hisses at you." Actually, the mere sight of Chris was enough to launch Brutus into full attack mode.

"I think he's afraid of the competition. See you tomorrow." He planted a kiss on the top of my head. "Don't work too hard."

It was another hour before I finished packing up and setting out materials for the next day. I pulled down the shades and turned off the fan, enjoying the unexpected silence that blanketed the room. I considered curling up under the desk and sleeping there so I wouldn't have to worry about getting to school on time.

I was bone-tired as I dragged myself downstairs to sign out. The office was nearly deserted. Shannon was slumped at her desk, staring at her cyber-aquarium in a state just this side of catatonia. She didn't even glance up when I walked in. Anna was leaning against the sign-in desk. One look at me sent her running for the chocolate.

"Rough start, huh? Can I help?"

"Only if you can transfer Michael Tayler out of my class."

"Get in line."

"The boy's got some serious issues. If he stays in my class, only one of us may come out alive."

Anna smiled at me the way my mother does when I'm being difficult. "Don't overreact. Remember last year? Andy Sellers? Danica Brown? You survived them. You can reach this kid."

The praise didn't make me feel much better. "I can't figure him out. It's like he's operating on a different wavelength than everyone else."

"Be patient. First day, new school. Bound to be adjustment problems. Probably just needs some friends."

Yeah, and a shot in the butt with a tranquilizer dart. "I don't think that'll happen anytime soon. From what I can see, he makes the other kids uncomfortable."

"Give him time. He'll straighten out."

If any of us live that long. "Okay, Anna, whatever you say. By the way, has Nancy left yet? I was hoping to catch her before she went home."

"Just missed her. She seemed rushed. Starts teaching those parenting classes tonight."

"I hope Michael Tayler's parents have signed up. They could use some tips on how to deal with a problem child."

As I plodded out to my car, I had the uncanny sense of reliving this morning in reverse slow-mo. The air was muggy and still. Tom was lowering the flag. The metal pulleys clanked against the pole.

"Hey, Jenna. Everything okay?" he asked.

"It will be when I get home."

"Yeah, I know the feeling. Have a good one."

I flapped him a listless wave as I trudged to the nearly deserted parking lot. Everybody else was probably on their third drink by now. I opened the car door and fell onto the seat. The trapped heat had softened the worn gray vinyl, and it burned the backs of my legs. I squirmed into a less painful position and searched through my purse for my key ring. When I turned the key in the ignition, a blast of hot air from the A/C vent hit me in the face, and Bruce Springsteen started singing about being born to run. If only I had the energy.

I drove the speed limit through the tree-lined streets, doing penance for the velocity of my morning commute. Even though I grew up five miles away in neighboring Hartfield, Morrisonville always felt like home to me. I spent enough time here to qualify for dual citizenship. A typical central New Jersey suburb, Morrisonville was a middle-class town with modest, well-tended houses that had been built in the early fifties. My grandparents moved there shortly after they were married, and my parents didn't stray too far afield. Now I had returned to the family homestead, completing the karmic circle.

I hung a right onto Sycamore Terrace and pulled into the driveway of my little brick rancher. After I killed the ignition, I sat for a moment, too tired to move. When I finally mustered enough energy to climb out of the car, Yin-Yang streaked across the lawn from her hiding place in the flower bed. Brutus screeched, and I could picture the cat chuckling as she dove through her pet door.

As soon as the lock clicked open, a throaty "Helloooooo" welcomed me home.

"Hello, Brutus." I dumped my tote bag and keys on the kitchen counter, narrowly missing this morning's half-filled glass of tea. "I'll bet you're not nearly as glad to see me as I am to see you. Wanna come out?" When I opened his door, he hopped onto my arm like an inmate who'd just been paroled.

I gave him a kiss. "Were you a good bird while I was gone?"

Brutus tilted his head, looking highly insulted by the question. I set him on his perch with a hazelnut while I washed the breakfast dishes. I'd just rinsed the last one when the phone rang. Since I couldn't locate a dishtowel, I wiped my hands on my dress and picked up the receiver.

"Hi, honey. How was your first day?"

"Hi, Mom. It was brutal. I feel like the walking dead."

"That bad, huh? Did you eat a good breakfast?" For some unimaginable reason, my mother thinks I don't get enough food.

"Yeah," I lied. "I guess I just have to get back into my school routine."

"How are your students this year?"

"Mostly okay. There's one who looks like he could be trouble. Nothing I can't handle, though"

"I'm sure you'll be fine. By the way, how's Chris?"

Less than a minute before she got around to that. Chris and my mother were new best friends. They bonded in her kitchen one Sunday when Chris came to dinner, and Mom's been his number one fan ever since. For his part, Chris thinks my mother's another Julia Child. He worships at her stove. I guess he figures if she's such a good cook, there might be some hope for me. I don't have the heart to tell him I didn't inherit my mom's cooking gene.

"Chris is fine. He brought me an apple."

"What a sweetie. You'll have to bring him over for dinner again soon. By the way, have you had dinner yet?"

"I was getting ready to cook when you called."

"Oh," she said, trying not to sound surprised. "What are you cooking?"

I pulled a Lean Cuisine out of the freezer and read from the box. "Meatloaf with Whipped Potatoes and Gravy."

"Sounds good. Be sure to have a green vegetable with that. Maybe a nice salad."

"I will."

"Well, I've got to get dinner for your father. Call me if you need anything."

"Okay. Talk to you later."

I hung up and put the Lean Cuisine in the microwave. Then I popped a can of beer and chugged it.

Brutus was balanced on one foot, preening his feathers.

"How'd you like to watch me grade papers?" I asked him.

Brutus continued preening as I dusted toast crumbs off the kitchen table and sat down to work. Most of the poems were about typical adolescent stuff: pets, music, sports, movie and TV stars. I read each one and commented on its merits, trying to find something positive to say even if I had to stretch the limits of my imagination.

When I was halfway through a gushy ode to a poodle named Fifi, the microwave signaled that dinner was ready. Brutus did a perfect imitation of the beep. After an unsuccessful search for a potholder, I opened the door and removed the plastic dish barehanded. Steam seared my fingertips.

"Goddammit!" I dropped the dish onto the counter.

"Dammit," Brutus repeated.

I glanced heavenward. "Sorry, Nana."

As I tugged the plastic film off the dish of meatloaf, some of the gravy sloshed over the side and pooled on the yellow Formica. After making a quick estimate of how many calories that would subtract, I decided to have another beer.

Since the food was too hot to eat, I returned to the poem about Fifi the Wonder Dog. I had slogged through six more cinquains before realizing that my eyes were moving but my brain had disengaged. It was time for a dinner break.

I handed Brutus an almond so I wouldn't have to eat alone.

"Good," he said.

After polishing off the meatloaf and potatoes, I tossed down a handful of wasabi peas so I wouldn't feel like I'd lied to my mother about the veggies. Then I switched on the six o'clock news, wondering what had happened in the real world while I was in school. A commercial came on, and Brutus bobbed up and down in time with the music. I was laughing when Nancy called.

"Hi, Jen. I wanted to check on you before I left for my parenting group. Sounds like you're in a better mood now, so I assume you survived the rest of the day. Did you get a chance to look at Michael Tayler's file?"

"Yeah. Now I'm really confused. Did you see his test scores and IQ? It doesn't make sense that he's such a poor student."

"A lot of things about this kid don't fit together. I'm going to do some digging and see what I come up with. Want to help?"

"Oh, sure. It's not like I have a hundred forty other students."

"I know, but you're a sucker for a challenge. Come to my office tomorrow. We'll do lunch."

"You've got a date, girlfriend."

I continued grading cinquains until the thought of reading about one more friendly puppy made me want to gouge out my eyeballs. Didn't any of these kids have a parrot? I pulled on an oversized Temple University t-shirt and a pair of striped boxers and tucked myself into bed. Soon I drifted off to sleep, where I dreamed of teaching a dog obedience class in my underwear. One of the dogs was a jumpy Irish Setter that bore a striking resemblance to Michael Tayler. He refused to sit, and when I tried to correct him, he lifted his leg and peed on my bare foot.

Chapter Four

It was shaping up to be another lunchless day. To make matters worse, I'd overslept again and had to skip breakfast. Even poor Brutus had to start the day without his toast. I grabbed a handful of animal crackers from the box on Nancy's desk.

Nancy took out a disciplinary referral form and wrote *Michael Tayler* at the top. "Now tell me exactly what happened."

Everything was fine in homeroom. Michael was jittery, but at least he wasn't acting out. Maybe Anna was right, and he was just stressed about being in a new school without a peer group. Since I had lunch duty, I checked to see if anybody was sitting at his table. There's nothing that spells "Loser" like sitting alone in the cafeteria. At first, Michael was the only occupant at a six-seater in the back corner. Then Jessica Corcoran came in with her friend, Chelsea Hopkins, and they sat on either side of him. Jessica is one of those kindhearted types who would probably take in a stray skunk. It must have bothered her to see Michael sitting by himself. All that female attention perked him up, and soon the three of them were chatting and laughing like old friends.

About five minutes before the end of the period, I was making a final clean-up check when I passed Michael's table. The girls had cleared their places, but the area in front of Michael was littered with crumpled food wrappers, a half-filled bottle of Snapple, an empty potato chip bag, and a pile of used paper napkins.

"Michael, the bell's going to ring soon. You need to throw away that trash."

I'd never seen someone look down their nose while looking up, but somehow Michael managed to do just that. "I think you've got me mixed up with the help," he said.

Help? If you don't lose the attitude, you'll need help picking your teeth up off the floor. I decided to count to three before I responded.

Jessica and Chelsea turned to him with identical, appalled expressions, but his eyes were fixed on me.

I glared back at him. "Unfortunately," I said, "in this school you're expected to clean up after yourself."

"Why?" he asked. "Isn't that what janitors are for?"

My fingers itched to slap his insolent face. Before I could respond, Jessica came to the rescue.

"C'mon, Michael. Chelsea and I will help you." She started gathering the paper napkins, and Michael's eyes broke away from mine just as the bell rang. He wadded the rest of the trash together, picked up the Snapple bottle, and followed Jessica to the trash can.

I didn't see him again until the kids were at their lockers. He was talking to Jessica when Bryan Grant and Alex Benitez came down the hall. They were horsing around like they always do, shoving each other as they walked. Alex pushed Bryan into Michael, and Michael dropped his binder. Papers went flying.

Bryan looked surprised. "Yo, dude. My bad." he said.

Michael spun around. "You stupid asswipe!" He punched Bryan in the chest, knocking him into the bank of lockers across the hall. Bryan didn't even have time to react. Alex dropped his books, ready to jump to his friend's defense.

I grabbed Michael by the shirt. "Michael, calm down."

"Let go of me, you bitch!" he shouted, trying to twist out of my grasp.

Wanna see a bitch? I'll show you a bitch. I tightened my grip on his shirt and yanked as hard as I could. Luckily, Charlie Donner was nearby. He helped me separate the boys before a full-scale fight broke out. Then we marched them to the office and turned the matter over to Don Clayton.

Don is the vice-principal in charge of discipline. He's an intense, quiet man, built like an NFL linebacker, with skin the color of mahogany. The students call him "The Enforcer." They'd be surprised to learn that he spends Saturday afternoons mentoring homeless kids. Don has one of the toughest jobs in the school. He spends half his time dealing with problem students and the other half trying to reason with irate parents who insist that their little darlings couldn't possibly be to blame. Talk about the job from hell. Whatever he gets paid isn't nearly enough.

Charlie and I left the boys with Don, and I went to the guidance office to file a discipline report.

Nancy finished writing. Then she pushed her glasses up onto her head and looked me in the eye. "So it's your opinion that Michael overreacted, and the other boy was not at fault."

"Seemed that way to me."

"You realize this could mean an out-of-school suspension for him."

Boo-freaking-hoo. Suspension was one of the most serious penalties in Morrison's discipline code, the result of a new "zero tolerance" policy enacted to eliminate school violence.

"I know," I said. "But as much as I'd love a few Michael-free days, I wouldn't let that color my judgment. Michael just lost it. Bryan and Alex may be itches, but they're relatively harmless. I've never known them to harass anybody. They're too busy annoying each other."

Nancy pinched the bridge of her nose. "Please don't think I'm questioning your judgment. I just want you to be certain of your facts. This could become a little—volatile."

"Meaning?"

"Do you recognize the name Bennett Tayler?"

My gurgling stomach was interfering with my brain's capacity for higher-level thought, so I popped another animal cracker to clear my head. "Sounds vaguely familiar. What's the connection?"

"Bennett Tayler is the president and CEO of TechTron Industries. He also happens to be Michael Tayler's father."

Bad news flash. The synapses in my brain started firing on all cylinders. TechTron was one of the biggest employers in Morrisonville. Bennett Tayler was one of our town's major VIP's.

"Bennett Tayler has friends in high places—including our school board," Nancy continued. "And judging from the info I've squeezed out of Elgin's guidance department, he takes a dim view of anyone who criticizes his son."

Just what we need around here. Another screwy parent. Suddenly I wasn't hungry anymore. "Now I see where this is going. But it doesn't change what happened. Michael was definitely the instigator. Bryan didn't even throw a punch."

"I'm not saying we should give Michael special consideration. You know me better than that. I just want to make sure you're protected in case this gets nasty." Nancy set her pen down. "It seems Mr. Tayler caused some massive headaches for the Elgin staff. One of Michael's teachers was even forced to resign. I couldn't get Michael's counselor to give me any of the details, but he hinted that it had something to do with a dispute between the teacher and Bennett Tayler. So I want you to go into this with both eyes wide open."

The animal cracker I was chewing had turned to sawdust in my mouth. I swallowed hard as I considered my response.

"Well, I saw what I saw. If Bennett Tayler wants to dispute that, let him try. I was there. He wasn't. And the day I bend over to some pushy parent is the day I hand in my chalk." With any luck, I sounded braver than I felt.

Nancy shook her head. "I knew you'd say something like that. But sometimes being right isn't enough. Can I give you some friendly advice?"

"I've never been able to stop you before."

"Start documenting every encounter with Michael. Get a notebook, and write down dates, times, places, and everything that was said and done. Start with homeroom yesterday, and try to remember every detail up to and including today." She shrugged. "Who knows? We may be lucky, and this whole thing will blow over. If that's the case, your notes might still be useful. Maybe we can find some pattern in Michael's behavior that will help us figure him out."

I took another handful of animal crackers and gave Nancy a hug. "You're the best. What would I do without you?"

"One thing for sure—you'd have to find another source for your animal cracker fix. Now get going or you'll be late for seventh period. We'll have to reschedule our lunch date, unless all those crackers you ate count as lunch."

I popped a lion into my mouth. Then I went back to my room and searched through my desk until I found a notebook I'd bought in Disney World. It had a big, grinning picture of Goofy on the cover. I opened to the first page and started writing.

The conversation with Nancy had unnerved me, so I had to force myself to stay focused on my last two classes. The seventh period kids were so bright and motivated, they didn't seem to notice. Michael Tayler was conspicuously absent from my eighth period class, and rumors were flying. *I heard the police took Michael away in handcuffs. Bryan had to go to the hospital—they think he has a concussion! Bryan's parents are suing the Taylers for everything they've got. Bryan's head was split open. There was blood everywhere! Alex and Bryan are gonna jump Michael on the way home from school. That'll teach him to mess with Morrison boys.*

Practically the only thing I didn't hear was that Michael was abducted by aliens, but I could understand why they wouldn't want him. Anyway, I knew better than to pay attention to the flurry of gossip. High school kids bore easily, and today's high drama would be tomorrow's old news. By the end of the week, everyone would most likely have forgotten the Michael Tayler affair. Everyone, that is, except me.

After the dismissal bell rang, I opened my Goofy book and checked that each detail I'd written was accurate. I was so lost in thought, I didn't hear Chris come in.

"Earth to Jenna."

I jumped as if he'd jabbed me with a cattle prod. "Dammit! You almost gave me a coronary."

"Hey, calm down. I didn't mean to startle you." He looked like a puppy caught chewing a new shoe.

"I'm sorry," I said. "It's not your fault. I've just got something on my mind."

"Want to tell me about it? Might make you feel better."

I considered that for a moment. "You know, it just might. I would like to talk, but not here."

"Why don't I cook up some dinner and bring it over to your place? We can talk while we eat. I've got a great new recipe I want to try, and I need a guinea pig."

"Where did you find a recipe for guinea pig?"

Chris laughed as he sat down on the corner of my desk. "Not what I meant, but I'll bet I could even make a guinea pig taste good."

"I may have skipped lunch, but I'm not *that* hungry."

"Probably because your stomach's full of animal crackers."

"So you've been talking to Nancy."

"I happened to pass her in the hall, and she said you needed feeding."

Nancy the Matchmaker strikes again. She's decided that Chris and I belong together, and she never misses an opportunity to pair us up. Not that I'm complaining.

"I need feeding, huh? What does she think I am—some kind of zoo animal?"

Chris stood up and looked at his watch. "I'll come by around seven. Make sure you throw a cover over Mongo the Killer Bird."

"Make Brutus an extra serving of whatever you're cooking, and I'm sure he'll do his best to tolerate you. And bring a bottle of wine. Or three. It's been a long day."

Chris arched an eyebrow. "This is beginning to sound promising. Shall I bring candles too? And massage oil?"

"Don't push your luck. Now go. I'm starving." I shoved him out the door, fantasizing about the massage oil.

Once I got home, I had to forget about Bennett Tayler. The house looked like the "before" version of a home makeover show. A film of dust dulled the hardwood. Fingerprints smeared the glass-topped coffee table. The tan microfiber sofa was barely visible under a heap of unfolded laundry. An impressive spider web adorned the ceiling fan, and unwashed dishes filled the sink. A nearly empty glass of root beer was stuck to the crumb-covered kitchen table. If my grandmother wasn't already dead, she'd die of shame.

To make matters worse, Brutus had expressed his indignation over missing breakfast by flinging parrot food onto the living room floor. The colorful pellets crunched under my feet as I walked toward his cage.

"Hey, buddy. Sorry I ignored you this morning. Want to come out and play?"

Brutus wasn't letting me off the hook that easily. He turned his back and gave a shake. One golden feather floated to the bottom of the cage.

"Come on. I said I was sorry." No response. This called for heavy artillery, so I reached for a walnut.

"Want this?" I wiggled the walnut under his beak.

"CRACKER." He stepped onto my arm, and all was forgiven.

"You are such a nut-whore," I told him. He looked at me and grunted.

"Now we have to have a serious talk. Chris is coming over tonight, and I want you to be nice to him." Brutus pretended to study the walnut. "I mean it. Chris is my friend, and you have to behave."

I carried Brutus into the kitchen and placed him on his perch while I performed my not-so-merry maid routine. He crunched into the walnut, crumbling shells onto the white linoleum. When I took out the vacuum cleaner, he froze.

"I know you don't like this, but you made a mess." As the vacuum roared to life, Brutus let out such a skull-splitting screech that I immediately switched it off.

"Okay, you win this time. But only because the last thing I need right now is a headache." I put the vacuum away and took out a nice, quiet broom. After sweeping the floor, I gathered the loose papers that littered the room and crammed them into my bottom desk drawer. Then I wiped the kitchen table, covered it with a flowered tablecloth, and set it for two. Not bad, even without the candles.

I was touching up my lipstick when I heard odd thumps coming from the front door. Yanking it open, I narrowly missed being kicked by Chris's left foot. His day-glo orange oven mitts cradled a steaming pot that released a heavenly fragrance. My salivary glands kicked into high gear.

Chris elbowed me out of the way. "Move over. I've got to put this down. These mitts are heating up."

I followed him into the kitchen like a bloodhound tracking fresh meat. "Smells great. What is it?"

Chris removed the mitts and rubbed his hands together. "Beef Bourguignon. It's a classic French stew made with burgundy wine. You said you wanted wine, right? And there's a bag in my car with a couple bottles of Chianti Reserve and a loaf of French bread. Could you get it? I have to put the finishing touches on the stew."

I hurried out to the car and wrapped my arms around the large brown bag in the passenger seat. It radiated warmth and a marvelous bakery aroma. I tried not to drool on it as I carried it inside.

"Okay, let's eat." I set the bag on the table.

"Don't you have a bread basket? I made this bread myself. It's too good to be served from a paper bag."

I rummaged around in the cabinet under the sink until I found a tired-looking wicker basket that once held a floral arrangement. "How's this?"

"It's not exactly what I had in mind, but I guess it'll have to do." He lined the basket with a white napkin. "There, that's better. Now where's the corkscrew? This wine has to breathe."

"Breathing wine? Sounds like something from a Stephen King novel."

Chris gave me the look he reserved for students who couldn't add. "Red wine needs to be uncorked for at least fifteen minutes to allow the full flavor to develop."

"Fifteen minutes? Are you kidding? I'll starve to death."

"Trust me—it'll be worth the wait. Have a piece of bread."

He ripped off a hunk of the warm, spongy bread and held it to my mouth. Before I could get my teeth into it, an angry tirade erupted from the living room.

"BAD. NO-NO-NO-NO."

Brutus's feathers were standing up like blue and gold daggers, and the pupils of his eyes had shrunk to pinpricks. Both wings were outstretched, and he was shifting from foot to foot as if to say, *Okay, pal, bring it on.*

"Oh, look," I said. "Brutus is saying hello."

Chris waved his arms at the infuriated bird. "Hi there, Psycho. Happy to see me?"

"DAMMIT," Brutus shrieked.

"Stop teasing him. Why don't you try to win him over instead?" I pointed to the bread.

"What? Give my gourmet creation to a bird?" Chris was interrupted by a high-pitched screech.

"Rather listen to that?"

Chris took the bread to Brutus's cage. Brutus hissed, eying it as if it were some kind of bird-eating snake.

"It's a peace offering," Chris said. "Want it or not?"

The aroma must have been irresistible because Brutus smoothed his feathers and poked the tip of his beak through the bars. Chris pinched off a small chunk of bread and gingerly passed it to him.

"There," I said. "Now you two can be friends." They both looked at me as if I'd beamed down from the Bizarro World. Then Brutus tore into the bread, and Chris hurried back to the kitchen.

"Dinner is served." Chris placed two steaming bowls on the table and handed me a glass of wine. I inhaled the rich, fruity fragrance and took a sip, feeling warmth kindling in my stomach. Then I dipped a chunk of bread into my bowl, blew on it, and took a bite. The burst of flavor made my eyes roll back into my head.

"Oooh, this is unbelievable. What's in it?"

Chris rocked back on his heels and smiled. "A good chef never reveals his secrets. But since this is just between you and me ..."

I listened in awed silence as he described the intricacies of French stew construction. Since my idea of cooking is nuking a frozen dinner, I'm fascinated by people who can prepare food from scratch.

When Chris finished, he sat down and smoothed his napkin onto his lap. "Now that I've told you my secret, tell me yours. What's bothering you?"

"Are you sure you want to hear about it? It'll probably spoil the mood."

"If things get too heavy, we'll have more wine."

I told him about Bennett Tayler, the fight, and the problems at Elgin. He listened without saying a word.

"So," I said, "now you've got the whole, ugly story. Any nuggets of wisdom to offer?"

Chris drained his wine in one swallow. "Jen, this isn't something to take lightly. You're not a tenured teacher. This kind of trouble could put your job at risk."

"Are you saying I should ignore the whole thing and hope it goes away, or blame it on another kid to keep Bennett Tayler off my back?"

"No. Just be cautious and logical. I know that's hard for you. Nancy gave you some sound advice. Document everything."

"Done."

"And try to keep out of Michael Tayler's way."

"How can I? He's in my homeroom and my English class."

Chris thought for a moment. "Keep your interactions with him to a minimum. Don't give his father any ammunition to use against you."

"You make this sound like warfare."

Chris refilled the wineglasses. "That's exactly what it might become."

After Chris left, I was too wired to sleep, so I decided to read for a while. Then I spotted a stack of ungraded papers on my desk—the cinquains from my eighth period class. I tossed my Dean Koontz novel onto the bedside table, figuring that poems about pet cats and dogs would put me to sleep a lot faster. I flipped the top paper over and, sure enough, the first line read, "My dog." Smiling beagles frolicked around the border, and my eyes started to glaze over.

After grading fifteen more papers, I felt like I had a head full of cotton balls, so I put my red pen down and called it a night. I was about to switch off the light when I noticed "Mike Tayler" scribbled across the top of a ragged-edged sheet of notebook paper. My curiosity got the best of me, and I pulled the paper free.

What I saw blew all the cobwebs out of my brain. The illustration at the bottom of the page showed a gaunt face surrounded by a mane of wild, red hair. Two tortured green eyes peered through splayed fingers. Spinning outward from the sides of the face were black, writhing tornadoes. Flecks of yellow swirled through the design like angry hornets. The motif snaked around the perimeter of the paper, its effect eerie yet strangely powerful. In the center of the page, written in Michael's barely legible scrawl, were these words:

My thoughts
Scattered, restless,
Bouncing, spinning, whirling,
Their static buzzes in my brain.
Mind-bits.

The raw intensity of the work hit me like a hammer to the chest. I couldn't tear my eyes away. I read the poem again. What was going on here? And as I read his words, Michael Tayler, the surly, irritating little brat morphed into a tormented, desperate boy crying for help.

Chapter Five

I arrived at school early after a restless night. I couldn't wait to show Michael's cinquain to Nancy. When I went to retrieve my mail, there was a Post-it stuck to the mail slot like a little yellow warning flag: *Please see me*, signed *Don Clayton*. This couldn't be good.

I poked my head into Don's office.

"Hi, Don. What's up?"

He looked up from his work. "Hello, Jenna. I'd like to speak with you if you have a moment."

I sat down in the heavy wooden chair across from his desk—the one usually reserved for unruly students.

"I got a call this morning from Bennett Tayler, Michael's father, concerning the incident yesterday involving his son and the other two boys. He's taking issue with the fact that Michael's been suspended, and he wants a conference with you, me, and Nancy Miller to discuss his concerns."

Uh-oh. I swallowed hard. "I'd be happy to tell him what I observed. When's he coming in?"

"He'll be here at three." Don took out a pad of paper. "I want you to fill me in on what happened yesterday. I read the discipline report, but I'd still like to hear about it firsthand."

Don's expression was unreadable as he listened. Every so often he'd jot something down. When I finished, he pushed his chair back.

"Well, that seems to cover everything. I'll see you after school in the conference room."

By the time I reached the guidance office, I felt as if a giant garrote had been tightened around my chest. Nancy was waiting by the door with a box of animal crackers.

"So you've heard about the conference," she said. "I know how you must feel, but try to stay calm. All you have to do is stick to the facts. And no matter how angry or abusive he gets, don't react."

I took a deep breath and blew it out slowly. "I can't say I wasn't warned. But I didn't expect things to happen so quickly. And check this out." I handed her the cinquain.

Nancy pushed her glasses down onto her nose. As she read, her eyes widened. "Wow. Where did you get this?"

"Michael wrote it in class. It shows he has some writing talent, but the mood is so—dark."

Nancy opened the top drawer of her filing cabinet and pulled out a packet of papers stapled at the corner. "I remembered this yesterday after we talked. It's from a workshop I went to last year. What do you know about Attention Deficit Hyperactivity Disorder?"

"The standard stuff. A couple of my college courses touched on it, but I didn't pay much attention."

Nancy raised one eyebrow. "Are you trying to be funny?"

It took me a second to get what she meant. "Sorry, I'm not that witty this early in the morning. I just figured ADHD was more of an issue for elementary school teachers."

"Considering what we've learned about Michael, I think this is worth a look."

"I don't know, Nance. I thought kids with ADHD can't focus. When Michael was writing that poem, he was focused like a laser. He didn't even hear the bell ring."

"That's called 'hyper-focus.' These kids can get so involved in something that interests them, they tune out everything else."

I took Michael's paper from her and looked at it again. "I think Michael has some serious emotional problems. His behavior's so weird. Just look at this picture."

Nancy nodded. "ADHD can cause all the things Michael's trying to express in this poem." She handed me the packet. "Read the articles, and see what you think."

I didn't get to the packet until lunch, but halfway through the third article, I decided that Michael could be the ADHD poster boy. It was all there: the disorganization, the forgetfulness, the irritability, the impatience, even the creativity. I stopped every few paragraphs and reread Michael's cinquain. My brain was whirling with ideas. *Could this be what it's like to have ADHD? How do these kids cope?*

I re-examined Michael's folder. The discipline problems, the inconsistency between his test scores and grades, his English teacher's comment—everything made sense now. His achievement was below his ability because something was getting in the way. Maybe that something was ADHD. And if Michael's problem had a name, there might be a way to get him some help.

I was about to lock up and go home when the wall speaker crackled to life. "Ms. Bianchi, please report to the conference room."

It all came back in a flash. I'd been so preoccupied with Michael, I'd forgotten about the three o'clock conference with his father. It was now three-fifteen. I pictured everyone sitting around the conference table, glancing at the clock. My stomach clenched like a fist as I scurried downstairs. Trying to hide my nervousness behind what I hoped was a perky smile, I opened the door. The scene was almost exactly as I'd envisioned it.

"It's about time." An impeccably dressed man in a charcoal suit was looking at his gold Rolex. He was tall and hawkish, with graying hair and piercing green eyes like Michael's. Next to him, a pudgy, balding man with thick glasses was tapping a slim, silver pen on a legal pad. He looked like Mr. Magoo.

"Sorry I'm late," I said, "but I had a few last-minute things to take care of before I could leave my classroom." *Okay, so I stretched the truth a little.* Nancy gave me a reassuring smile as I slid into the molded plastic chair next to hers.

Don looked around the table. "Mr. Tayler has some questions about the incident that led to his son's suspension. He requested this conference to clear things up."

"Actually," Mr. Tayler interrupted, "I want to know why my son has been excluded from school for such a minor infraction. This"—he pointed to Mr. Magoo—"is my attorney, Stanton Hawthorne. He has agreed to sit in on this meeting to make sure none of Michael's rights are violated. My son is entitled to an education which the public schools are required to provide. Right now, you are depriving him of that education."

Don pushed back in his chair. "Mr. Tayler, it's not our intent to deprive Michael of anything. However, to ensure a safe, orderly environment for all our students, we have a discipline code that must be respected. Part of that code states that there will be zero tolerance for any kind of physical violence."

"I'd hardly consider Michael's good-natured roughhousing physical violence. I believe you singled him out because he is new to the school, and you wanted to make an example of him. Why weren't the other boys suspended?"

"I think we should hear Ms. Bianchi's account, since she was the teacher who witnessed the incident." Don turned to me.

Stanton Hawthorne gave me a strange look when I took out my Goofy notebook. Goofy's grin seemed oddly out of place, but I made a mental note to thank Nancy for her good advice. Having all the information in writing bolstered my confidence. My hands wanted to shake, so I rested them on the table. I tried to keep my voice calm and decisive, ignoring Stanton Hawthorne as he scribbled notes. When I finished, Mr. Tayler fixed me with an intimidating stare. I returned his stare with a self-assurance I didn't feel. The only sound was the muffled hum of the fluorescent lights in the ceiling.

Nancy finally broke the silence. "I think it's clear that Ms. Bianchi's actions were appropriate. She was looking out for the safety and welfare of all the students involved."

"I disagree with your assessment." Mr. Tayler's tone was thick with hostility. "How do I know her version of the events is accurate? It differs in many respects from what Michael told me. Are you expecting me to believe this teacher over my own son?"

Of course not. That's what a sane person would do. I disregarded Nancy's under-the-table kick. "Mr. Tayler, I resent your implying that I would lie about a student. What possible motive could I have?"

Bennett Tayler glared at me. "According to Michael, you showed an unprovoked dislike of him from the moment he walked into your classroom. That hardly seems like professional conduct. I realize you are an untenured teacher," he said, the threat undisguised, "but your lack of experience is no excuse. In fact, it's further reason for me to doubt your interpretation of yesterday's incident."

Why, you pompous jackass! A wave of outrage swamped me as I searched for the perfect rebuttal. I wanted to crawl across the table and slap that superior expression right off his face.

Don leaned forward and folded his hands. "Mr. Tayler, Ms. Bianchi is one of our finest young teachers. I have every confidence that she handled the situation the way any of our veteran teachers would have."

"Be that as it may," Mr. Tayler said, "I don't feel that she is in a position to make an impartial judgment. And given this fact, I insist that Michael be permitted to return to school immediately. If not, I'm afraid I will be forced to take legal action." He looked at Stanton Hawthorne, who gave a terse nod.

Nancy put on her sympathetic face. "I understand your feelings. After all, we're talking about your son, and like any good parent, you want to protect your child. But teaching Michael that there are consequences for inappropriate behavior is an important life lesson. You'd be doing him a disservice to let him think he can behave any way he likes."

Mr. Tayler raised himself up to his full height. "Don't you dare presume to tell me how to discipline my son. This conversation is over. From now on, you may communicate with me through my attorney." He turned to Don. "I will be waiting to hear when Michael can return to school." With that, Bennett Tayler strode out of the room, the silent Mr. Hawthorne scuttling after him.

The three of us stared at the open door. Then Nancy took off her glasses and began polishing them with a tissue. "We've just seen living proof that the nut doesn't fall far from the tree."

Don chuckled. "Yeah, he's a real piece of work. You did well, Jenna."

"Thanks." *Now if I could just lose the urge to vomit.* I unclenched my hands and wiped the perspiration from my lip.

Don stood up and cracked his neck. "Go on home now. Put your feet up and watch something mindless on TV. Leave Mr. Tayler to me."

"Sounds good," I said, "but I need to talk to Nancy first."

"Then I'll leave you two to your talk. I have some calls to make—the first one to the school board's attorney." Don slumped a little as he walked to his office.

Nancy turned to me. "So what did you want to talk about? Bennett Tayler and the principles of positive parenting?"

"What a horse's ass," I said. "With a father like that, it's no wonder Michael's got problems."

"Speaking of problems, did you get a chance to read those articles?"

"That's why I wanted to talk to you. Michael fits the profile of an ADHD kid to the letter, no pun intended. What can we do to help him?"

"Not a whole lot. ADHD is a medical diagnosis. Michael would have to be examined by a neurologist to find out if he has it. And for that to happen, you'd need cooperation from his parents."

I had a quick vision of pigs flying. "Mr. Tayler hardly seems like the cooperative type."

Nancy yawned. "Well, they say the longest journey begins with a single step. And I think we took that step today. Let's go. I've had enough excitement for one afternoon."

After dinner, I wrote a detailed account of the conference in my Goofy notebook. It was surprisingly therapeutic. Then I took out my laptop, typed "Attention Deficit Hyperactivity Disorder" in the keyword box, and hit "Search." Information poured onto the screen. Recalling what Nancy said about a journey beginning with one step, I clicked on the first link.

Three hours and four cups of tea later, I had printed out a formidable stack of information. I turned off the computer and dumped the last of the tea into the sink. Then I said goodnight to Brutus and headed to my room, armed with a pile of papers and my handy yellow highlighter.

Thanks to the caffeine, I wasn't sleepy. I started reading an article entitled "Helping the ADD/ADHD Student in the Classroom." By the time I finally clicked off the light, I'd made up my mind to do just that.

Chapter Six

The morning dawned warm and foggy. Sounds seemed to move in slow motion through the soupy air. It had been too long since I'd had a solid eight hours of sleep, and the inside of my head was as hazy as the world outside the window. I sleepwalked through my morning routine, bumping into walls and knocking things over. Because it took me so long to get myself together, I only had enough time to grab a granola bar for breakfast. I broke off a piece for Brutus, who was unnaturally quiet as he watched me stumble around the house. Then I crammed Michael's folder, the ADHD articles, and all the Internet printouts into my tote. I was about to lock the door when I realized my keys weren't in my purse. After a frantic ten-minute search, I found them in my jacket pocket.

The drive to school was like snaking through a sauna. Every now and then, a large drop of water plopped onto the windshield from an overhanging branch. When I flicked on my headlights, the fog glowed a sickly yellow. My skin felt clammy as I hurried into school, praying that my hair hadn't frizzed to Bozo the Clown dimensions.

The air hung in my classroom like a mildewed cloak. When the fan didn't relieve the suffocating closeness, I opened every window. Not that it helped. I found myself longing for an air-conditioned prison cell.

I stood by the window and rested my head against the pane. The scene outside resembled a watercolor painting, soft and blurry around the edges. The trees looked like shrouded giants, and it was hard to tell where the gray sky ended and the ground began. I was watching a vein of water pulse down the glass when I felt someone's eyes on me.

Chris was leaning against the doorjamb, his head cocked to one side. "You're only wearing one earring. Going for the buccaneer look?"

I grabbed an earlobe with each hand and removed the single silver hoop. "Guess I wasn't paying attention when I got dressed."

"You look pretty good to me," he said.

"Frizzy hair, puffy eyes, and one earring. You must have lowered your standards."

He closed the door and crossed the room. "What's up?" he asked, looping his arm around my neck. His hand dangled tantalizingly close to my left breast.

Besides my pulse rate, you mean? I rubbed my cheek against his wrist. "I may have pissed off the wrong person." I told him all about the conference. He frowned when I got to the part about Mr. Tayler's pet lawyer. His frown deepened when I explained my ADHD research and what I planned to do.

When I finished, Chris raked his fingers through his hair. "Do you really think that's a good idea? Tayler sounds like a serious control freak. I doubt he'd take kindly to you telling him something's wrong with his son."

"I don't plan on telling him anything of the sort. At least not yet. And if he sees that I'm helping Michael, I'm sure he'll change his attitude toward me."

"Jenna, please stop being stubborn and think this through. Do you know the kind of trouble this could cause for you? The guy's way out of your league."

I turned away from him. "Don't worry about me. I can take care of myself."

Chris pulled me back until my face pressed against his chest. I felt his pecs tighten. "I know," he said, his voice soft against my ear. "But you trigger my protective instinct." He slid his hand up my back, and I fought a sudden urge to rip off his shirt.

Then the bell rang. *Dammit!*

Chris released me and straightened his tie. "Talk about lousy timing," he said. The next thing I knew, he was disappearing into a noisy sea of teenagers.

The morning announcements had just ended when the door burst open and Michael sauntered in. He tossed a late pass onto my desk and announced, in an unnecessarily loud voice, "I wasn't due back till tomorrow, but my dad had a talk with Superintendent Dimmit. He let me off with time served." Then he strolled to his desk and flopped into his seat.

And good morning to you, too, Mr. Cocky. I ignored his snotty attitude and gave him my brightest smile.

"Well, it's good to have you back," I said. In spite of my annoyance with Timothy Dimmit, our notoriously weak-willed superintendent, I was kind of glad to see Michael. He seemed confused by my reaction, and, for the first time, didn't try to have the last word.

By lunchtime, the news of Michael's premature return had swept through the school. I sat with Nancy at a beat-up wooden table in the corner of the faculty room. She was trying to control her outrage as she ripped into a peanut butter and banana sandwich.

"I can't believe that Dimwit Dimmit went over Don's head. Don tries so hard to be fair. What message does it send when a kid gets special treatment because his father's rich and connected? It undermines our whole discipline code."

I swallowed my last bit of grilled chicken and sipped some Diet Snapple. "I hear you, but I'm glad Michael's back. Now I can start working on him." I grabbed a handful of Nancy's animal crackers, figuring the diet drink would cancel out the cookie calories.

Nancy raised her eyebrows. "You've sure changed your tune since the beginning of the week. I seem to remember you begging Anna to get Michael out of your class."

"That was before I got into all the ADHD stuff. I've been doing some research, and I think I can help this kid."

"The accepted treatment for ADHD is medication. That can't be done without a doctor's diagnosis which can't be done without Michael's mommy and daddy."

"I know, I know. But I'm working on some strategies that don't involve meds—things I can do in my classroom."

Nancy balled up her napkin and stuffed it into her lunch bag. "I think you're playing with fire. It'll be even worse now that Tayler's got Dimwit in his corner."

"If my plan works, I'm sure Mr. Tayler will see things my way. And if not, there'll be no harm done." Little did I know.

I could hardly wait until eighth period. When the students began ambling in, I craned my neck to catch a glimpse of Michael. He was at the end of the line, walking close to Jessica.

I started class by returning the cinquains. "I really enjoyed reading these. Some of your poems show a lot of creativity. Are there any brave souls who'd be willing to read their cinquains to the class?"

One way to guarantee silence in a classroom is to ask students to volunteer for something. The kids slid down in their seats and avoided my eyes, thinking this somehow made them invisible. Then they began casting hopeful looks at one another. I knew if I waited long enough, the tension would become unbearable, and someone would raise a hand.

"Come on," I urged. "Don't be embarrassed." Jessica gave a tentative wave. *Bingo!*

Jessica's poem was one of the better pieces, which wasn't surprising. Jessica was a talented writer and one of the editors of the school newspaper. She stood up and read in a clear, melodic voice. When she finished, the class broke into applause. A few others found the courage to volunteer, but Michael remained slouched in his seat, silently studying his left thumbnail.

I finally gave up on him. "Thank you all for sharing," I said. "Now that our poetry reading is over, you can continue working on your peer interviews."

Michael straightened up, his eyes darting around the room, and I remembered that he'd been out on suspension when I assigned the project. He started drumming on his desk with a pencil.

Remember what the article said. Singling him out will only make his behavior worse. Then I had an idea.

"Jessica, since your interview is almost finished, would you please partner with Michael and fill him in on what he missed?"

Jessica brightened. "Sure."

Michael put his pencil down and glanced at her. Then he shrugged and opened his notebook. By the end of the period, he'd caught up with the rest of the class.

I had an announcement to make before dismissal. "Just a reminder that the first meeting of the school newspaper staff will be tomorrow after school. I encourage all of you to join us. It's a great learning experience, we have lots of fun, and if that's not enough, I'll bribe you with doughnuts."

While the students were packing, I walked over to Michael's desk. "I'd like to talk to you before you go."

He turned on me like a cat with its back up. "Why? What did I do now?"

"Nothing. At least nothing bad." The bell rang, and he rose to leave. Time for some fast talking. "I just wanted to tell you how impressed I was with your cinquain. It was one of the best in all my classes. You have quite a talent for writing."

Michael was half out of his seat, staring at me as if I'd suddenly started speaking in tongues. His expression reminded me so much of Brutus that I began to smile.

Michael flushed an angry scarlet. "Are you jerking me around? Did my father tell you to say all that stuff?"

"Oh, Michael, no." My smile evaporated. "I'm being totally honest. Your writing has real depth and maturity, and your artwork is excellent. Actually, I wanted to ask you to join the newspaper staff. We could use someone like you."

Michael looked down at his scuffed sneakers. He rolled a discarded pencil back and forth under his shoe; then he kicked it across the room. "Do I have to decide right now?"

"No. Go home and think about it. Talk it over with your parents. You can let me know tomorrow."

"Okay," he mumbled, and shuffled out to his locker.

The drive home was invigorating. The sun had burned away the last shred of fog, and the air had that fresh linen smell that follows the rain. Everything looked crisp and well-scrubbed. The leaves on the trees seemed to glow as I drove through the sun-dappled streets. Kids rollerbladed along the sidewalks and shot hoops in driveways. It was one of those afternoons that made me long for a convertible. I cranked up the CD player, and joined The Boss in a chorus of "Jersey

Girl." I had just finished the last *sha la la la* when I pulled into the driveway. Even my house looked shiny and clean. From the outside.

Brutus greeted me with a loud whistle when I stepped through the door.

"Hi there, handsome," I said. "Miss me?"

He responded with a kissy sound. I took him out of his cage and set him on the kitchen sink.

"How about a little shower?" This was Brutus's favorite leisure activity. I guess it had something to do with being a rainforest bird.

"WOOO-WOOOOOO." He fluffed his feathers and flapped his wings as I spritzed him with water from a spray bottle. Then I carried him to his perch and took out an animal cracker I had pocketed at lunch.

"This is from Aunt Nancy."

"Cracker?"

"Yep." Sometimes Brutus makes me forget I'm talking to a bird. Just then, my cell phone chirped.

"Hello," Brutus and I answered in unison.

"Is this Jenna Bianchi, patron saint of wayward students?"

"Hi, Chris. What's on your mind?" *Me, I hope.*

"Rumor has it Dimwit caved and let the Tayler kid come back early. True?"

"True, and I think I'm making some progress with him. I asked him to join the newspaper staff, and he's considering it."

"What about his father? Anything new?"

"Uh-uh. And no news is good news. Maybe he took his little troll lawyer and crawled back under his bridge."

"Ah, Jenna—always the optimist. One of the many things I love about you."

Love? Did he say LOVE? Before I had a chance to respond, Chris stammered, "Uh, listen, I've got something on the stove. Talk to you later."

I stared at the silent phone as I flipped it closed. What the heck was that all about? But I couldn't dwell on Chris's weird behavior when I still had Michael's weird behavior to figure out. My thoughts were interrupted by a sexy, "Hellooo, baby." Brutus was hanging upside-down from his perch, his wings outstretched and chest puffed out.

"Not you, too," I said. "I've had enough male weirdness for one day."

"Michael, don't keep me in suspense. What have you decided?"

Eighth period was over, and he hadn't given me a clue.

When he looked up at me, his face was a mixture of bewilderment and suspicion. "Why're you so hot about me working on this paper? I know it's not because of my grades. So what's the deal?"

I perched on the edge of his desk. "I'm not convinced your grades give an accurate picture of your ability. Someone who could write a poem like yours shouldn't be getting Cs in English. I'm always on the lookout for talented writers, and I think you could make a significant contribution to the newspaper."

I waited for him to respond, but he kept his eyes focused on his hands.

How about we go at this from a different angle? "We have a great group of kids," I said. "Ask Jessica. It would be good for you to meet them and maybe make some new friends, and it would be good for them to have someone on the staff with your gift for writing and art. Seems like a win-win proposition."

Michael began picking at the corner of his notebook. He seemed to be searching for an excuse to leave when Jessica came and stood beside me.

"Come on, it'll be fun," she told him. "If you don't like it, you can always quit."

Michael looked up at the clock. "But I'll miss my bus."

"No problem," Jessica said. "Take the late bus home with me."

That did the trick. "I guess I can try it."

Jessica pretend-punched his arm. "Great. Come with me to get the doughnuts."

"You're pretty pushy for such a short person," Michael said. He tried to look indignant, but his grin broke through.

I stood up and checked my watch. "Let's get this show on the road. I'll meet you in the computer lab."

Jessica and Michael walked off, their voices echoing in the empty corridor. I gathered my things and raced down the hall. The meeting should have started five minutes ago. I opened the door to a chorus of voices.

"WHERE ARE THE DOUGHNUTS?"

"Thanks for the wonderful greeting." I hoped my sarcasm wasn't lost on them. "The doughnuts are on the way. In the meantime, everybody can sign in." I took out a blank sheet of paper. "Write down your first and last names and your homeroom numbers."

"Should we write down our middle initials too?" Alex Benitez was the class comedian.

I rolled my eyes. "Alex, if it makes you happy, you can write out your entire middle name. All of them." Because of Alex's Hispanic heritage, he had several surnames and liked to brag that he had the longest name in the school.

"Muchas gracias, profesora." Alex gave an exaggerated bow, and I swatted him with the sign-in sheet. Everyone was laughing when Jessica walked in, followed by Michael hiding behind three orange and white doughnut boxes. Alex's wide grin melted into a scowl. I had almost forgotten his role in the dispute between Michael and Bryan. Damage control time.

"You can all relax now," I said. "The doughnuts are here, along with a new staff member. For those of you who haven't met him, this is Michael Tayler. He's new to Morrison, so I know I can count on you to make him feel welcome." I fired Alex a this-means-you look.

Alex pretended to be concentrating on the sign-in sheet, but the scowl didn't leave his face. I decided to avoid an uncomfortable scene by getting everyone busy, so I gave an overview of the different committees and asked the kids to sign up for whichever best suited them. Michael stood off to the side, looking like he wanted a sinkhole to swallow him. I sidled over.

"Have you given any thought to the type of work you'd like to do?" I asked.

"No clue."

"Since you have a flair for writing, why don't you join Jessica's group?" *Jessica. You know. The cute little girl you've had your eye on?* My guess was the idea of working with Jessica would appeal to him. And Alex would be on the other side of the room working on graphics. This would give both boys some breathing space until I could negotiate a truce.

Michael shrugged. "Whatever."

"Come with me, and I'll introduce you to the rest of your team." As we crossed the room, several kids shot meaningful glances at one another. Jessica and Chelsea were sitting side-by-side, their backs to us, when I heard Jessica say, "I'll bet he's a real hottie under all that red hair." One glance at Michael told me I wasn't the only one who'd overheard. His face and hair were now the same color.

I cleared my throat, and Jessica whirled around. She turned scarlet when she saw Michael. *How adorable! A matched set.*

"I've asked Michael to work with you because he's a good writer. I think he'll be a valuable addition to your group."

Michael stood there, face glowing and feet shuffling, until Jessica patted the chair next to hers. "You can sit here," she said. Michael stopped shuffling and sat down. It took the glow a while to disappear.

On the opposite side of the room, Alex and three other boys were hunkered over a computer. It was obvious from their expressions they weren't discussing graphics.

"How's it going over here?" I asked, feigning cheerfulness.

Alex swiveled his chair around to face me. "Ms. B., what's that freak doing here? You saw how he went off on Bryan. Then he got off suspension 'cause his father's some rich corporate dude."

Well, you're right about that, but—"Come on, Alex. Give him a break," I pleaded. "It was his second day in a new school, and he was probably tense and uncomfortable. Don't you remember how you felt when you moved here from New York? And it's not his fault that his father's wealthy. I'd consider it a personal favor if you'd give him another chance."

"You're not being fair, Ms. B. I'd love to help you out, but Bryan's my buddy, and Tayler tried to mess him up."

Oh, that's right. The male bonding thing. "It was a misunderstanding. Michael didn't know that you two were only fooling around, and he reacted without thinking. Haven't you ever done that?"

Alex admitted that he had, and one of the other boys mumbled in agreement.

"Can I count on you then?" I asked. "I'm not expecting you to become buddies. I'm only asking you to coexist. Please?"

Alex shrugged. "Okay, you got it. But if he tries any more of that psycho crap, all bets are off."

Whew! Another catastrophe averted.

As the students filed onto the late bus, Michael lagged behind. He turned to me and looked down at his untied shoelaces.

"Thanks for talking me into this," he muttered. "It was fun."

I patted his shoulder. "I'm glad you liked it. I hope you'll feel the same way when we're down to the wire trying to make our deadline."

"Yeah, well—later." He climbed onto the bus, taking a seat next to Jessica. It was only after the bus pulled away that I allowed myself to relax. Thank God it was Friday!

Chapter Seven

I drove to school on Monday morning replaying the weekend in my head. I spent Saturday catching up on paperwork, doing laundry, and getting my house semi-clean. Chris and I went to the mall for drinks and a movie on Saturday night. We're both horror movie buffs, and this one was a real nail-biter. On Sunday after-noon, I had dinner with my parents. My brother, Anthony, was home from college for the weekend, and Mom had killed the fatted calf. Or, in this case, pig. She'd made a honey-glazed ham, Anthony's favorite, and mashed sweet potatoes studded with little marshmallows. She also made a broccoli-cheddar casserole in an effort to get some green vegetables into me. As usual, there was way too much food, and the remnants now resided in my freezer. My mother always sends me home with enough leftovers to get through the first half of the week. I suspect she does this out of pity, having unsuccessfully tried to pass her cooking secrets on to me.

On Sunday night, I worked on what I'd come to think of as "Project June Bug." From my research, I compiled a list of strategies known to have helped people with ADHD. I planned to try each one with Michael. If the strategy worked, I'd mark it with a plus. There was already a big plus next to #1: *Don't take Michael's impulsive behavior personally.* I was still working on #2: *Involve Michael in activities that will boost his self-esteem.*

As I turned into my parking space, Nancy pulled up beside me. She'd been away all weekend, and I hadn't had a chance to tell her about Michael and the newspaper meeting. By the time we got to the main office, I'd brought her up to speed.

"I'm glad you broke the ice between Alex and Michael," she said. "I've sched-uled a conflict resolution session for those two and Bryan during second period today."

"Great idea. Tell me how it goes." If the conflict resolution was successful, I could put a plus next to Strategy #5: *Help Michael learn to express his feelings more appropriately.*

"Any fallout from the Bennett Tayler conference?" she asked.

"No lawyers have come knocking on my door. Maybe he's backed off."

"He doesn't strike me as the type who gives up that easily. If I were you, I wouldn't let my guard down." She turned down the hall to her office.

When I opened the classroom windows, I could smell autumn coming. The muggy warmth of last week had been blown away by a brisk breeze scented with apples. There was even a subtle change in the color of the leaves on the sugar maples that lined the school driveway. Soon they'd be blazing like a row of orange candles. Plump pillows of yellow chrysanthemums ringed the flagpole. A chevron of Canadian geese sliced through the clear sky, honking like an airborne traffic jam. I pulled the cool, spicy air deep into my lungs.

When the homeroom bell rang, Michael was one of the first through the door. I looked at him and did a double-take. *Wow! Zero to GQ in one weekend.*

His hair had been cut and styled so he no longer looked like the Lion King. He was wearing a striped polo shirt and a pair of jeans that were actually the right size. Even the laces on his new running shoes were tied. I didn't want to draw attention to him by staring (Strategy #3: *Don't embarrass Michael by singling him out*), so I just smiled and gave him a thumbs up. I was elated when he smiled back.

On my way to lunch, I stopped by Nancy's office to find out how the conflict resolution had gone.

"I hardly recognized Michael when he walked in," she said. "What did you do at that newspaper meeting—give him a makeover?"

"I was as surprised as you. Much as I'd like to take credit for his new look, I think the real motivation is Jessica Corcoran."

"Ah, love is in the air—and it isn't even spring."

"Sure seems that way. How did Alex and Bryan react?"

"Bryan was hostile at first. Alex was quiet. That chat you two had on Friday must have made an impression. After Michael explained why he reacted the way he did, Bryan softened a little. Then Alex told Bryan he understood how Michael could have misinterpreted their actions. Michael finally apologized and all three shook hands. They may never become friends, but I don't think we'll see any more battles in the halls."

Chris was waiting for me in the faculty room. "Where've you been? I almost gave up and ate this myself." He handed me a foil-wrapped packet.

"I had to talk to Nancy. What's this?"

"A beef empanada."

"Say what?"

"It's a little meat pie. A Latin American recipe I was fooling around with yesterday."

I opened the packet and sniffed. "Smells yummy."

"Didn't want you to have to eat the cafeteria's mystery meat. And speaking of mysteries, I've been nosing around to see what I could dig up on Bennett Tayler."

"And?" I asked, taking a bite of the empanada.

"Charlie Donner knows a guy who teaches math over at Elgin. Michael was in his class last year and drove him nuts. He warned Charlie to stay out of Bennett Tayler's way. Told him to just pass the kid and keep his mouth shut."

"Oh, real professional. This is delicious, by the way."

"Don't try to change the subject. Charlie said Michael's history teacher decided to play hardball. He told Tayler that Michael was failing and would have to go to summer school if he didn't shape up."

"I'll bet that went well."

"Not for the teacher," Chris said. "He isn't working there anymore."

Michael's behavior during class that afternoon was as changed as his appearance. The obnoxious, scruffy brat had been replaced by a likeable young man. I wondered if the new and improved Michael had an evil twin hidden in his closet.

I spent the period reviewing for a test—not, I'll admit, the most captivating lesson I'd ever taught. Every time I glanced at Michael, he was staring out the window. Time to try another strategy.

I walked around the classroom as I talked. When I was standing beside Michael, I tapped on his desk as if to emphasize a point. He turned from the window to look at me. Then he continued following me with his eyes. *The discreet signal scores a plus.*

At the end of the period, Michael stayed behind as the other students funneled into the hall. I sensed there was something he wanted to tell me. Sure enough, when everyone was gone, he came over to my desk.

"Um—can I talk to you for a minute?"

"Sure. What's up?"

"I was wondering …" He hesitated, then looked at the floor. When he looked up, I knew the moment had passed. "It's, um, about the test tomorrow. Do we have to do any revising?"

"There's one revise-edit item, nothing you can't handle. Just review your class notes and you'll be fine."

"Well, uh—okay. I gotta go or I'll miss the bus."

"Then I'll see you tomorrow. And Michael," I added, "if you have any other questions, or if there's anything you need to talk about, I hope you'll feel free to come see me."

He nodded and hurried out to his locker, almost colliding with Chris.

"Sorry," Michael mumbled.

Chris watched from the doorway until Michael disappeared down the hall. Then he turned to me, his eyes like chips of blue ice. His usual smile was gone.

"I can see how seriously you took our little lunchtime chat," he said. "I thought I made it clear to you that you shouldn't be getting involved with that kid." His overbearing tone made me bare my claws.

"Oh, really?" I asked. "So sorry, but I didn't realize you were my keeper. I guess I was under the mistaken impression that I'm in charge of my own life. Silly me."

Chris set his lips in a grim line, and I saw a little muscle jump in his jaw. I instantly regretted having been so spiteful, but I'd gone too far to back down now.

"Are you honestly naïve enough to think that you can tweak the nose of a man like Bennett Tayler and get away with it?" he asked. "Can you possibly be that clueless?"

Clueless? I'll show you who's clueless. "Well, since I'm so damn clueless, maybe you should take your infinite wisdom and shower it on someone more deserving. Or somebody who gives a shit."

We stared at each other in glacial silence, neither of us wanting to blink first. Finally, Chris pulled his eyes away.

"Do whatever you want," he said, all the emotion gone from his voice. "You will anyway." He turned his back on me and walked out the door.

"That's the first sensible thing you've said since you came in here," I called after him.

When my adrenalin rush had worn off, I wanted to sit at my desk and have a good cry. What the hell had I done? Chris was only trying to look out for me. Why did I have to be such a bitch? A sob caught in my throat, and I decided to find him and see if I could smooth things over.

By the time I reached the math department, I knew it was a lost cause. The corridor was dark and still. The only sound was the echo of my footsteps as I walked to Chris's classroom and tried the doorknob. It was locked.

"Mom? I wanted to make sure you were home. I'm on my way over." I know it's lame, but after the fight with Chris, I had an uncontrollable urge to run home to Mommy.

"Sure, honey. I'll put on some tea. Is something wrong?"

"Tell you when I get there. I don't want to get pulled over for talking on my cell phone."

I flipped the phone closed and tossed it onto the passenger seat. The CD player changed tracks, and Bruce started singing "Waitin' On A Sunny Day." My throat tightened. I switched the music off, but not before my eyes misted over.

I blinked to clear my vision and made the turn onto Hartfield-Morrisonville Road, the two-lane that linked my old hometown to my new one. I found myself behind a mammoth white Cadillac Eldorado that appeared to be driving itself.

The right-hand turn signal was blinking, but the car crept along the straightaway at a steady thirty in a forty-five no passing zone. My hand itched to lay on the horn, but I didn't want to startle the little old lady in the driver's seat. From what I could see of the top of her head, she looked kind of like my Nana. And I didn't need any more bad karma at the moment, thank you very much.

I followed Granny for two more miles, that damn turn signal mocking me with every blink. When she reached the stop sign where the road intersected with SR 23, she hung a left and continued on her way, the right blinker still winking merrily like a bad practical joke.

I turned right and followed the road into Hartfield. My parents' house was just across the town line, about as close to Morrisonville as you can get. It was as though Mom and Dad wanted to stretch their parents' apron strings without snapping them. My maternal grandparents had also lived in Morrisonville, across town from the Bianchis. They died before I was born, and my mother adopted her in-laws as surrogate parents. An unusual relationship, but one that worked.

I turned onto Poplar Lane and pulled up to the curb in front of the gray and white colonial where I grew up. My mother was waiting by the front door. Her willowy shadow fell across the flagstone walk.

"Jenna, you had me worried. What happened?"

"It's a long story."

I followed her into her spotless kitchen.

"Something smells great," I said. I opened the oven and peeked inside. "Is that eggplant parmigiana?"

"Yep," Mom answered. "There was a sale on those Japanese eggplants at the Acme today. They're not as bitter as the Sicilian kind, so they make the best parmigiana."

Another subtle cooking lesson wasted on me. I pulled out one of the four captain's chairs that circled the table and dropped onto the ruffled blue seat cushion. Mom placed a matching blue placemat in front of me. The Tiffany lamp that hung over the kitchen table cast a soft glow on the polished oak. Not a crumb in sight.

"Tea's ready." Mom set a steaming stoneware mug on the placemat, and I read the tag that hung from the teabag's string. *Celestial Seasonings Tension Tamer.* Good old Mom. She poured herself a glass of San Pellegrino water and squeezed in a wedge of lime. Then she sat down across from me, her tawny eyes searching my face.

"So what's the problem?" she asked, lifting the lid off the Capodimonte cookie jar in the center of the table.

I reached inside, feeling around until my practiced fingers recognized a homemade biscotti. I pulled it out and dunked it into the tea. "I might have really screwed things up with Chris."

"Oh, dear. What did you do?"

"We had a fight over this kid in my class." I told her about Michael, Project June Bug, and Chris's reaction. During my non-stop monologue, she merely nodded, gave an occasional "Mm-hmm," and sipped her sparkling water. To her credit, my mom has always been able to listen without inserting editorial comments. A trait not shared by my dad.

"I know I overreacted," I said. "But Chris was so patronizing. Like I was some kind of helpless nitwit. He got on my last nerve."

My mother chuckled and shook her head. A strand of auburn hair pulled loose from her barrette, and she tucked it back in. "I always said you were your father's daughter. You seem to have inherited the Bianchi disposition. In Italian, it's called 'arrabbiato.' The closest English translation is 'fiery.' Your Grandpop Bianchi was the same way." She put her hand on mine. "Nana and I used to say that life with a Bianchi was never boring."

I sighed. "If I keep this up, the only one who'll want to share my fiery life will be Brutus. I really don't want to mess up what Chris and I have, but I can't let him think it's okay to boss me around."

"Honey, you have to learn the difference between bossing and caring. Sure, Chris may have come on a bit strong, but it's because he has strong feelings for you. He's afraid you might get hurt."

I wasn't ready to let him off the hook yet. "That doesn't give him the right to tell me how to do my job."

I could tell from Mom's silence she had something to say.

"What?" I asked, trying not to sound defensive.

She studied me a moment longer. "Chris may have a point about this Michael business."

"Oh, no. Not you, too."

"Just consider the possibility. Chris has more experience than you have. And it makes perfect sense for you to keep a low profile until you get tenure."

"And does it make perfect sense for me to ignore a student who needs my help?" I knew I was getting snippy, but, as usual, I couldn't stop myself.

"Jenna, Jenna. Always fighting dragons. Someday that stubborn streak is going to get you into trouble."

"God, I hate it when Chris's words come out of your mouth. What is it with you two? Some kind of weird culinary mind-meld?"

She smiled and patted my hand. "Nothing paranormal. Just a common desire to keep you from self-destructing. And there are a lot worse things than having people who care about you."

I couldn't argue with that. "I know, I know." My hand went back into the cookie jar and came out with a coconut macaroon. "I just can't figure out how to fix things with Chris without looking like a total wuss."

"You two need to sit down and have a serious talk. Set some parameters for your relationship so you understand where the boundaries are. But first, you should both take some time to cool off. Especially you."

I was actually beginning to feel a bit cooler. I wasn't sure if the tea had tamed my tension, or if it was all the carbs from the cookies.

"Yeah, you're right," I said. "We haven't discussed any serious stuff yet. And I know I can be pigheaded. But Chris has always been so mellow. I guess I took it for granted that he'd take whatever I dished out."

Mom stood up and started clearing the table. "He's a good man, Jenna. But he's a man, and that means he won't always know what you're thinking. It's the Mars-Venus thing. Take it from somebody who's been there. The first year we were married, your father bought me a vacuum cleaner for Christmas when I'd been hinting for jewelry." She laughed. "Men are a lot of work, but the right one's worth the effort."

As if on cue, the door swung open and my father walked in. Or burst in. Dominic Bianchi was one of those larger-than-life guys. Definitely not your typical accountant-type. In spite of his stocky, compact body, he seemed to fill a room. He was Robert De Niro to Mom's Diane Keaton.

His face lit up with his trademark killer smile when he saw me.

"Yo, Mighty Mite! What're you doing back at the old homestead? Miss your Pa?" He put down his briefcase, strode over to the table and gave me a bristly kiss. One whiff of his English Leather, and I was five years old again.

"Hi, Daddy. I came over to talk to Mom. Girl stuff."

"Uh-oh. Here comes trouble." He turned to my mother and gave her a playful slap on the butt. "Hey, Frannie. How's my favorite lady?"

She kissed his cheek. "Hi, Dom. Dinner's almost ready. Jenna's eating with us."

Uh, well—okay. That was my cue to start setting the table.

"Something smells great," Dad said, opening the oven door. "Eggplant parm?"

I guess I am my father's daughter.

Chapter Eight

When I got home, I ran to the answering machine to see if Chris had called. A red zero glowed in the message window. "Dammit," I whispered, hoping Brutus didn't hear. Despite the jab of disappointment, I wasn't really surprised. If Chris wanted to reach me, he would've called my cell. We have each other on speed dial. Or had.

I put the Tupperware container of leftover eggplant parmigiana in my freezer and refilled Brutus's water bowl. Then I thought about calling Nancy, but I wasn't in the mood to hear someone else tell me how unreasonable I was. I already knew that. What I really needed was a way out of the mess I'd gotten myself into.

I took Brutus out and sat down to watch TV, switching channels until I found a rerun of an old *Seinfeld* episode—the one where Kramer accidentally kills Fredo the Parrot. I positioned Brutus with his back to the screen so he wouldn't be offended. When the program ended, I was no closer to fixing my love life, but at least I'd had a good laugh.

I returned Brutus to his cage, hearing a muttered "dammit" when I covered him for the night. Then I sat down at the computer to check my e-mail. Maybe there'd be something from Chris. I scrolled through the messages. Just a bunch of forwarded jokes and some spam, so I deleted everything and logged off. The phone stayed stubbornly silent, no matter how hard I willed it to ring. I couldn't help wondering if Chris was doing the same thing.

By the time I got to school the next morning, some of my regret had turned to annoyance. How dare he not call me to apologize! After all, I wasn't the one who came to his classroom and started pushing him around. I buried my mother's advice under a thick layer of righteous indignation and stomped into the office. Chris had already signed in, so I knew he was around somewhere. Maybe he planned to stop by and apologize in person.

When the homeroom bell rang and Chris still hadn't made an appearance, I revised my expectations. Downward.

As the kids dribbled in, I tried to re-focus on teaching English. Michael walked past my desk and flashed me a quick smile. I was taken aback for a second. Then I returned his smile, my spirits rising.

"All ready for the test today?" I asked him.

He shrugged. "Guess so." He smiled again, and headed back to his seat.

So there. In spite of what Chris believed, I was making some headway with this kid.

After the lunch bell rang, I hurried down to the faculty room. On Mondays, Tuesdays and Thursdays, Chris and I shared a common lunch period, and we had a standing date. I opened the door and looked over at our usual corner table. Empty. My heart plummeted to my shoes as I crossed the room and sat down. I was unpacking a sandwich when Charlie Donner walked in. Suddenly, I thought of a way to get the skinny on Chris.

"Hey, Charlie, have a seat." I pushed out a chair with my foot.

"Thanks," he said, setting down his cafeteria tray. It held a dried-out burger, a handful of ketchup packets, and a mountain of French fries on a Styrofoam plate. "Be right back. Want something from the soda machine?"

"Could you get me a Diet Coke?" I fished around in my purse and handed him a dollar, but he waved it away.

"My treat," he said.

He returned with two cans. He placed the Coke in front of me and set a ginger ale on his tray. Then he looked at it and sighed. "Wish this was a Heineken."

"Rough day in the math department?"

"No rougher than usual. I think I'm just getting too old for this." He patted his balding head. "Used to be covered with hair." Then he tore open a packet with his teeth and squeezed a flat ribbon of ketchup onto the fries.

I popped open my soda. "How's Michael Tayler doing in your class? Any improvement?"

Charlie took a bite of his burger, made a face, and put it back on the tray. "The kid's no math whiz, but at least he doesn't look like a derelict anymore." He picked up a fry and pushed it into his mouth. "He's quite the wacko. One of the reasons I crave beer. Or something stronger."

I laughed. "Yeah, we really lucked out this year. How did you get stuck with the low-level classes? Piss somebody off?"

He shook his head. "No. All the math teachers drew straws, and I got the short one."

Aha! A perfect opening. "That's too bad. Chris seems pretty happy with his classes. By the way, have you seen him today?" I tried to sound casual.

"Uh-huh. He's eating lunch in the math office. I think Terri's with him."

I almost choked on my ham and cheese sandwich. *That skank!* Terri Rexhall was the faculty Paris Hilton. She taught sophomore and junior English on Chris's side of the building and had dated him for a while before I came to Morrison. Since she still ogled Chris like a jackal in heat, I surmised that she wasn't quite ready to give him up. T-Rex and I had a relationship that could best be described as mutually antagonistic. Luckily, we didn't cross paths too often.

Charlie had the look of someone who'd accidentally stepped in something nasty. I took a swig of soda and smiled at him. "Chris must have a lot to do today," I said, trying not to picture him doing those things with T-Rex.

Charlie pounced on that like a quarterback on a fumble. "You're right. He's really tied up. We're working on curriculum revision, and it's due next week. There's a lot of paperwork to wade through. You know how Superintendent Dimmit can be when he doesn't get things on time. Nobody needs that kind of aggravation. I'm sure Chris just wanted to get a jump on it." Having managed to expel the foot from his mouth with a blast of chatter, Charlie stuffed some fries in.

I hope curriculum's the only thing Chris is jumping on at the moment. "Well, when you see him, tell him I missed him at lunch." There. I held out an olive branch. Now to see if Chris would take it.

"Five minute warning."

Several students were still working on their tests. Michael was one of them. He bent low over the desk, his nose almost touching the paper. I walked over to check on him. He was about to start the final item

The silence in the room was suddenly broken by sounds of a touch football game floating through the open window. Michael turned toward the window and stared out. I tapped his desk with a pencil, and he looked up at me. Then I pointed at the clock, and he went back to work. The bell rang just as he put his pen down.

As the students filed out, grumbling about the difficulty of this or that test item, Michael was gathering his things.

"Michael, can I see you before you go?" His first reaction was a look of alarm. I hoped a smile would reassure him. Sure enough, his face relaxed.

"You seemed a little distracted during the test."

He flushed. "I couldn't help it! There was a gym class outside."

"I understand that, and please don't take this as a criticism. I thought it might help if we changed your seat. There'd be a lot less distraction on the other side of the room. I could switch you and Chelsea. Then you'd be right up front in the row by the wall."

Michael was silent for a moment. "I guess that'd be okay."

"So we have a plan. Tomorrow I'll ask Chelsea to trade seats with you. I'm sure she'd be thrilled to sit next to Jessica."

From the look on Michael's face, he'd just discovered a major flaw in the plan. Before he could change his mind, I added, "Maybe this will help you bring up your English grade."

He shrugged. "Yeah, that'd be great." When he was almost out the door, he stopped and looked over his shoulder. "Thanks, Ms. Bianchi."

"You're quite welcome, Mr. Tayler," I replied.

After dismissal, I hung around on the off chance that Chris would show. When I ran out of busywork, I locked up and went down to the office. And just in case I didn't feel crappy enough, there was T-Rex. She was bent over the sign-out sheet, her tight skirt stretched across her butt. Somebody should tell her she can't pull off spandex.

She turned as I walked up to the desk, almost knocking me over with her expensive breasts.

"Oh. Hi there," she said, grinning like a crocodile.

"Hi," I muttered, wanting to slap that smile right into her cleavage.

She handed me the pen. I tried to ignore her as she watched me jot down my initials.

"How're things going?" she asked, still grinning.

"Great," I answered. I clenched my teeth and grinned back at her.

She gave a toss of her over-processed hair. "Same here. Couldn't be better."

If I didn't get away from her soon, they'd be pulling those silicone implants out of her ass.

"Well, that's good to hear." I pushed past her and didn't look back until I was locked in my car, calling her every variation of *tramp* I could think of. When I calmed down enough to get the key into the ignition, I revved the engine and took one last look at the building. Suddenly, the door opened, and out walked Chris. My stomach did a quick flip. This had to be some cosmic sign. I was about to kill the motor when the door swung open again, and T-Rex came scurrying down the walk. She caught up with Chris and latched onto him like a bleached-blonde vampire bat. Before they could see me, I hit the gas and sped out of the parking lot.

On the way home, I stopped at Domino's and picked up an extra-large stuffed crust pizza with mushrooms, olives, and double-cheese. Some women eat ice cream from the carton when they're upset. With me, it's pizza with extra cheese. And beer.

When Brutus saw the box, he started bobbing up and down.

"Cracker. CRACKER."

"Give me a chance to unload this stuff." I unwound my tote from my wrist and dropped the pizza onto the kitchen table. When I lifted the lid from the box, the scent of tomatoes and oregano filled the room, and my stomach gave a low growl. So did Brutus. I opened the refrigerator and grabbed a can of Miller Lite. Then I pulled out a slice of pizza and bit off the point, tugging with my front teeth as a hot string of cheese trailed onto my chin. I gulped some of the cold beer to prevent third degree pizza palate. I had enough problems as it was.

"CRRRRAAAAAACKERRR."

"Okay, okay." I cut off the crust and gave it to Brutus. Pizza crust is one of his favorite treats.

I finished off the first slice and started on my second. "Men suck," I said to Brutus. I chugged the rest of the beer and ripped the top off another. "All they want is some brain-dead bimbo with big boobs who'll flutter her eyelashes and do whatever they say."

Brutus didn't disagree, so I gave him another piece of crust. We stuffed ourselves until we were both practically comatose.

After dinner, I wanted to curl up on the sofa like a big, self-pitying wad of dough. But I needed a diversion to get my mind off Chris. And T-Rex. Fortunately, there were tests to grade, and I was curious to see how Michael had done. I corrected his first, circling the errors with a red pen. Holding my breath, I calculated the score. Seventy-nine. I marked "C+" at the top of his paper, resisting the urge to draw a big smiley face. Instead, I wrote "Good job!" I was as proud as if I'd earned the grade myself. In a way, I felt I had.

When the next day went by without a Chris sighting, I began to suspect that he was dodging me. So I tried to fill the big hole in my life where Chris used to be by throwing myself into work.

Nancy was waiting for me in the faculty room at lunchtime. She'd brought along a box of animal crackers, but she didn't look happy.

"Is something going on between you and Chris?" she asked.

"Nothing good." I filled her in on everything that had happened, including the part about Terri the Slut.

When I finished, she drummed her fingers on the table. "So what do you plan to do? Are you ready to give up on him?"

"If that's what he wants."

"You know perfectly well that's not what he wants. And he doesn't want Terri, either, in spite of what she may think."

I shrugged. "Even if he does, I don't see what I can do about it. He's been avoiding me like the plague."

"And don't you feel even the teensiest bit responsible for that?" she asked.

Ouch! "Well, maybe. But I'm not going to lie down and let Chris walk all over me. And I'm not going to stop working with Michael, especially now that I'm making some progress."

Nancy shook her head. "You and Chris have something special. Don't blow it by being obstinate. Talk to him. I'm sure you can work this out." Then she added, "Before it's too late."

At the beginning of eighth period, I pulled Chelsea aside. "Would you mind trading seats with Michael Tayler?"

Chelsea chewed her lower lip. Then she snickered. "Oh, I get it. You want to move him away from Jessie."

I laughed. "No, it's nothing like that. This isn't meant to be a punishment."

"Jessie might not see it that way." She was trying not to grin.

"Those two really seem to be getting along," I said. "I'm glad Michael's making some friends. It's tough being the new kid in school."

"He's not so bad. Since the fight with Bryan, a lot of kids are mad 'cause he only got suspended for one day. They say it's because he's rich."

"You sit with Michael at lunch. Do you think things are improving for him?"

Chelsea nodded. "Yeah, for sure. He used to have a pretty bad attitude. Now he's a lot nicer." She added, with a smile, "Especially to Jessie."

"Then you don't mind switching seats with him?" I asked.

"Nuh-uh. It'll be fun sitting next to Jessie."

"Not too much fun, I hope."

Michael seemed more focused sitting away from the window, and since he was in the front of the room, I could stand near his desk while I taught. This helped him stay with me, and I was close enough to give him the desk tap if his attention wandered. When I returned his test, he stared at it. Then he turned to Jessica and gave her an air-five.

At the end of the period, they left together, Michael beaming as Jessica examined his paper. I was erasing the board when I heard a soft knock. I looked up, hoping to see Chris.

"Hi, Michael. Forget something?" I tried to mask my disappointment with a smile.

"No, um—it's nothing like that. It's just—well—there's something I wanted to tell you."

"I'm listening."

"It's, uh—it's about the fight. You know—with Bryan—out in the hall—" He hesitated, knotting his hands together.

"But that's all been settled. Mrs. Miller told me you straightened everything out during conflict resolution."

He shook his head. "No—um—you don't understand. It's not about Bryan. It's about you."

Now it was my turn to be tongue-tied.

Michael took a deep breath. "I—want to apologize for what I called you when you broke up the fight. I didn't mean it. I was so—well—mad at Bryan and all. I just mouthed off without thinking." His voice dropped to a whisper. "That happens to me a lot." The tops of his ears were flaming, and my throat tightened with sympathy.

"Michael, I understand, really, and I didn't take it personally. We all say things in anger we're sorry for later." *Speaking from personal experience.* "You've shown a lot of maturity by coming to me and taking responsibility for your actions. I accept your apology."

He looked up at me, his ears returning to a more normal color. "Thanks," he said. "See you tomorrow."

After Michael left, I sat at my desk for a while, thinking about what I'd said to him. Now I knew what I had to do. I clicked the e-mail icon on my computer and typed in Chris's address. Then I typed "SORRY," hit SEND, and said a little prayer.

I had just changed into my nightclothes and was drying my hair with a towel when someone knocked at the door. It was after ten, too late for company. I tiptoed into the darkened living room and pulled the baseball bat out of the closet. Then I switched on the porch light and pressed my eye against the peephole. There was Chris, holding a bouquet of daisies.

I dropped the bat, threw the door open, and held out my arms. He walked into them and buried his lips in my damp hair. "You smell good," he whispered, his breath tickling my ear.

I wrapped my arms around his waist and kicked the door shut. Then I pressed my face against his throat, and he rested his chin on my head. We stayed that way for a moment before walking wordlessly to the sofa. After Chris set the daisies on the coffee table, he sat down and patted his lap. I curled up on it, wound my arms around his neck, and kissed him. I couldn't get enough of his lips. His hands slid under my t-shirt and up my back, pulling me so close to his chest I thought I'd come out the other side. I turned my face away and tried to catch my breath.

"Let's never fight again," he murmured. "Okay?"

"Okay," I said, and meant it.

He stared into my eyes. "What we have is too good to throw away."

I nodded, unable to speak.

"I know I went a little overboard," he said. "But I can't help it. Something about you brings out my caveman side."

I swallowed hard. "And I know I can be a little stubborn." *Okay, more than a little.* "My mother says it's because of the fiery Bianchi gene."

He laughed and squeezed my shoulders. "I guess that's what makes you so irresistibly hot."

We spent almost three hours getting our relationship back on track. I remembered my mother's advice about boundaries and parameters, and Chris and I finally reached a compromise we could live with. He promised to curb his protective impulses, and I promised to try not to overreact. Although we still differed on the subject of Michael, Chris agreed to respect my decision. And I didn't mention T-Rex, figuring it wasn't his fault that she couldn't get over him. If she wanted to keep chasing him, so be it. I'd never let her catch him.

By the time we finally kissed goodnight, the big hole in my life had filled back up.

Chapter Nine

The next morning, Chris and I drove into the school lot at the same time, bleary-eyed but smiling. He parked in his spot and came over to my car. When I opened the door, he extended his hand and pulled me to my feet.

"Sleep well?" he asked.

"Well, but not nearly enough."

"That's what you get for staying up until two on a school night."

"I know," I said, "but I was having so much fun."

"Then we'll have to do it again soon." Chris gave me a look that sent my heart into overdrive.

We held hands as we strolled toward the building, and I secretly hoped T-Rex was watching. Nancy was in the office. She chuckled when Chris and I came in. Then she gave us a once-over.

"This is more like it," she said.

T-Rex was nowhere to be found. Probably asleep in her coffin. Or hanging upside-down in a belfry. Chris walked me to my classroom and waited while I unlocked the door.

"See you at lunch," he said.

"You bet."

He kissed me and headed down the hall. I switched on the lights, went to my desk, and turned on the computer. When I checked my e-mail, I found a reply to the message I'd sent to Chris. It was dated yesterday afternoon, only twenty minutes after mine. I clicked on it and smiled at the words that filled the screen: I'M SORRY TOO.

Anna came into the faculty room while Chris and I were eating lunch. She was looking for me. I waved her over to our table, and she sat down.

"Tayler called. He wants weekly reports on Michael. Didn't say why. Sounds like the lawyer's idea. Probably wants a paper trail."

I sneaked a glance at Chris. He pressed his lips together and pushed his chair away from the table. "Anyone want something from the snack machine?"

"No. Thanks," Anna answered. I shook my head.

After he'd gone, I turned to Anna. "I don't have a problem with a weekly progress report. It might turn out to be a good thing. Michael's doing better in my class."

"Charlie's too. Haven't talked to the others."

"Maybe this will satisfy Mr. Tayler, and he'll ease up."

Anna shrugged. "Who knows? Guy's a fruitcake. Just watch your back."

By the time Chris returned with a bag of Doritos, Anna had gone. He sat down, avoiding my eyes.

"Go ahead," I told him. "I know you want to say something."

Chris clapped the bag between his hands. It opened with a pop like a rifle shot. Heads turned, and the hum of conversation stalled.

When Chris looked at me, his expression was veiled. "I'm going to take the fifth this time. You're a big girl. I have to assume you know what you're doing."

Victory is mine! "I do," I said, stealing a Dorito. "Please don't worry. Everything will be fine."

By the end of the week, I was so encouraged by the success of Project June Bug that I had to share it with someone. Since Chris and I had agreed to disagree on the subject, Nancy was the next logical choice. I decided to invite her to lunch. This would involve food preparation, but I didn't let that deter me. I needed a place where we could talk without being interrupted. With any luck, Brutus would cooperate.

Early Saturday morning, I headed straight for the Shop-Rite. It was already warm. The New Jersey summer was refusing to let go, even though Halloween decorations were appearing in store windows and pumpkins were sprouting on porch steps. I walked up and down the bright supermarket aisles, listening to Beatles-lite and trying to maneuver my cart in spite of its wobbly front wheel. I tossed in a frozen spinach quiche, a jar of diet peach iced tea mix, a plastic bag of baby field greens, a gourmet-sounding raspberry vinaigrette dressing, and a container of Ben & Jerry's Chunky Monkey. On the way to the checkout lane, I grabbed a bunch of cut chrysanthemums for the center of the table. Might as well do the whole Martha Stewart thing.

I was waiting in the endless checkout line when I heard a voice I couldn't quite place.

"Yo, Ms. B. What's happenin'?"

I turned around and immediately connected the voice to the face. "Danica! It's so good to see you. How've you been?"

Danica Brown had been in my third period class last year. A cute little girl with a giant chip on her shoulder, Danica was my very first June Bug. Although she was bright and had a lot of potential, she hid it under a thick crust of attitude. By the middle of the year, I'd managed to chip enough away to expose the innately talented writer that lived inside. We spent many after-school detentions talking about her life and her future, and by the end of the year, she made the honor roll. But it was a tooth and nail battle all the way. Danica made my first year of teaching an adventure, to put it mildly.

She gave me a toothy smile that was dazzlingly white against her dark skin. Things're good, real good." She turned to the heavyset, gray-haired woman standing beside her, holding a gallon of milk and a carton of eggs.

"Grandmom, this here's Ms. Bianchi. She was my English teacher last year. You remember—the one I tol' you 'bout."

The woman gave a slight nod, passed the eggs to Danica, and extended her hand. "I'm pleased t'meet you," she said. She had a smooth, mellow voice, like maple syrup.

I took her hand and shook it. Her grip was firm, but her knuckles were rough and calloused. "You have a fine granddaughter," I said. "I'm expecting big things from her."

Grandmom's face broke into a carbon copy of Danica's smile. "Thank you kindly. Danny's a good girl, but she sure can be headstrong at times." She chuckled and tugged on Danica's earlobe.

Danica rolled her eyes. "Now c'mon. You know I been bein' good."

"How're your classes this year?" I asked. "I never see you, now that you're over on the other side of the building."

"Everything's cool. Got Miss Rexhall for English. She's not near as good as you."

Hee-hee-hee. "Well, I hope you're not giving her a hard time." The enormity of that fib almost made me gag. "You're much too smart to let your behavior get in the way of your education. I want to see your name on the honor roll again this quarter."

"I know, Ms. B. I'm rememberin' all the stuff you tol' me last year. I need to do good on the SATs. I wanna apply to Montclair. See if I can get a scholarship."

Grandmom was beaming. "She'll be our first college girl. She's gonna make us proud."

I made a mental note to ask Nancy for scholarship information. "If there's anything I can do to help, be sure to come see me. I can write you a letter of recommendation or help you with your application."

Danica took that in. "Y'know, it'd be great if you could look over the essay I gotta write. I'm tryin' to write it like you taught me, but I'd 'preciate it if you could check it out."

"I'd be happy to. I'm sure it'll be great. Like I told you last year, you've got the makings of a good writer."

She grinned at her grandmother. "See. I tol' you I could write a book some-day." Then she turned back to me. "I was thinkin' of maybe bein' a teacher. Like you."

I wondered if my head was visibly swelling. "You'd make a terrific teacher. All you have to do is stay focused. You've got the brains to do anything you set your mind to."

By then, I'd reached the cashier. I was placing my groceries on the moving belt when Danica tapped my shoulder.

I turned and looked into her large, solemn eyes.

"Y'know, Ms. B, I been wantin' to tell you that I feel real bad about bein' such a pain last year. In the beginnin', anyway. You're the best teacher I ever had. No lie."

Grandmom was nodding, her face a picture of quiet dignity. "You sure made a big impression on this child," she said. "I thank you."

The only thing that kept me from skipping back to the car was the heavy grocery bag I carried. It's amazing what a little stroking can do to a teacher's ego. Now I was even more firmly resolved to move ahead with Project June Bug. Who could tell? By this time next year, Bennett Tayler might be the one singing my praises.

I felt all housewifely as I eased the quiche into the oven. Thirty minutes at three hundred twenty-five degrees—even I could manage that. While the quiche baked, I wiped the crumbs from the kitchen table and arranged the chrysanthe-mums in a tall porcelain vase that held Chris's daisies. I covered the table with a woven yellow tablecloth that belonged to Nana and set the vase in the center.

I was admiring my handiwork when Brutus started to shriek. He was staring out the window with a murderous look in his eyes. Yin-Yang was sunbathing in the middle of my front lawn. I rapped on the window, but she didn't even lift her head.

I turned from the window and surveyed the living room. It needed some serious work. I took a bottle of Windex and a paper towel from the pantry and scrubbed the smears and dried gunk off the coffee table, wondering what mental aberration made me buy one with a glass top. Then I swept up the parrot food and stray feathers around the birdcage.

"You are one messy bird," I told Brutus. "My next pet will be something low-maintenance, like a goldfish."

He eyed me with open contempt. "Good Brutus," he growled.

"We'll see about that. You have to behave when Aunt Nancy comes. No screeching, okay?"

Brutus's gaze was inscrutable. Maybe he was doing some serious thinking about the goldfish.

I was stirring the pitcher of iced tea when Nancy arrived, holding a round cake with animal crackers pressed into the chocolate frosting. One of the great ironies of my life is that I'm surrounded by fantastic cooks.

"Dessert," she announced.

"Why wait till dessert?" I asked. "This would make a great lunch."

Nancy went into the kitchen and placed the cake on the counter. Then she headed for Brutus's cage

"How's my big boy?" she asked, in an exaggerated, high-pitched voice.

Brutus danced back and forth. "Hi! Hi! Hellooooo," he crowed. Nancy is definitely one of his favorite humans. He poked his beak between the bars, waiting for a pat.

Nancy pulled a small plastic bag of animal crackers from her pocket and held one out to him. "Look what Aunt Nancy brought for you."

"GOOD. Good cracker." Brutus took the cracker in his beak and crunched it with enthusiasm.

"What a good, good bird. Here, have another."

"You're going to spoil him," I said.

"Too late. Seems you've already done that." She turned toward the kitchen and sniffed. "Is something burning?"

"Omigod! The quiche." I ran to the oven and opened the door. A wisp of smoke floated out.

"Dammit," I said.

"Dammit," Brutus echoed.

Nancy laughed. "You've been a bad influence on that bird. Your grandmother's ears must be burning."

"No, that's our lunch."

The quiche's crust was the color of burnt toast. I was engaged in a frantic search for my pot holder. It was nowhere to be found, so I pulled my shirtsleeves over my hands and removed the smoking quiche. I dropped it onto the table a second before my sleeves scorched.

Nancy shook her head. "It's a good thing Chris can cook. You'd better snag that guy before he gets a chance to see you in the kitchen. You're not exactly a domestic goddess."

I plunged my hands into the dishwater. "The only domestic thing you can say about me is I live in a house."

Nancy poked at the quiche. "I think we can salvage this if we cut off the crust. The filling looks fine."

While Nancy performed the crustectomy, I mixed the salad and set the table. I doubted even I could mess that up.

"So," she said, as we sat down to eat, "what's the big secret? It must be a matter of great importance if you felt the need to cook."

"It is. It's about Michael Tayler."

"Why am I not surprised? Then I take it you aren't going to give this up."

"Just the opposite. I've been doing a lot of reading about ADHD, and I've found some ways to help him."

"Is Chris okay with this? He was pretty worried about you tangling with Michael's father."

"He's not thrilled. But he knows how important this is to me, so we've declared a truce."

I told her about the strategies I'd been using and how Michael had responded. "He's averaging a high C in English, and his class work has really improved. He still makes some careless mistakes and has problems with homework, but his attentiveness is better. And the best thing is the change in his attitude. He's made some friends, and he even apologized for calling me a bitch."

"No offense, but I have known you to be a bit bitchy at times." Nancy took a forkful of quiche. "You know, this isn't bad. It has a nice, smoky flavor."

I ignored that. "So what's your opinion of Project June Bug?"

Nancy paused, savoring the quiche. "You seem to be doing some good things, judging by Michael's improvement." Then she pointed her fork at me. "But be careful about assuming he has ADHD. Remember—you're not a doctor."

"I don't have to be a doctor to know when a kid needs help."

"I'm not saying that. Just don't be so quick to conclude that ADHD is the cause of all Michael's problems. And I know this is a touchy subject, but his father seems to have a few screws loose, and he's not too fond of you."

"I don't give a rat's ass what Bennett Tayler thinks of me. It's pathetic, the way he tries to push his weight around. The man is pompous, arrogant, and pretentious—and those are his good qualities."

"My, my, my," Nancy replied. "And I was just saying you could be bitchy. What was I thinking?"

Okay, guilty as charged. "Well, call me a bitch, but I won't ignore a kid who's in trouble to avoid being hassled by a pushy parent."

"Your dedication is admirable. Just be a little cautious. To tell the truth, I'm pretty impressed with what you've done." Nancy forked the last bit of quiche into her mouth. "It might be a good idea to share your strategies with Michael's other teachers. From what I hear, they're still having problems with him. I'll see if I can arrange a meeting one day next week."

We were interrupted by a plaintive voice.

"Good Brutus. Good, GOOD bird."

Nancy grinned. "I hear you, buddy. It's time for dessert." She took the bag of animal crackers into the living room.

"Dessert sounds good to me, too," I said. "I'll clear the table while you feed that bottomless pit of a parrot."

"Don't insult my pal Brutus. Didn't you hear him? He's a good, GOOD bird." Nancy's imitation was perfect.

After giving Brutus his dessert, Nancy cut two thick slabs of cake and topped each with a hefty scoop of Chunky Monkey. I finished every bite, but I washed it down with diet iced tea. After all, I have to watch my calories.

Chapter Ten

With the teacher's meeting scheduled for Wednesday, I thought it would be a good idea to try out some new strategies. The first opportunity came sooner than I expected.

When Michael came to class on Monday, he couldn't find his homework. He rummaged through his binder, pulling out handfuls of God-knows-what.

"I know it's in here somewhere. I finished it last night right before I went to bed." A few crumpled papers tumbled to the floor.

It didn't take a degree in quantum physics to figure out what was causing the problem. The binder was an organizational nightmare. Papers were randomly stuffed inside, and the binder was so overfilled, it couldn't be zipped shut. I visualized Michael's homework falling out and being eaten by a dog. Time to implement Strategy #7: *Give Michael some help getting organized.* Here was a problem I could relate to.

While I got the rest of the class started on a writing assignment, Michael continued a futile search for his homework. He didn't see me walk over.

"Your binder reminds me of my desk at home."

His head jerked up. A broken pen, poised on the edge of his desk, plunked onto the floor.

"I'm famous for not being able to find things," I told him. "I keep swearing that I'll get organized, but I never get around to it."

"Yeah," he said. "You should see my room. My mom's afraid to go in there." He picked up the pen and placed it on top of the heap of papers covering his desk. It rolled off and landed back on the floor.

"I can't help you with your room, but we can do something about this binder." I pulled the trash can over to his desk and handed him five folders, each a different color. "Label a folder for each of your subjects. Then go through your papers one at a time. Put the papers you need in the folders, and throw away anything you don't want. Like this." I held up a tattered lunch menu from the first week of school.

He looked at the other students. "But what about my class work?"

"I think the binder is more important right now. We don't want any more of your work disappearing into that black hole."

By the end of the period, the binder was empty, the trash can was full, and Michael had five folders of neatly-stacked papers. He waved a wrinkled sheet at me. "Here's my homework."

I took the paper and gave him a large metal clip. "You can use this to clip all your homework papers inside the front cover of your binder. Then you won't have to go searching for them every period."

"That's a pretty good idea. I can never find my homework when I need it. This'll make it a lot easier."

"Now the real challenge will be keeping the binder organized. Think you can manage?"

"I'll do my best." He transferred the folders to the proper sections of his binder and zipped it shut as the dismissal bell rang. "Hey," he said, as he turned to leave, "it's too bad you don't make house calls."

I was locking up when Chris stopped by. "Hi, stranger," he said. "Where've you been hiding?"

"I've been working on my top secret project. Have you missed me?"

"Every moment we spend apart is sheer torture. Can you tear yourself away long enough to have dinner with me?"

"Depends on what you have in mind. Big Macs and fries?"

"I'm feeling more Italian tonight. You have that effect on me." He winked, and a little shiver squirmed up my spine. "How'd you like to go to Bacio? The special is seafood risotto."

Seafood risotto at Bacio? Kiss my diet good-bye. "You've made me an offer I can't refuse. When do we go?"

"We have a reservation for six o'clock."

"You made the reservation already? Pretty sure of yourself, aren't you?"

"Not as sure as I am of you. The odds of Jen Bianchi passing up seafood risotto are slim to none."

I poked him in the ribs. "Mr. Holloway, you know me so well, it's scary."

Bacio is one of my favorite restaurants. It's not fancy, but the atmosphere is intimate and the food is to die for. We sat at a cozy table lit by a single, flickering votive candle. The air was heavy with the scent of herbs and simmering sauces. Chris ordered a bottle of Chardonnay. I reached for the warm foccacia the waiter brought, but Chris intercepted my hand.

"Aren't you afraid that'll spoil your appetite?"

I pulled my hand away, enjoying the pleasant warmth his fingers left behind. "Have you ever known me to have a spoiled appetite?"

"Now that you mention it, no." He pushed the bread basket toward me. "Here. Now tell me what you've been up to."

"Bribing me with foccacia? You're not playing fair. I guess I'll have to divulge the details of Project June Bug."

Chris frowned when he heard the name. "The Michael Tayler thing?"

I was certain I could change Chris's mind about "the Michael Tayler thing" if I could show him how well it was working. I described the strategies I'd been using and how Michael had responded. When I got to the part about the binder, Chris almost choked on his wine.

"What's so funny?" I asked.

"Oh, come on. Don't you find it kind of ironic? You, of all people, giving pointers on being organized? It's like a frog giving singing lessons."

"I'll admit it's a little out of character. But you have to admit my ideas are good ones."

Chris let that slide. "Now if we could only get you to take your own advice. Ah, here's the risotto."

The waiter set down two heaping platters. Inhaling the steam was enough to cause a five-pound weight gain, but after the first forkful, I forgot about carbs and fat grams.

"You know," Chris said, as he swirled his wine, tilting the glass to the light, "you should give Michael a daily planner like mine. It has a *Things to Do* page and a calendar. In fact, I may have an extra one lying around somewhere. I'll bring it in tomorrow."

As far as I was concerned, this was the equivalent of a papal blessing. I wanted to throw my arms around Chris's neck and liplock him right there in the restaurant. "Thanks, Mr. Wonderful," I said. "I should have known you'd be the person to talk to about getting organized."

"Only one of my many talents." He caressed my knee under the table, and I took a big gulp of wine.

The next morning, Chris brought the planner to my classroom. "Now you owe me," he said.

"Sure. I'll make you dinner sometime."

"On second thought, never mind. Consider it a gift."

I ran my hand up his arm and caressed the back of his neck. Then I gave him a quick kiss. "This means a lot to me. Especially considering your feelings on the subject. I appreciate you doing this for Michael."

"Not for him. For you. And my feelings on the subject haven't changed."

Not yet, anyway. "Well, I still think you're pretty great." I kissed him again, and he kissed me back.

I couldn't wait to give Michael the planner. I caught up with him on the way to the cafeteria.

"How's the binder holding up?"

"Pretty good so far. And the clip works great. I found all my homework today."

"That's terrific. If you're interested, I have another suggestion."

I showed him the planner and explained how it worked. "You can slip this right into your binder, and since it's big, it'll be easy to find. If you remember to write everything down and cross things off as you finish them, it'll be easier to keep on top of all your assignments."

"Hey, thanks a lot." He tucked the planner under his arm and joined Jessica and Chelsea at their table.

When I assigned homework to the eighth period class, Michael took out the planner and copied the assignment on the *Things to Do* list. I gave myself a mental high five.

As I watched my colleagues file into Nancy's office on Wednesday, I wondered how they'd react to taking suggestions from a second-year teacher. I'd brought my list of strategies, many marked with red plus signs. When everyone was seated, Nancy passed around the animal crackers.

"As I told you all on Monday," she began, "I thought we should meet to discuss Michael Tayler. He is, to put it kindly, one of our more challenging students."

"He's challenging all right," interrupted Jack Bateman, the science teacher. "He's challenging my sanity. What's that damn kid doing in a regular ed classroom? Don't we have special classes for problem students like him?"

Here we go. I knew Jack would be the hardest to convince. He was a staunchly traditional teacher who resisted anything new. Although he knew a lot about science, he showed little personal interest in his students. I often heard kids complaining that they couldn't ask questions in his class for fear of being ridiculed.

Charlie Donner spoke up. "I agree that Michael can be a real pain in the butt, but every so often he shows flashes of intelligence. Sometimes, I wonder what he's doing in the low level math class."

"I know what you mean," Helen Rafferty said. "During our current events discussions, he's made some comments that show a good deal of insight. I just wish he could learn not to interrupt every time an idea strikes him."

"In Spanish, his biggest problem is being able to sit still and listen," Marita Lopez added.

"And he makes a lot of careless mistakes," Charlie said, "like skipping a test item or not going back to check his work when he's finished. And he can never seem to find things." Charlie's eyes cut to me. "Jen, do you think he learned that in your class?" The man had an innate talent for comic relief.

I made a face at him, and he grinned. "Seriously," he said, "Michael seems to understand the material. He could do a lot better in math if he'd get his act together."

Jack gave a loud grunt. "Just be thankful you don't have him in a science lab. He refuses to follow directions. Struts around like the rules don't apply to him. Must've learned that from his rich old man. I'm waiting for him to screw up an experiment and blow us all to hell and back."

Maybe you should just blow it out your—

"So what I'm hearing," Nancy said, "is that we have a kid who's performing below his ability because of problems like disorganization, lack of focus, impulsiveness, and distractibility. Sound to anybody like an undiagnosed case of Attention Deficit Hyperactivity Disorder?"

"That crossed my mind," Helen said. "But how could Michael have gotten to tenth grade without anyone noticing? Most of my ADHD students were diagnosed in elementary school."

"According to his records, he hasn't stayed in one school long enough to be evaluated," Nancy told her.

Jack snorted. "Attention Deficit Disorder. Another excuse for a kid to act like an ass and get away with it. I'm sick to death of all this psycho-babble. What that boy needs is a good, swift kick in the pants. I bet that'd get his attention."

A good, swift kick wouldn't do you any harm either. I opened my mouth, but Charlie spoke up before I had a chance to rip into Jack.

"I don't know, Jack. It makes some sense to me. Michael fits the profile so well that I have a hard time believing it's pure coincidence."

"And ADHD would explain so many puzzling aspects of his behavior," Marita said.

Nancy looked over at me. "I think it's time we heard from Jenna. She's been trying some things you might find interesting."

I took a deep breath. "I know how you all feel about Michael. No one was more upset with him than I was. On the first day of school, I even begged Anna to get him out of my class."

"So you got to her before I did?" Charlie asked. "Where's your respect for seniority?"

I told them about the research I'd done and the success of the strategies I'd been trying. Although Charlie, Marita, and Helen seemed receptive, Jack's body language indicated that he was having none of it. He sat with his legs crossed and arms folded, his eyes fixed on the ceiling. When I finished, he looked down his nose at me.

"Jenna, with all due respect to your youthful idealism, this kid doesn't need mothering. He needs someone to make him straighten up and fly right."

And that would be—ah—who? "Really, Jack? How do you propose we do that?" I tried to keep from sounding too sarcastic.

Helen squirmed in her seat. "I honestly don't see what harm could come from trying the things Jenna suggested. I, for one, would welcome anything that would make it easier to deal with Michael."

"And a lot of Jenna's strategies are just good, sound teaching practices," Marita added.

Jack looked at his watch. "I've got to go. I'm officiating a football game today." He stood and pushed in his chair. "And you four can baby this kid all you want, but in my class, he'll be treated like everybody else—disordered or not." He marched out of the office without bothering to shut the door.

Nancy thanked everyone for coming. Charlie told me how impressed he was with my ideas, and he, Marita, and Helen agreed to give them a try.

When the two of us were alone, Nancy turned and handed me an animal cracker.

"Well, kid," she said, "three out of four ain't bad."

Chapter Eleven

When I got home, there was a message on my answering machine from Marian Molino, my college roommate. She was in Philadelphia for a three-day conference and wanted to get together for drinks and dinner at The Waterworks. I knew this would be pricey, but considering all I'd been through, I figured I deserved an upscale girls night out. After confirming that there was a positive balance in my checkbook, I called Marian back and agreed to meet her at seven. Then I searched my closet for something dressy. I settled on the black silk, scoop-necked sheath I'd bought for my cousin's wedding, and my pride and joy—a pair of strappy black Dolce & Gabbana slingbacks. In a moment of unbridled excess, I blew my first real paycheck on these, and I saved them for special occasions. They hurt like hell, but they always made me feel affluent. I slipped a sterling bangle onto my wrist, fastened silver studs onto my ears, and latched a chain of oval silver links around my neck. No way was I meeting Marian looking like a schoolmarm.

Marian and I met during our sophomore year at Temple. She was a pharmacy major, so we weren't in the same classes. But we were both Italian girls from New Jersey with a common passion for Seinfeld reruns, cheesesteaks, Bruce Springsteen, and Miller Lite. As a result, we became good friends and shared a room in an off-campus house until graduation. Then Marian got a job as a drug rep for Merck and moved to Newark, and I went home to Morrisonville to look for a teaching position. I last saw Marian in June when I stopped by her apartment on my way to pick up my brother at NYU. By then, her salary had topped eighty thousand a year. Mine just hit forty-one. But whenever we got together, we were nothing more than two good-time Jersey girls.

When I turned into the lot at The Waterworks, I decided against valet parking. My Neon would look out of place lined up with all the Beemers, Mercedes, and Lexuses at the entrance. I smoothed my dress and checked my make-up in the rear-view, rubbing a lipstick smudge off my front tooth. Then I tottered toward the huge glass doors, hoping everyone would be too busy admiring my shoes to notice the pained expression on my face. The maître d' directed me to the bar. Fashionable patrons chatted over drinks at small, round tables overlooking the Schuylkill River. Lights from the expressway cast silvery ripples on the water, and the tiny white lights along Boathouse Row gave the night an ethereal quality.

Marian was sitting in one of the high-backed barstools, sipping a martini and watching the fish in the enormous saltwater aquarium behind the bar. She looked every inch the yuppie in her slinky beige halter dress. When she tossed her head, her sleek black hair skimmed her shoulders and fell back into place like a dark curtain. Her eyes sparkled. None of this was going unnoticed by the bartender, a dead ringer for Brad Pitt. He stood across from her, polishing the same glass over and over.

I stood on tiptoe and waved. Marian saw me and broke into a blinding smile.

"Jenna, I've really missed you. You look great." She gave me a big, Chanel-scented hug.

"Look who's talking. Little Miss Executive. Love the hair."

"Thanks." She patted her head. "A girl must keep up appearances when she's pushing drugs. What're you drinking?"

I ordered a chocolate martini, and she laughed. "We still think alike." She held up her empty glass. "Just finished one. So how's the family? Anthony still up at NYU?"

"Everybody's fine. Dad's still accounting, and Mom's still the kitchen queen. Anthony has another year to go. And I still live with Brutus."

"I can't believe you haven't lost a finger to that parrot," she said. "He's crazed. I'd be afraid to get near him."

"It just takes him a while to warm up to people. Actually, he's pretty good company. His vocabulary's limited, so he can't talk back much. Although I'm finding I have to put a lid on the swearing when he's within earshot."

Brad Pitt set my martini down. Marian tapped her glass, and he went running for a refill.

When he returned, I held up my drink.

"To the Jersey Girls."

Marian clinked her glass against mine. "If we were down the shore at Maloney's, I'd climb up on the bar and start singing. *Sha-la-la-la-la-la-la-la.* Springsteen rules. To The Boss."

I took a sip, and it slid down my throat like liquid satin. "Yeah," I said, "those were some good times. We sure have come a long way."

Marian giggled. "Remember when we got so shitfaced we had to call my brother to take us home? God, was he pissed!"

"Speaking of Joey," I said, "what's new and exciting at the Molino house?"

"Joey's still working for the city. He and his wife are expecting again. My sister just got accepted into Rutgers. It was her first choice, and she's thrilled. And my parents just celebrated their thirtieth. Married thirty years—can you imagine?"

She shook her head. "I'd be happy to find a guy who didn't drive me crazy after a month. And speaking of guys—still dating that hot blonde?"

Before I could answer, the maître d' announced that our table was ready. We followed him into the dining room and were escorted to a table by the window. A waiter materialized almost immediately. He filled our water glasses and recited the evening's specials, all of which made me salivate.

Over dinner, Marian and I swapped stories about our love lives and our jobs. I'd ordered a butter-poached striped bass with vanilla bean risotto, and if I hadn't been in such a trendy restaurant, I might have licked the plate. While we shared a chocolate lava cake that should have been illegal, I told Marian about the work I was doing with Michael.

"You're not going to believe this," she said, "but Joey's kid was just diagnosed with ADHD. You remember him—little Nicky, the one who always acted like he had snakes in his shorts? We babysat for him once."

"How could I forget? He trashed your bedroom."

Marian sniggered. "Yeah. Never did find my leopard-print thong. I worried for a long time that he'd turn out to be a perv. Anyway, Nicky's in first grade now, and his teacher told Joey to have him checked for ADHD. Sure enough, the little bugger's loaded with it."

"So what did they do?" I asked.

She spooned the last bit of dessert into her mouth and licked her lips. "The doctor wrote him a script for a new medication. Comes in an extended release patch. Just stick it on his little butt once a day and he's good to go. A lot easier than trying to cram pills down the throat of a wriggly kid."

"I thought they used Ritalin for ADHD."

"Still do. But they keep coming out with new treatment options all the time. There's a huge market out there. You can't believe how many kids are diagnosed every year. Adults, too. In fact, I have my suspicions about Joey. You know how squirrely he is." She laughed. "My mom always swore that someday Joey'd have a kid just like him. Turned out, she was right. Anyway, there's a lot of research being done."

I pushed my chocolate-smeared plate away, calculating the number of sit-ups it would take to work off the half-dessert. "Well, I guess Project June Bug could qualify as research. Michael seems to be improving without the meds."

After we paid the bill, we walked out to the parking lot and said our goodbyes. Marian promised to send me some information on the latest ADHD studies and new medications.

"Let me know how your project plays out," she said. "I think what you're doing is terrific—even if it cuts into my drug sales."

After spending the evening with Marian, I felt in need of some serious body maintenance. Jogging would have been smart, but I opted for a manicure. It would feel nice to be pampered for a while, and my cuticles were looking pretty ratty. On the way home from school, I pulled into a strip mall and scored a spot right in front of the nail salon.

A soft chime rang as I opened the salon door. The air was scented with vanilla and lavender from an aromatherapy candle that burned on the front desk. The girl behind the desk took my name and led me to a free station. As I settled into the upholstered chair, listening to the soothing sounds of soft rock that floated down from the wall speakers, I could feel myself slipping into relaxation mode. I scanned the rack that held bottles of nail polish in every imaginable color. Who, in their right mind, would want iridescent green fingernails?

Before long, the manicurist appeared and took her place across from me. She was a pretty Asian girl, with onyx eyes and straight, ebony hair that curled just below her chin. She greeted me with a smile and pushed a small glass bowl of soapy liquid toward me. I dunked my right hand into the bowl, soaking my fingers as the girl readied her files and buffers.

"What kind manicure?" she asked.

"French. And could you please use OPI polish?"

The girl nodded and smiled again. She lifted my fingers out of the bowl and dried them with a soft white towel. Then she massaged my hand, kneading my palm and working her way down each of my fingers. When she squeezed the pressure point at the base of my thumb, all the tension drained out through my fingertips.

She was filing my chipped thumbnail when an attractive woman with long, ash-blonde hair and sunglasses sat down at the station next to mine. As she turned to look at me, we connected in a moment of mutual recognition.

"Dianna? I can't believe it!"

Dianna's family lived down the block from my parents. We played together as kids and were in a lot of the same high school classes. We kind of lost track during college, but reconnected after graduation when we discovered we'd both gone into teaching. Dianna had taken a job at St. Paul's, a parochial school in Hartfield, and moved into an apartment on the other side of town. We ran into each other every so often when we were both visiting our parents.

"Jenna, it's been forever. It's so good to see you." She took off her sunglasses and put them in her purse.

"Same here. How've you been?"

"Great." Her amber eyes sparkled. "In fact, I'm here to get my nails done because of this." She held up her left hand and wiggled her ring finger. A beautiful, princess-cut solitaire winked from a narrow platinum band.

"Omigod! You and Allen finally got engaged." I reached across with my free hand and examined the ring. "It's gorgeous. Congratulations."

"Thanks. It sure was a long time coming."

Dianna had been dating Allen McCartney since their senior year in high school. They were voted "Cutest Couple" in the yearbook, and everyone assumed they'd marry someday.

"So when's the big day?" I asked.

"We have to wait till June when school's out. Allen just landed a great job with NFL Films, so we can finally afford a wedding." She did an exaggerated eye-roll. "God knows, we'd never be able to swing it on my salary."

"So you're still at Saint Paul's?"

"Yep. Seventh grade science. In fact, I heard that one of my ex-students is going to Morrison now. A kid named Michael Tayler."

I almost yanked my hand away from the manicurist. She tightened her grip and continued brushing on base coat.

"You're not going to believe this, but he's in my homeroom and my English class."

Dianna looked toward heaven. "God help you. I only had him one period a day, and that was one too many." She looked back at me. "We were all lighting candles and praying that he'd leave. The church must've collected a fortune from the offering box during the two years we had Michael. There was dancing in the halls when he finally transferred to Elgin." Her eyes narrowed. "Have you met his father yet?"

I shuddered. "Unfortunately, yes. Quite the wack-job."

Dianna didn't smile. "You'd better watch out. He's a real shark. I heard a rumor that he bought his kid's way into Saint Paul's with a hefty donation to the playground fund. Guess he thought a few swings and jungle gyms gave him the right to push us around. Almost gave Michael's social studies teacher a nervous breakdown. The poor woman retired at the end of the year." Dianna shook her head. "That man even managed to intimidate Sister Margaret Mary."

"Attila the Nun? You've got to be kidding." Sister Margaret Mary was a local legend. She had the reputation of being God's answer to Saddam Hussein.

Dianna hitched forward in her chair. "About a week after Michael came to Saint Paul's, he started mouthing off to his teachers. We kept sending him down to the office. Sister tried to talk to him, but he mouthed off to her, too. And nobody mouths off to Sister Margaret Mary."

"So I've heard."

"Anyway," Dianna continued, "Sister decided to suspend him for insubordination. So Mr. Tayler brought some lawyer to school—Hawthorne, I think his name was—and threatened to go to the diocese. It was the first time I saw Sister get really shook up. She's usually the shaker, not the shakee."

"And did she back down?" I asked.

"Folded like a beach chair under a sumo wrestler. It was a historic first at Saint Paul's."

"Then why did Tayler take Michael out?"

"I think it had to do with his grades. By the end of eighth grade, the kid was flunking practically everything, and it looked like he'd have to be retained. Tayler wanted him to go to high school, so he bought him a place at Elgin."

I thought for a moment. "What about Michael's mother? Ever meet her?"

Dianna nodded. "She showed up at Back to School Night and a few parent-teacher conferences. Never said much. She seemed like an okay lady, but her husband's definitely the lord and master in that relationship."

This conversation was making me decidedly uncomfortable. I squirmed a little. All my tension had returned, and not just to my hands. At this rate, I'd need a full-body massage.

"My advice to you," Dianna continued, "is to stay away from Mr. Tayler. Whatever he wants, give it to him. He'll wind up getting it anyway, so you might as well save yourself the aggravation."

"You dry now." The manicurist pointed to the nail dryer at a table across the room.

I looked down at my hands. My nails were finished, the white tips curving in slim, flawless crescents across the transparent pink polish. I spread my fingers and stood up, holding my hands out in front of me.

"Well, it was great seeing you," I told Dianna. "Tell Allen I said congratulations. And thanks for the info."

"No problem. We'll have to get together for a few drinks. Toast my entry into the ranks of Bridezillas."

As I rested my fingers under the dryer's ultraviolet light, listening to the whir of its fan, I mulled over my conversation with Dianna. I knew she was a good teacher, and I respected her opinion. But a kid can change a lot in three years, and that middle school period is rough under the best circumstances. Maybe Michael was just rebelling against the strict structure of Catholic school. I could understand a kid like him having problems in that environment. And now that most of his teachers would be using my strategies, Michael should start doing better. Then his father wouldn't have any reason to give me grief. My mental spin machine revved into high gear, trying to rationalize away every doubt that had wormed itself into my brain.

When the buzzer signaled that my nails were dry, I tipped the manicurist and paid the girl at the front desk. She opened the door for me and waved as I walked out to my car. I was so preoccupied with thoughts of Michael that I creased a nail opening the car door.

Dammit!

Chapter Twelve

With the strategies in place in four of Michael's five major subjects, I hoped to see some improvement in his grades. Sure enough, as the days stretched into weeks, Michael's averages inched upward. By the time interim reports were issued, he was averaging a C minus in social studies, Cs in math and Spanish, and a B minus in my class. He was even passing science. His behavior had improved as well, and he'd even made a few guy friends. Damien Roberts and Paul Sysak had joined his table at lunch, and I often saw the three of them walking together in the halls.

The first hint of a problem came the week before Halloween. The kids were buzzing about the Halloween dance, the first big social event of the year. I'd signed up to oversee the decorating. Jessica was on the decorating committee, and she talked Michael into volunteering. I wondered if Michael was going to ask her to the dance. He seemed more distracted than usual, so I figured he might be trying to work up the nerve. I cornered him after the newspaper meeting.

"Michael, you did a great job on the interview with Tom. I especially liked the part of the article where you appealed for funding for new lockers."

"Thanks. Hope it'll do some good."

"Never underestimate the power of the pen." *Now on to more pressing matters.* "By the way, you seemed to be daydreaming during class today. Prepositions may not be the most exciting things in the world, but we're having a test on them next week. I'd hate to see you ruin your average."

Michael's foot started jiggling. "Guess I had some other stuff on my mind."

"Anything I can help you with?"

"No. I've gotta work it out on my own."

"Okay, but don't forget to put in some extra study time on those prepositions."

He nodded and went out to the bus.

The next day, Charlie flagged me down in the hall and gave me some troubling news. There seemed to be something brewing between Michael and two other boys in the low level math class—Jason Hawkins and Hank Spears. Charlie happened to be in the gym, shooting the breeze with the health teacher, when he overheard the three boys arguing. Although Charlie didn't catch what it was all about, he heard Jason mention Jessica's name. He said that Michael got pretty hyper. When Charlie asked the boys what was going on, Jason laughed and said they were only ragging Michael about his girlfriend. Michael didn't say a word, but Charlie could tell from the look on his face that this wasn't just good-natured male ribbing.

I thanked Charlie for the heads-up and asked him to keep an eye on them. Jason and Hank were tough customers. Jason, a muscular, good-looking boy, was always in trouble. He was one of the regulars on the "call down" list of kids who had to meet with Don Clayton for disciplinary problems. Hank Spears, a Jason wannabee, followed Jason around like a loyal pet hippo. Both boys were on the varsity football team, and, judging from their academic performance, had taken too many hits to the head. But what they lacked in brains, they made up for in brute strength, so they generally went unchallenged by the other kids. There are a lot of similarities between the behavior of high school students and pack animals in the wild.

Knowing how volatile Michael could be, I was worried that he'd do something stupid, like getting involved in a two-on-one with Jason and Hank. Aside from the fact that he could sustain some serious physical damage, it would be a shame for him to get in trouble now that things were going so well. The situation would require careful monitoring. In circumstances like this, I could appreciate the logic of having in-school surveillance cameras.

Two days later, I passed Jessica on my way into the cafeteria. Jason was talking to her, one arm on the doorjamb right above her head. He leaned in close as she tried to inch away. Jessica's lips were stretched in a false smile that was almost a grimace. When she saw me, she gave a desperate wave that I took for a distress signal.

I stopped just inside the cafeteria door. "Jessica, could I see you for a minute? I need to ask you about the dance decorations."

"Sure thing, Ms. B." Her whole body relaxed. "Talk to you later, Jason."

When Jason had gone, Jessica turned to me. "Ms. B., you saved my life."

"I don't know about that, but it looked like you were caught in an awkward situation. Want to tell me about it?"

"Jason's been dogging me to go with him to the Halloween dance. I hate to hurt his feelings, but he's really not my type." She blushed. "And there's somebody else I'd rather go with."

A long, tall redhead, maybe? "I think I understand. This 'somebody else'—has he asked you yet?"

"No, but I think he's going to." She looked across the room to the table where Michael was sitting. He waved at her. She smiled and waved back. "And even if he doesn't, I'd rather go with my friends than with Jason. But I don't know how to say no without making him mad."

"It's a sticky situation. But the longer you wait, the more annoyed he'll be when you finally tell him. Want some advice?"

She looked at me and nodded.

"Thank Jason for asking, and say you've already made other plans you can't change. Don't be more specific than that. This way, he can get away with his ego intact." *Although with Jason's ego, it'd be hard to do any serious damage.*

"That's a great idea. I'll tell him after lunch. Thanks!" She dashed into the cafeteria and joined the others at Michael's table.

A little later, I noticed her chatting with Michael by the snack machine. Her face suddenly lit up like someone had switched on an internal floodlight. My hunch was that Michael had popped the question. When Michael turned to go back to the table, Jessica looked at me with a hundred-watt smile. I smiled back and pretended to applaud.

At the end of the period, Jessica lingered in the cafeteria after her friends had gone. Then she squared her shoulders and walked over to Jason, who was surrounded by four other boys from the football team. She glanced at me.

No-no-no! Don't shoot him down in front of his buddies. To my great relief, Jason waved his friends away and walked off with her. They talked for a few minutes, Jessica maintaining that faux smile. Then Jason shrugged and rejoined his friends. I wanted to ask her how it went, but I was already late for my next class.

On the day of the Halloween dance, the decorating committee transformed the gym into a haunted house complete with jack-o'-lanterns, red-fanged bats, and a replica of that ghoul from the *Scream* movies. A life-sized scarecrow wearing a bloodstained hockey mask lurked in the corner next to the water fountain. Synthetic cobwebs dripped from the light fixtures and basketball nets, and a disembodied plastic hand lay next to a rubber axe on a hay bale by the door. Three boys were testing the rented smoke machine that was hidden under the bleachers, and a spooky mist swirled on the polished wood floor. It was like walking around in a Wes Craven film.

I looked up at the clock where a tissue-paper ghost spun lazily in the draft from a heating duct. Then I clapped my hands.

"Okay, everybody. Time to wrap this up. The late bus will be here in fifteen minutes."

There was a final burst of activity as the volunteers packed things away. I crossed the gym to a corner where Jessica and Michael were putting the finishing touches on a cardboard witch.

"Come on, you two. If you miss the bus, you won't have time to get ready for the dance. Have you decided on your costumes?"

Jessica wiped her hands on her jeans. "It's a surprise. You'll have to wait till tonight."

I picked a flake of cardboard out of her hair. "But how will I recognize you?"

"She'll be with a guy who looks like me," Michael said.

I was in the parking lot, searching my purse for my car keys, when two arms slipped around my waist. "So how's my hot dance date?"

Since Chris and I had both signed on as chaperones, we decided to go together. I turned around, and Chris hooked his thumbs in my waistband. Then he pulled me against him until our pelvic bones touched. I felt a tingle in a very private place.

"I don't feel all that hot at the moment," I lied. "Just tired and hungry."

"Want to stop for something to eat before the dance?"

"Only if you're buying."

"Before I agree to that, tell me—exactly how hungry are you?"

"Since we got paid today you should have enough to cover the bill."

Chris unhooked his thumbs and checked his watch. "I'll come by around six. It'll give me time to stop at the bank."

I could hear Brutus screeching as soon as I opened the car door. Yin-Yang was rustling around in some dead leaves under my juniper bush. As I trotted up the walk, she shot across my path with something hanging from her mouth. Probably a defenseless baby bird. No wonder Brutus was upset. It must have been like watching some horrible avian version of *CSI*.

The screeching changed to a cheery "hi" as soon as I opened the door.

"Hi, Brutus. Did that evil cat scare you?"

Brutus climbed down from his swing and began rattling the cage door with his beak.

"Okay," I said, opening the door. "Come on out."

After settling Brutus on his perch with a grape, I poured myself a glass of iced tea and tidied up. I didn't want Chris to think my housekeeping skills were in the same category as my culinary expertise. Even though they were.

When the house looked fairly presentable, I changed into my new black jeans and a bright orange sweatshirt that said "THIS IS MY COSTUME" in big black letters. I rummaged around in my sock drawer until I found the pair of orange and black striped trouser socks I'd bought for a Halloween party last year. I pulled them onto my feet and slipped on my black Bass loafers. Then I went into the bathroom and fluffed my hair with the blow dryer, hoping to remove any stray bits of leftover Halloween decorations. After freshening my makeup, I fastened smiling pumpkin earrings onto my ears.

"Helloooooo, baby," Brutus called from the kitchen. I guess he was feeling neglected.

I went to the sink and rinsed my iced tea glass. According to Felix the Cat, it was five-forty. I had just enough time to play with Brutus before Chris arrived.

Brutus was sitting on my shoulder, batting my earring with his beak, when the doorbell rang.

"Come on in," I called. "The door's unlocked."

Brutus hissed when he saw Chris.

"I almost tripped over that cat on your front step." Chris's eyes travelled up and down my body, stopping at chest level. I couldn't tell if he was reading my shirt or admiring my anatomy. "Nice costume," he said. "I'd never have guessed it was you."

I carried my hissing parrot back to his cage. "At least I made an attempt. Where's your Halloween spirit?"

Chris pointed to a plastic ghost pinned to his collar. "Watch this." He pulled a string and the ghost's eyes glowed red.

"Cute," I said. "Looks like me after my third margarita."

We stopped at Bennigan's and shared a rack of ribs and a pitcher of beer. Ribs and beer are one of my favorite combos. The ribs were succulent and sticky, and that first icy beer went down like silk.

"Too bad we have to chaperone," I said. "I could stay here eating these ribs all night."

Chris refilled my pilsner glass. "And I'd love to sit here and watch you. You look really cute with that little glob of sauce on the tip of your nose."

I swiped at my nose with the napkin.

"Still some there," he said. "Want me to kiss it off?"

"Not here in the middle of the restaurant. Maybe later." I dipped the corner of the napkin into my untouched glass of water and scrubbed the end of my nose. "Gone?"

Chris nodded. "You're no fun," he said.

I was sucking the last bit of barbecue sauce from under my fingernails when I noticed Chris leering at me. "Need some help with that?" he asked.

"What is it with you tonight? Somebody spike your beer with Viagra?" I hoped there were no visible signs of the warmth rising into my face.

He gave me a wicked smile. "With you around, who needs Viagra?" Then he tapped his watch. "I hate to interrupt you when you're so obviously enjoying yourself, but we've got to get going."

"Okay, but first I have to make a pit stop and wash up."

"Why bother?" he asked. "You were doing such a great job with your tongue."

I pushed away from the table and looked at his spotless hands. "You know," I said, "it's a sign of an aberrant personality to be able to eat ribs and stay that clean."

We arrived at school as the first carload of students pulled up.

"I'll stay out here and keep an eye on the kids as they come in," Chris said. "Why don't you go on inside? I'll join you later."

Nancy and Don were standing by the gym entrance. Nancy wore a black academic robe and was pulling an oversized witch's hat onto her head. She waved when she saw me.

"The gym looks great," she said. "You did a fantastic job with the decorations."

"The kids did most of the work. I just gave them a few pointers."

"Where's Chris?" she asked, looking over my shoulder.

"On parking lot detail. He's in rare form tonight."

Nancy cut her eyes to me. "Lucky you," she said.

Don watched a mummy, two girls in togas, and a Darth Vader pass by. "I hope we don't run into any problems. Most of these kids are fine, but there are always a few bad apples."

My mind flashed on Jason Hawkins.

Nancy and I followed the first groups of students into the gym. The deejay was checking the sound system, and a loud, high-pitched squeal made me wince. I spotted Alex Benitez and went over to greet him.

"Alex, I love the bullfighter costume. It's so you."

"Gracias, Ms. B. It's authentic. Belonged to my great-uncle."

"Well, you look dashing." I turned to the dark-eyed girl holding his hand. "And who's the pretty flamenco dancer?"

"This is Angela Gonzalez. She goes to West Catholic."

Angela smiled and extended her hand. "Nice to meet you. Alex talks about you a lot."

"Uh-oh," I said. "Since you're a guest in our school, I won't press you for any incriminating details."

Alex laughed. "Come on, Ms. B. You know it's all good stuff. Hey, there's Bryan and Carol."

As Alex pulled Angela toward a pair of soldiers in camouflage fatigues, I caught sight of Jason Hawkins decked out in his football uniform. With all the protective padding, he looked more intimidating than ever, and I was hit with another bad vibe. It was obvious that he hadn't wasted any time pining over Jessica. His arm was slung around the neck of a perky blonde dressed as a cheerleader. She was gazing up at him with the rapt admiration of a dog that had just found its long-lost master.

A few minutes later, I heard someone call my name. I turned to see two shadowy figures gliding toward me. When they emerged into the light, I recognized Jessica and Michael, both dressed as vampires. Their faces were coated with white greasepaint, their mouths darkened with black lipstick. They wore matching sets of plastic fangs. Michael was dressed entirely in black and sported a long, swirling cape lined in red satin. He'd even sprayed his red hair black and had slicked it down with an abundance of hair gel. Jessica had donned a long ebony wig and a slinky black gown.

"You two look terrific," I told them.

"We got the idea from an old horror movie," Jessica said.

"Let me guess. Bride of Dracula?"

Jessica's eyes grew wide. "How did you know?"

"Oh, I doubt you could name a horror movie I haven't seen," I said.

Michael gave a low whistle. "I never would've thought you were a horror movie fan. You sure don't seem like the type."

Just then, the deejay announced a slow song. "C'mon, Mike, let's dance." Jessica pulled him by the hand, and they disappeared onto the crowded dance floor.

I turned and almost bumped into Chris. He was carrying a cup of apple juice and two gingersnaps.

"Since we didn't have time for dessert, I thought you'd like these."

I grabbed the cookies. "You sure know the way to my heart."

We patrolled the perimeter of the gym, looking for anything out of the ordinary. Jason was keeping his distance. No one had tried to spike the apple juice. There was no detectable odor of smoke, tobacco or otherwise. We checked all the darkened nooks and crannies, but found no overly-amorous couples to pry apart.

Jessica and Michael passed by and waved. They'd been joined by Chelsea and Damien, dressed as Raggedy Ann and Andy.

"Look at those two," Chris said. "It must be true love if she was able to talk Damien into wearing that get-up."

"How do you know it wasn't his idea?" I asked.

Chris chuckled and shook his head. "Are you kidding? They'll be calling that poor boy 'Andy' for the rest of his life."

The dance was winding down when I felt a tap on my shoulder. It was Jessica, her white forehead creased with worry lines.

"Ms. B., have you seen Michael? Chelsea and I went to the bathroom, and when we came out, he was gone. Damien said he was talking to Jason."

Mental alarm bells started clanging, but I tried not to let on. "He probably got sidetracked by a friend. Why don't you check around in here, and I'll have a look outside."

I headed out the side exit. The night was overcast, the only light coming from a single bulb in a metal cage above the gym door. My breath made smoky phantoms in the chill air as I walked along the side of the building. Suddenly, I heard angry voices rise up from the athletic fields behind the gym. I hurried toward the sound. When I rounded the corner, I saw the hazy outlines of two figures on the running track.

"You goddamn son-of-a-bitch, if you bother her again I'll kick your fat ass!" Michael's voice echoed in the still night air.

"Oh, yeah, shithead? I'll show you whose ass is gonna get kicked." Jason's disdainful laugh was followed by a series of muffled thumps and grunts.

"What's going on back here?" I shouted. "Jason! Michael!" There were more grunts. I started running and reached the track in time to see Jason's fist connect with Michael's face.

Michael reeled, falling backwards onto the ground. Cinders crunched under his body. Then Jason marched up to him and kicked him solidly in the ribs. I heard a sickening *thunk* as his heavy shoe connected with Michael's side. Michael's body contracted into fetal position as Jason drew back his foot for another kick.

"Jason! Back off now," I yelled. Jason wheeled around. He looked from me to Michael and took off across the football field. For one crazy moment, he seemed to be running for a touchdown. Then he disappeared into a stand of pine trees that bordered the end zone.

I looked down at Michael. He was bleeding from an ugly gash on his cheekbone, the blood a garish red against his stark white makeup. His head wobbled as he tried to sit up, and his eyes looked dazed. Then he leaned over and vomited, barely missing my shoes.

I moved away from the steaming puddle and knelt down beside him.

"Michael, look up at me." I took hold of his bloody chin and turned his face toward mine, forgetting all the warnings I'd been given about bodily fluids and latex gloves. He clutched his side and moaned. Blood ran down his cheek and dripped onto his black pants.

As I searched my pockets for a tissue, I heard the rapid thump of approaching footsteps.

"Jen, is that you? What's wrong?" I was never so happy to hear Chris's voice.

"I'm over here. There's been a fight, and Michael's hurt."

Chris crouched down. He folded his handkerchief into a thick square and handed it to Michael. "Here. Press this as hard as you can against your face." Then he turned to me. "Was it Jason?"

I nodded. "He ran off when he saw me. I wish I'd come out here a minute sooner."

Chris rested one knee on the ground. "Go back to the gym and get Don. I'll stay with Michael." I stood up and raced toward the gym door. "And Jen," he called, "I think you'd better phone for an ambulance."

As the strobing lights and wailing siren faded into the darkness, Chris put his arm around my shoulders. I wiped Michael's blood off my hands with the germicidal towlette Don had given me. The night had grown damp, and the antiseptic smell mingled with the acrid odors of exhaust and vomit that lingered on the frosty air, making me slightly queasy.

"You all right, champ?" Chris gave me a squeeze.

"I'm fine. I just hope Michael will be. That cut on his face looked pretty bad. Thank God he didn't lose an eye."

"He'll probably need some stitches. He's lucky you got out here when you did. The kid may be tall, but he's no match for Jason Hawkins."

Don walked toward us from the gym office. "I've contacted Mr. Tayler. He's on his way to the hospital to meet the ambulance. Needless to say, he's not too happy."

"I can understand that," I said. "If it were my son, I'd be upset too. It's good that Nancy rode with Michael in the ambulance. She'll be able to keep everybody calm."

Don nodded, but he seemed preoccupied. Before I could ask him if something else was wrong, he said, "I think we should all go home. We've had enough action for one night."

"That's for sure." Chris took my hand. His fingers were warm and strong. "Come on, Jen."

As I followed Chris to his car, I heard something crack under my shoe. I looked down to see Chris's little ghost pin, smashed to bits on the blacktop.

Chapter Thirteen

The ringing phone wrenched me from a dreamless sleep. I fumbled for the receiver.

"Jen, did I wake you?"

My eyes flew open, and I sat up, squinting at the bright stripes of sunlight that framed the window shade.

I coughed and cleared my throat. "That's okay, Nance. What happened at the hospital?"

"First of all, Michael's all right. It took nine stitches to close the cut on his face. He'll probably have a scar, and he has some scrapes and a bruised rib, but at least there weren't any broken bones or internal injuries. The hospital released him just after two."

"How did Mr. Tayler take it?"

"That's the other reason I'm calling. The man went ballistic. He got the police chief out of bed and had him come to the hospital to file charges against Jason."

"Well, I'm certainly no Bennett Tayler fan, but you can hardly blame him. His son's face had to be stitched back together. My dad would have pounded Jason into the ground."

"But here's the really bad news. Tayler's demanded an emergency meeting with us at nine o'clock Monday morning."

I fell back onto my pillow to the sound of shit hitting the fan. "Somehow that doesn't come as a big surprise. What about my nine o'clock class?"

"Anna's arranging coverage for you. I think it'd be a good idea to write down everything you remember about last night while it's fresh in your mind. Mr. Tayler's bringing his lawyer."

I squeezed my eyes shut. "Terrific. Why do I have the feeling a giant load of crap is about to be dumped right on my head?"

"Don't panic. He may feel differently once he's had a chance to calm down."

"Yeah, and someday I may fit into those size three jeans in the back of my closet."

I hung up the phone and pulled the covers over my head. Unfortunately, Brutus realized he'd overslept.

"HELLOOOOOO. Good, good bird. Step up." This was followed by a deafening scream. Translation: Time to get up. I shuffled into the living room and uncovered the cage. Brutus was hanging upside down, banging his beak against the bars. Being fluent in bird language, I knew this meant "Let me out," so I opened the door. He hopped onto my arm and gave me a kiss.

I set Brutus on his perch and took a box of Eggos out of the freezer. There were two left. After dusting off the ice crystals, I dropped the waffles into the toaster and put on water for tea. By the time I sat down to eat, little gremlins with pickaxes were at work in my brain. I swallowed an aspirin along with my tea.

"Cracker. CRACKER."

No translation needed. I broke the corner off a waffle and gave it to Brutus. Then I drowned the remaining waffles in Aunt Jemima Lite.

After breakfast, I wiped the sticky table and took out my Goofy notebook. I turned to a fresh page and began writing a detailed play-by-play of last night's incident. The way things were going, I'd soon have enough material for a novel. *Misery* would be the perfect title, but it was already taken.

As I reread what I'd written, I discovered a big problem for Michael. I couldn't deny that both boys had been fighting. According to our discipline policy, they were equally at fault. The penalty for fighting on school property was an automatic ten-day suspension. *Freaking great.*

The gremlins traded their pickaxes for sledgehammers. I took another aspirin and pressed my thumbs against my temples. It was bad enough that Michael had been hurt, but missing two weeks of school would set back all his progress. Brutus whistled an off-key tune, and I looked up at him. His waffle was gone.

"What should I do, buddy? This really sucks." Then I had an idea.

Chris answered the phone on the third ring, sounding out of breath.

"I was running on the treadmill," he puffed. "What's up?"

"Exercising on a Saturday morning? You are truly demented. Have you talked to Nancy yet?"

"She called me around eight. I told her to wait until later to call you in case you were sleeping."

"She did and I was. Have you heard about Monday's meeting?"

"Nancy filled me in."

"I need your advice. I'm positive both boys were fighting. I heard them when I came around the corner. Even though I only saw Jason throw a punch, I'm sure Michael was more than an innocent bystander."

"Then that's what you tell Mr. Tayler."

I blew out a frustrated sigh. "But if I do, Michael will be suspended. It doesn't seem right. From what I heard, he was trying to defend Jessica. I'd hate to see him suspended now that he's doing so much better."

"I can appreciate that, but it's not your decision. You have to stick to the facts. The rest is up to Don."

"I know, but that doesn't make it any easier."

"Nobody ever said being a teacher was easy."

On Monday morning, I came to school feeling like a kid about to rat out her best friend. I'd decided to take Chris's advice: tell the truth and hope for the best.

At nine o'clock, I entered the conference room, clutching Goofy to my chest like a shield. It was déjà vu all over again. Everyone sat around the table in the same seats as before. Don's face was grim. Nancy gave me a shaky smile. Stanton Hawthorne's silver pen was poised over his legal pad. Mr. Tayler looked like a tick ready to pop.

"So you're involved in this," he snarled, as I slid into a chair. "I should have known. You've been nothing but trouble for my son since he came to this school."

Oh, and meeting you has been such a transcendent pleasure for me. I felt myself shift from flight to fight mode. Nancy glared at me and gave her head an imperceptible shake.

Don held up his hand like a crossing guard stopping traffic. "Excuse me, Mr. Tayler. I cannot allow you to make unfounded accusations against a member of my staff. The purpose of this meeting is to discuss the events surrounding your son's injury, not to assign blame."

Just then, the door clicked open. Chris walked in and sat next to me.

"Now that all the involved parties are here, I think we're ready to begin," Don said. "Ms. Bianchi, please tell us what transpired during the dance."

I opened my notebook and started reading. When I got to the part about hearing Michael and Jason scuffling, Stanton Hawthorne broke in. His voice was high and reedy.

"So you didn't actually see the boys fighting. You only heard what you assumed were the sounds of a fight."

"I guess you could say that," I told him. "It was pretty dark."

"And you naturally assumed the worst because of your hostility toward my son," Mr. Tayler added.

"Just a minute, Mr. Tayler," Chris said. "Ms. Bianchi's attitude toward your son has been anything but hostile. She's treated him with consideration and fairness that go way beyond what's required. Her biggest concern when I arrived on the scene was your son's welfare. In fact, if it hadn't been for her stopping the fight when she did, things might have been much worse for Michael. You should be thanking her, not criticizing her."

My hero. I sneaked my hand under the table and gave his thigh an appreciative squeeze.

"I'll thank you to stop telling me what I should or should not be doing." Mr. Tayler's eyes narrowed to slits, and a vein on his forehead began to pulse. I had a sudden mental picture of his head exploding. It was an extremely satisfying thought.

"If you teachers had been doing your jobs," he continued, "my son would not have been assaulted. Isn't it your responsibility as chaperones to supervise these students?"

"Please try to be sensible." Don struggled to keep his voice level. "When teachers volunteer to chaperone a school function, they are expected to provide reasonable supervision. They can't be watching every student every minute."

"I disagree with how much supervision you consider reasonable. As a parent, I should be able to send my son to a school-sponsored dance and have him return unharmed. That seems reasonable to me, Mr. Clayton."

"I think we can leave it to the courts to determine how well the students were supervised," Stanton Hawthorne piped in. "I've advised Mr. Tayler to press charges against these teachers for negligence."

My heart lurched. I looked at Chris, too shocked to speak.

"Furthermore"—Mr. Tayler's voice dripped venom—"I intend to tell Superintendent Dimmit that I want official letters of reprimand placed in the files of both Ms. Bianchi and Mr. Holloway."

I swallowed the lump that had risen from my stomach and blinked back the tears that pushed into my eyes. *No way. I won't give that bastard the satisfaction of seeing me cry.*

Nancy looked from Stanton Hawthorne to Bennett Tayler. "I think you're overreacting. These two teachers did everything possible to help Michael. Ms. Bianchi intervened to stop the fight, and Mr. Holloway aided your son until the ambulance arrived."

"If they had been conscientious in carrying out their duties," Mr. Tayler sneered, "there would have been no fight, and my son wouldn't have needed an ambulance. As a result of their poor judgment, my son will be scarred for life. I hardly think I'm overreacting."

Stanton Hawthorne placed his hand on Mr. Tayler's arm. "I think we've said all that needs to be said about this. Now we must discuss Michael's return to school." He turned to Don. "We'd like this to happen as soon as Michael's physician feels the boy is well enough."

Don responded with a stony glare. "I'm afraid that won't be possible. According to our discipline policy, any student who engages in a fight on school property faces a mandatory two-week suspension. Neither Michael nor Jason will be permitted to return before then."

Mr. Tayler rose to his feet. "We'll see about that. Superintendent Dimmit may have a different opinion. I will await his decision. We have nothing more to discuss here."

It was only after the door slammed shut that I gave in to the tears I'd been holding back. Chris took my hand.

"Jen, don't cry. You didn't do anything wrong. No judge in his right mind would find us negligent."

"But I don't have tenure," I sobbed. "I'll never have my contract renewed with this legal mess hanging over me. And a letter of reprimand in my file will make it impossible for me to get another teaching job."

Nancy took off her glasses and set them on the table. "Things aren't that hopeless. Your evaluations have been outstanding. You have a wonderful reputation with the kids and the parents. I don't think the school board will overlook all that because of one disgruntled lunatic."

I took a ragged breath. "But Mr. Tayler isn't your garden variety lunatic. He's a really influential one. Everybody warned me that he'd be a dangerous enemy, but I never thought it would come to this." Nancy offered me a tissue, and I wiped my eyes.

Chris massaged the back of my neck. "Don't blow this out of proportion. Anyone with two functioning brain cells can see the man's out of control. Even Dimmit."

I looked up at Chris, and my eyes filled again. "Go ahead. Say it. You know you want to."

"Say what?" he asked.

"'I told you so.' You were right about this from the beginning, but I was too stubborn to listen." I sniffled and blew my nose.

Chris took my hand and rubbed it between both of his. "Jenna, that's the last thing I want to say to you. Your stubborn streak's part of your charm."

"Yeah," I said. "My charm has gotten us slapped with a lawsuit."

Nancy pushed her chair back and stood up. "You were just trying to help the man's kid. I'm sure he's not too far gone to understand that. Most likely, he's just blowing off steam because he's upset about the fight. And now that he's kicked us around and proven he's the alpha dog, he'll probably drop the whole thing."

Don rubbed his forehead. "Jenna, I want you to take the rest of the day off. I'll get someone to cover your classes. There's nothing more you can do about this, so leave things in my hands. That's why I get paid the big bucks."

I managed a watery smile. "Thanks, but I have tests scheduled for all my classes, and I need to be there. It's bad enough that I've missed one class already. Just give me a few minutes to pull myself together."

"Are you sure?" Don asked.

"I'm positive. The best thing I can do is keep busy." As I looked around the table, my throat tightened. "I'm so grateful to be working with all of you."

"The pleasure's ours," Chris replied.

Going back to work was a smart decision. I was too busy to obsess about Bennett Tayler, and by the beginning of eighth period, I had accumulated a sizable stack of test papers that needed grading.

At dismissal, I called Jessica up to my desk. Her usually shiny hair hung in limp strands, and the shadows under her eyes looked like faint bruises. I asked her about Michael.

She fingered a strand of hair. "Damien and I went to his house yesterday, but he wouldn't come out of his room. He let Damien in, but not me. Damien says it's because his face looks so bad. And he feels really lame because he didn't even get one good shot at Jason." She wound the length of hair around her finger. "Are they really going to suspend Michael?"

I looked away. "I'm afraid so. That's the penalty for fighting."

Jessica pulled her finger free, leaving a loose curl. "I can see why Jason's suspended, but not Michael. Isn't it bad enough that he's been hurt? Jason walked away without a scratch."

"I understand how you feel, but according to our discipline code, everyone involved in a fight gets suspended. It doesn't matter who wins or loses."

"Well, it isn't fair." Jessica shook her head as she walked to the door. "It really isn't fair."

Life's not always fair, kid, I thought. *Get used to it.*

When I got home, I threw myself on the sofa, wiped out and dying for some quiet time. As usual, Brutus had other ideas.

"Hi, baby," he crowed, flapping his wings. When I ignored him, he ramped up the volume until I took him out and sat him on my lap. He settled in and fluffed his feathers.

"I've had a terrible day, pal. I'm in the middle of a shitstorm, and all you care about is having your head scratched."

He took my finger in his beak and made kissy sounds, and I felt a smile tickling its way out. This crazy bird could always make me feel better. I was staring out the window, rubbing Brutus's little blue head, when the ringing phone brought me back to earth.

"Hello," I said.

"HELLO," Brutus echoed.

"Hey, sweetie." Chris sounded like a parent trying to coddle a crying toddler. "I looked for you after school, but you'd already signed out. How's it going?"

"Okay, I guess. Brutus is trying to cheer me up."

"Bet I can do a better job. I'll even bring dinner."

"I'm not very hungry."

"What? You, not hungry? Now I'm really worried. I'll be right over." He hung up before I had a chance to argue.

I put Brutus in his cage, ignoring his mumbled "Dammit." Then I returned to the sofa and unfolded the cherry and white afghan that was draped over the armrest. Nana had crocheted it for me in Temple's school colors the summer before I left for college. It had comforted me through many sleepless nights of homesickness, broken romances, and cramming for exams. After Nana died, I liked to wrap it around me and pretend she was giving me a hug. I cocooned myself in the soft wool, feeling like Linus with his security blanket. *If I start sucking my thumb, I'll know it's time to check into the rubber room.*

I closed my eyes, trying to forget the quagmire I was in. My head began to feel light and fuzzy, and I had the pleasurable sensation of drifting away. The next thing I was aware of was an insistent knocking on the front door. I heaved myself off the sofa and stumbled over to open it. There was Chris, holding a covered casserole dish. A girl could really get used to this.

I rubbed my eyes and pointed to his big orange oven mitts. "This is like a sitcom rerun."

He gave me a strange look. "What kind of greeting is that?"

"It's the best I can do." I yawned. "I must have dozed off. I'm feeling a little woozy."

"Then I've got just what the doctor ordered. Wait'll you taste this." He carried the casserole into the kitchen and set it on the table. "It's four-cheese lasagna."

"When did you have time to make that? Are you some kind of magician?"

"While I do have certain superpowers, I have to admit I had this in my freezer. For emergencies."

"I guess this qualifies as an emergency. After all, it isn't every day you find out you're being sued." I didn't even try to keep the bitterness out of my voice.

Chris removed the cover from the casserole. "One taste of this and you'll forget all about Bennett Tayler. Let's get the table set."

I put out the plates and forks, and Chris filled two glasses with Miller Lite. "I would have preferred a fine Cabernet," he said, "but this was all you had in the fridge. We'll have to make do."

Chris scooped the gooey lasagna onto my plate. He took a big forkful, blew on it, and held it to my lips. "Now close your eyes, and empty your mind of all negative thoughts. Open wide—you're in for a real treat."

When the lasagna hit my mouth, my taste buds broke into *The Hallelujah Chorus.* "Oh," I groaned, "this is fantastic. I feel better already."

"That's why it's called comfort food. Have some more."

I didn't need persuading. After my third helping and fourth beer, I pushed back from the table. My waistband was screaming for mercy, but there'd been a significant improvement in my mood. I stood up and teetered a little as I unzipped my slacks.

"Whoa," said Chris. "I know my cooking is good, but I didn't realize it was *that* good."

I shot him a "get real" look. "How can you even think about sex when your stomach's so full?"

"My stomach has nothing to do with it."

It was time to change the subject. "Chris, I need to talk to you about something."

"Okay." He pulled me by the wrist. "Come sit on my lap, and we'll talk about the first thing that pops up."

I rolled my eyes. "Did anyone ever tell you that you have a one-track mind? Oh, yeah. That was me." I settled onto his lap and rested my head on his shoulder. "Try to stifle the testosterone for a second. I need you to give me an honest opinion."

"Honestly? Those black lace bikinis you're wearing are really hot."

All righty, let's try this one more time. "No, seriously. How do you see this lawsuit playing out?"

Chris nuzzled my neck. "I have to admit, I'm not thrilled at the prospect of being hauled into court. But I don't think it will go anywhere. We haven't done anything wrong. The judge will probably decide the suit's frivolous and refuse to hear it."

"What if the judge is a friend of Bennett Tayler's?"

"Worst case scenario? If the suit goes to court, we're covered by the district's liability insurance. Even if the judge were to somehow rule against us, Tayler couldn't harm us financially."

"Maybe not. But I'm non-tenured. I could lose my job."

"Even idiots like Timothy Dimmit have to see that this lawsuit is bogus. And you have friends who will stand by you." He brushed his lips against mine. Then he slid his hand up the inside of my leg. "Forget about Bennett Tayler."

Bennett who? I looked into Chris's eyes. God, what a gorgeous shade of blue.

"Thanks for coming over tonight." I caressed his hand. "I feel almost human again."

"Actually, it wasn't me. It was my magic lasagna."

"Then thank you both." The sound of my laughter surprised me.

"If you really want to thank me, I can think of a much better way," he whispered. I slid my hands up his back and around his muscular shoulders. Then he slipped his fingers into the waistband of my black lace bikinis and gave me a kiss that was even better than the lasagna. Which is saying a lot.

Chapter Fourteen

The next morning, I felt refreshed and ready to take on the world. I was a fine teacher with a really hot boyfriend, loyal friends, supportive students, and a highly intelligent parrot. Let Bennett Tayler do his worst. It would take more than an overblown bully and a sniveling little lawyer to get the best of Jenna Bianchi. I walked through the parking lot with a jaunty bounce.

"Jen. Wait up." Nancy was trotting toward me, juggling a stack of books.

"Need some help with those?"

"As a matter of fact, I do." She stopped and let me remove the top two. "Yep, that's definitely better." Then she gave me an appraising stare. "You certainly look perky. I came by to check on you last night, but Chris's car was parked in front of your house. I figured three would be a crowd. Judging from the way you look this morning, I'd say Chris gave you all the consolation you needed."

"We had a long talk and an amazing lasagna. I feel like a new person."

"Love will do that to you."

I could feel my face heating up. "Hold on a minute. It's quite a leap from lasagna to love."

"All I know is you're positively glowing. I never heard of lasagna that could put color in your cheeks."

"That's because you haven't tasted Chris's. It's the stuff of which legends are made."

"I'll just bet it is," she said.

In the office, Anna and Don were behind the sign-in desk, huddled over a pile of crumpled chocolate kiss wrappers. Not a good sign.

Nancy looked from the wrappers to Anna to Don. "What's wrong?"

Anna unwrapped another chocolate kiss and poked it into her mouth. Then she offered the jar to Nancy and me. Nancy declined, but I took a handful, sensing trouble on the horizon.

"Dimmit called," Anna said, moving the chocolate kiss into her cheek. "He revoked Michael's suspension. Kid's coming back Thursday."

Don's eyes were stormy. "I'd like someone to explain to me why we need a discipline policy if it only applies to students whose parents don't have full-time attorneys. The whole thing's a sham. How can we expect the students to respect our rules if our own superintendent doesn't?"

Nancy slammed her books down. A chocolate kiss wrapper fluttered to the floor. "How in the world did Dimmit justify his decision?"

Anna picked up the wrapper and rolled it into a tight silver ball. "No proof that Michael was fighting. Jenna didn't see him. It's legally shaky."

I was experiencing a strange mixture of outrage and relief. Although it bothered me that Bennett Tayler was getting his way, I was thrilled that Michael would be coming back. I excused myself, muttering that I had some work to do, and realized I was whistling as I climbed the stairs.

On Thursday morning, the normal hum of homeroom stopped dead as the door opened and Michael walked in. He looked like he'd gone one-on-one with a semi. The right side of his face was completely distorted. An angry red gash on his cheekbone was crisscrossed with knotted black stitches. The bridge of his nose was swollen and purple. A bruise painted his cheek in shades of green and brown. His Hugo Boss sunglasses couldn't hide the swelling around his right eye. He ducked his head as he walked to his seat in the stunned silence. I needed a diversionary tactic. Fast. In desperation, I searched the morning bulletin for something to read.

"Could I have your attention for a moment?" All eyes turned from Michael to me. "Class pictures will be taken on Monday. Please make a note of this in your assignment books." As the students began to write, I continued reading as if announcing a sign of the apocalypse. "You'll need to have your order form completely filled out before your picture can be taken. And remember to dress appropriately. I'm sure you'll want to look your best in the yearbook."

Duh! I gave myself a mental head slap. That was probably the last thing Michael needed to hear. Before I could wedge my foot any further into my mouth, I was saved by the bell.

As the students spilled into the hall, Jessica linked her arm through Michael's and whispered something in his ear. He glanced over his shoulder at me, and I wiggled my fingers in a little wave.

During lunch duty, I decided to do some cafeteria surveillance to see if there was any resentment brewing over Michael's early return. As I passed the table where Jason usually sat with his gang, Hank Spears was ranting about the unfair advantage Michael had been given. Every so often, he'd pound his beefy fist on the tabletop. I crept closer.

"Jason said Tayler started it. Assface was pissed off at him for comin' on to Jessica."

"Yeah, right," said Andrew McKinley, varsity linebacker and full-time pain-in-the-ass. "Like he'd have a shot if Jason really wanted to hook up with her." The other boys snickered.

"His old man called the cops," Hank said. "Might get Jason kicked off the team."

"And we play Woodfield on Saturday," added Bruce Crutcher, the team's star tackle. "If we lose, we're out of the playoffs."

"That pencil dick deserved everything he got, and more." Hank's face was florid. Veins bulged in his thick neck. "If it wasn't for his old man's money, he'd be home, same as Jason."

Bruce gave a humorless snigger. "Fuckin' A. Rules change when you flash the cash. I say we teach the geeky bastard a lesson."

Then Hank noticed me. He nudged Bruce and pointed, and their conversation dropped to a whisper. So much for my stealth operation.

I went to check on Michael. He was sitting next to Jessica, facing the wall.

"So how're you feeling?" I tried to keep my tone light.

His hand went up to his stitched cheek. "I'm okay. Can't wait to get these stitches out."

"I'm glad you're all right," I said. "I've been worried about you."

He shrugged. "The doctor said I'll just have a thin scar that'll fade after a while."

"I think it'll make you look tough," Jessica told him. "Like Van Damme."

Michael flashed her a lopsided grin. As I started to walk away, he called me back.

"Thanks for helping me out the other night," he said. "If it wasn't for you—well, I really appreciate it." The way he emphasized *I* made it clear he was thinking about his father.

"That means a lot to me," I said. *It's not your fault your father needs intravenous antipsychotics.* "Just try to stay out of trouble. And keep your eyes open. Some of Jason's buddies are pretty angry with you."

A shadow of fear flitted across his face, and Jessica put her hand on his arm.

"No problem," he said. "I can handle those guys."

"I'm sure you can, one at a time," I lied. "But they tend to travel in a pack, so be careful."

Jessica turned from Michael and looked up at me. "I'll make sure he stays far away from those idiots. I promise."

I hoped that was a promise she could keep.

To be on the safe side, I filled Don in on what I'd overheard. He nodded as I spoke, jotting down the names of the boys.

"Michael's trying to act like he doesn't care," I said, "but I can tell he's worried."

"I'd be worried too if half the football team was out to get me." Don tapped the list with his pen. "Thanks for letting me know about this. I'll handle it from here. Rest assured there will be no more problems from the Jason Hawkins gang." When I rose to leave, Don stopped me. "By the way, I think it's admirable of you to be so concerned about Michael in light of his father's behavior toward you. It shows you're a true professional."

Coming from Don, a man of few words, this was high praise. I smiled. "Truth is, I really like Michael. It's to his credit that he's such a neat kid in spite of having a screwball for a father."

Don chuckled. "I wish I had a dollar for every screwball I've had to deal with since I took this job. I'd buy that yacht I've had my eye on."

During class, Michael slouched in his chair, staring glassy-eyed at something in La-La Land. High school teachers are accustomed to looking out at a sea of deadpan faces, but this was beyond the pale. Even my little desk-tapping trick didn't get his attention, so I scrapped my plan to have him make up his preposition test. I found myself mentally calculating the number of times he yawned.

After the bell rang, I called him over and asked him why he seemed to be lost in space. He stifled another yawn—by my count, number twenty-two—and told me he was having a hard time staying awake. So kill me, but this made me a tad defensive. My eyebrows involuntarily shot up, and Michael turned scarlet. I felt kind of guilty when he hastily explained that his spaciness was due to painkillers. Relieved that my teaching hadn't become coma-inducing, I asked him when he'd be ready to take his test. I was hoping to get all the tests graded and recorded by Friday so I could have a paper-free weekend.

Michael agreed to take the test during class on Friday afternoon since he'd be off the heavy meds by then. That was cutting it pretty close, but if I worked straight through my lunch period and stayed after school to grade his paper, I'd have enough time to get everything into the computer before I went home.

It was nearly four o'clock by the time I'd logged the last set of preposition tests. Michael had scored a ninety on his make-up test, and I couldn't resist the urge to draw a smiley face (a small one) in the corner of his paper. I shut down the computer and pulled the shades. Then I picked up my atypically empty tote and pulled out my key ring.

The clinking of my keys seemed magnified in the silence of the deserted corridor as I locked the classroom door. The building cleared out fast on a Friday afternoon, and the emptiness was kind of spooky.

I jumped when Chris called my name. He had just turned the corner at the far end of the hall. Sunlight from the window was at his back, and I could only see the outline of his body as he walked toward me. I put my keys in my pocket and leaned against the wall, watching him. There was something in his stride, a kind of casual, masculine grace that made my pulse race.

"I didn't think you'd still be here," he said. "Nice surprise."

I smiled up at him and pulled on his tie until our noses touched. "I've missed you, too," I said, kissing his lower lip. "I hate it when we have different lunch periods."

"Well, you know what they say about absence." He cupped my face in his hands and kissed me full on the mouth. "Makes the heart grow fonder and all that." We laced out fingers together and walked to the office hand-in-hand, like two high school kids.

"Why don't you come to my place tonight?" he asked. "It's Friday, so we can stay up as late as we want. I'll make pizza, and we can have some wine and rent a scary movie. And after that, we can share our fondness."

Fondness sharing? Is that what they're calling it now? "Sounds good to me. Shall I bring anything?"

"How about those black lace bikinis?"

I shoved him with my hip. "I mean food. I can pick up something on the way."

His lips curved in a suggestive smile. "Then pick up a pair of edible panties."

Chris's townhouse is on the outskirts of Hartfield. It's a two-bed, two-bath model in one of the new developments along the river, and you can see the water from the little balcony on the second floor. The rooms are sparsely furnished with sleek, contemporary pieces made of leather, glass, and chrome. A fifty-inch plasma TV dominates one living room wall. Chris's bedroom has a king-sized bed and one triple dresser. The second bedroom serves as a study with a computer center and a large bookcase. While the décor in Chris's place is minimalist at best, he spared no expense when it came to the kitchen. The cabinets are light oak with black granite countertops. Black and white ceramic tiles cover the floor. A black granite breakfast bar and four white barstools with black seat cushions take the place of a kitchen table and chairs. All the appliances are stainless steel, institutional-quality models polished to a mirror finish. The room has the feel of an upscale commercial kitchen. The Vulcan stove has four massive burners with a separate side grill, and you could bake a small child in the oven. Chris's pride and joy, a freestanding wine cooler that holds one hundred bottles, stands against one of the white walls. Next to it is a Sub-Zero side-by-side refrigerator. A five-quart mixer, a high tech espresso/cappuccino machine, and a fifteen-piece set of top-of-the-line Henckels knives in a maple block sit on the counter over the Bosch dishwasher.

By the time I arrived, Chris was getting ready to remove a pepperoni pizza from his humongous oven. He had made it from scratch, sauce and all, and the whole place smelled like a pizzeria. The pizza was baking on a thin slab of stone that fit on one of the oven racks. Chris deftly slid a wooden pizza paddle under the crust and transferred it to an acrylic cutting board. Then he sliced it into eight precise triangles with his high-carbon German steel pizza cutter. Chris has every kitchen gadget known to man.

"Look," I said, showing him a square white box tied with twine. "I stopped at DeLeo's and picked up some cannoli. Ricotta, with mini chocolate chips."

He removed the twine and peeked under the lid. "They look great, but where are the panties?"

I licked my thumb and rubbed a smudge of flour from his cheek. "Sorry. The porn shop was in the opposite direction."

I opened the refrigerator and put the box inside. When I closed the door, it made a soft "whoosh" as the vacuum seal settled into place. I wiped my fingerprints off the shiny handle. Then I sat down at the breakfast bar and helped myself to a slice of pizza while Chris filled two delicate stemmed glasses with wine.

"I called a lawyer friend of mine today," he said, placing my wineglass on the countertop. "I told him about Tayler and the fight, and he agrees that this lawsuit is going nowhere."

"That's good to hear." I sipped the wine. Lately, the mention of Bennett Tayler made me crave alcohol. "But what about the letters of reprimand? Having one of those in my file could really screw things up for me."

"He said that could be a little more complicated. Courts tend to defer to the superintendent when it comes to personnel issues. My friend suggested we check with our association rep to see if we have any recourse through union channels. So I called Marita, and she promised to look into it."

Leave it to Chris to get all his ducks lined up. Mine too. Since we were lining up ducks, I told Chris about Michael's preposition test.

"I knew I was making progress with him," I said, as I picked a piece of pepperoni off his plate. "And now I have hard evidence to show that my strategies are working. Hit me with more of that Zinfandel."

Chris refilled my glass and touched it with his. "Here's to being proven right. Maybe it'll make an impression on his crazy old man. Get him to rethink the lawsuit."

I frowned. "Doubtful. But at least I have the satisfaction of knowing I helped Michael. That's the best thing about this job."

Chris pursed his lips in a pretend pout. "Hey. I thought meeting me was the best thing about this job."

I leaned over and kissed him, flicking his lower lip with my tongue. "Well, let's just say you finish a close second."

When nothing was left of the pizza but a lingering aroma and a delectable memory, Chris suggested that we take our dessert up to the patio to watch the moon rise. He climbed the circular stairs, balancing two steaming cups of cappuccino and a bottle of anisette, and I followed him with liqueur glasses and the box of cannoli. After we set everything down on the little patio table, I folded myself into one of the two cedar Adirondack chairs and tucked my legs under me. The chill night air carried an almost imperceptible hint of wood smoke that blended deliciously with the coffee-cinnamon scent of the cappuccino. Chris pulled his chair close to mine. We sipped cappuccino and ate our cannoli as a beautiful harvest moon rose over the trees like a fat, orange bubble, turning the river to liquid amber. When the coffee was gone, Chris filled the two liqueur glasses with anisette and handed one to me.

"To us," he said, holding his glass out.

"Cent'anni," I answered. *A hundred years.*

We watched in silence as the moon ascended into the black sky, shrinking and brightening until it became a cold, round pearl floating high over our heads. The inky heavens were dusted with starlight, and the only sound was the chirping of an unseen cricket choir. I exhaled a sigh, and Chris took my hand.

"Beautiful, isn't it?" he asked.

"Mmmm," I answered, pressing his hand to my cheek. "It's magical. I only wish you had a loveseat out here. It's getting chilly, and you'd be so nice to cuddle up to."

Chris pushed himself up from the chair and grasped both my hands. "I can fix that," he said, pulling me to my feet. I followed him through the sliding glass door that led into his bedroom. The room was swathed in darkness, except for the ambient moonlight and the flickering of a pillar candle on the dresser. I inhaled the fragrance of sandalwood mingled with an undertone of Polo Blue aftershave. The anisette, coupled with my raging hormones, made me a little lightheaded, so I plunked onto the edge of the bed. Chris knelt in front of me. I heard his breath catch as he reached under my sweater and slid it up my sides and over my head. His cool hands against my warm skin made me shiver. My trembling fingers fumbled with the buttons on his shirt until he finally stood up and shucked it off. Then he gently pushed me onto my back. I could see the outline of his body above me, silhouetted in the moonlight. He lowered his face until it was inches from mine.

"Cuddle time," he whispered.

When we came back downstairs, I stretched out on the soft leather sofa in the living room. I felt loose and relaxed, as if all my joints had come unhinged. Chris slipped a disc into the DVD player. Then sat beside me, lifting my head and setting it in his lap.

"I rented *Halloween*," he said. "The original John Carpenter version. I know how much you like it, and I love the way you get all snuggly during the scary parts."

"It'll take a lot more than that to frighten me," I told him. "Lately, I feel like my whole life's turning into a horror movie. And Bennett Tayler's a hell of a lot scarier than some knife-wielding lunatic in a William Shatner mask."

Chris smoothed my hair back from my forehead. "Don't worry about him. I won't let him hurt you."

I looked into his eyes and saw that he was serious. He bent his head down and kissed me. Then he hit the PLAY button on the remote.

By the time the movie ended, I was hanging onto Chris like grim death. I looked at my watch. It was after one. I had to get going, so I peeled myself off him and stood up.

"Are you sure I can't convince you to stay over?" he asked. "There's plenty of room in my bed."

Although I would have crawled on my belly over broken glass for the chance to spend the night spooned next to Chris in that big, warm bed, I decided to overcome my baser instincts and be the responsible adult.

"As good as that sounds, I have to get home to Brutus. I feel guilty enough about leaving him alone all day. I wouldn't want him waking up to an empty house."

"What about me? Doesn't it bother you that I'll be here all by my lonesome?"

"Just be grateful you're not locked in a cage."

"Sounds kinda kinky. Maybe we should give it a try."

I swatted him with my purse and shrugged into my jacket. The night had grown damp, and I suppressed a shiver as I stepped out into the darkness.

Chris walked me to my car and kissed me goodnight. "Be careful driving," he said.

As I navigated the long, gloomy stretch of road back to Morrisonville, that eerie *Halloween* theme music kept playing in my head. I turned on a CD, hoping Springsteen's voice would drown it out. Then I glanced in the rear view mirror, and goose bumps rose on my arms. I don't know if I was still terrified from the movie or experiencing the residual effects of the anisette and wine, but I had a chilling certainty that Bennett Tayler's sinister face would be staring back at me.

By the time I got home, I was so creeped out that I practically scorched a path into my darkened house. I yanked the door closed, clicked the lock, and twisted the deadbolt. Then I took a deep, steadying breath and switched on the light. Brutus blinked at me and croaked.

"Sorry I woke you," I said. "I know it's late. Let me tuck you in."

He fluffed his feathers as I threw the cover over his cage. Then I noticed the blinking red light on my answering machine. One message. I pressed the button.

BEEP. *"Hiya, Jen. It's Marian. I was hoping to catch you home, but oh, well. Just wanted to let you know I overnighted you a bunch of ADHD stuff. Hope it helps. By the way, I really enjoyed seeing you. Can't wait to get together again. Maybe you can come up some weekend, and we can go into the city. That is, if you can tear yourself away from Chris the Hottie. Give him a big, juicy kiss for me. Bye now."*

I deleted the message and switched off the light. Before long, I was lying in my lonely bed, staring at the ceiling and wishing Chris was beside me.

Chapter Fifteen

Someone was at the door. I rolled over and looked at the clock. It was after nine. Brutus screeched as I hurried into the living room. An UPS delivery guy with really nice legs was standing on my doorstep, holding a thick envelope. I rubbed the sleep out of my eyes, fluffed my hair, and opened the door.

The UPS guy looked slightly unnerved. He craned his neck to peer into the living room. "Is everything okay in there?" he asked.

I was puzzled until Brutus fired off another shriek, and Mr. UPS took a step back.

"Everything's fine," I assured him. "That's my watchbird. He overslept this morning."

The deliveryman cracked an uncertain smile and handed me the envelope. I thanked him, admiring his firm little butt as he hurried back to his truck. Then I pulled my eyes away and looked at the return address. It was from Marian.

I took the envelope into the kitchen and tossed it onto the table before going over to uncover Brutus. He yawned and shook himself.

"Good morning, sleepyhead," I said. "Did I keep you up too late last night? I'll have to do that more often."

Brutus climbed off his swing and took a sip from his water bowl. Then he let loose with an impressive dropping, looked out the window, and froze. Yin-Yang was skulking across the lawn, probably searching for another small, helpless animal to rip apart. Brutus exhaled a long, snakelike hiss, and all his feathers stood on end. I opened the cage door and stuck my arm inside before he could start screeching again.

"C'mon, buddy. Just ignore her. Step up, and I'll make you breakfast."

"Okay!" he said.

Brutus and I were sharing a sesame bagel when I opened the packet from Marian. Inside were research reports and a bunch of fliers with all kinds of technical information about different brands of ADHD medication. It didn't take me too long to realize this was not good recreational reading. Figuring it would be best to take this pharmaceutical stuff in small doses, I crammed the papers into my bulging ADHD folder and shoved it into my tote. Not, as it turned out, a very smart move.

Mom and I had agreed to meet for lunch at the mall, so I showered and pulled on my good jeans and my L.L.Bean fisherman's sweater. It was chilly, but the sun was bright so I didn't bother with a jacket. When I got to the car and checked my purse for my key ring, I remembered that I'd left it in my jacket pocket. Since I was now locked out, I had to search under the bushes for the fake rock that held my spare house key. I dusted off the dirt, removed the key from the hidden compartment, and unlocked the front door. By the time I pulled out of the driveway, I was already ten minutes late. I called Mom on my cell to let her know I was on the way.

The mall was crowded, typical for a Saturday. I pulled into a space in front of Bahama Breeze and hurried inside. Mom was waiting for me in one of the tropical print chairs by the hostess desk. The hostess, a spunky girl with Jennifer Anniston hair, led us to a sunny table by the window. When our waiter appeared, we ordered two mojitos.

"Sorry I'm late," I said. "Forgot my keys."

Mom smiled and shook her head. "I can't understand why you don't put a little hook by the front door. If you hung your keys there, you wouldn't have to spend so much time tracking them down."

"You remind me of myself giving advice to this student I've been working with," I said. "I guess it's a case of 'Do as I say, not as I do.'"

"Are you talking about the boy with the attention problem? The one who's father's been giving you a hard time?"

"Mm-hmm. But things have been getting better. Michael even got an A on a test."

"Well," she said, "that should make his father happy."

"I hope so. The man's been making my life pretty miserable."

The waiter came with our drinks and took our food order. I chose a salad with grilled chicken, dressing on the side. After all the pizza I ate at Chris's, I had to be good.

"I can't understand these parents," Mom said, sipping her drink. "When you and Anthony were in school, your dad and I would never have dreamt of telling your teachers how to do their jobs."

"I wish there were more parents like you."

"Things have certainly changed since I was in school. If a nun ever complained about me, there would have been hell to pay from my parents."

"Maybe I should have become a nun." An idea that didn't seem too appealing last night.

Mom laughed. "Sorry, honey, I don't think you have the temperament. And I'm sure they have the same problems in Catholic schools. Nowadays, if a child misbehaves, it somehow becomes the teacher's fault."

"That's because people seem to think anybody can get up in front of a classroom and teach," I told her. "You know the saying. 'Those who can, do …'"

"'Those who can't, teach.' Yes, I've heard that before. I guess it's just a question of respect. Dad and I have always held teachers in high esteem."

"Maybe that's why I wanted to become one. Although lately, I've been questioning the wisdom of that decision." I stirred my mojito with the straw, pushing the mint leaves to the bottom of the glass.

Mom gave me her stern look, the one that told me a lecture was on the way. "Don't ever doubt how important your job is. Teaching is one of the most difficult occupations out there. It takes a special kind of person to do it well. And you're very good at what you do."

"You've got to say that. You're my mother."

"That's not the point. Anyone can see how much this profession means to you, and how much you care for your students. No matter what that boy's father does, your dad and I are really proud of you. We think you're a terrific teacher."

I looked away, wondering if she'd still be able to say that a year from now.

As the days passed, Michael gradually got back to normal. Or normal for him. His bruises faded and disappeared. Even his scar thinned to a fine red line. Not quite Van Damme, but who was I to judge? While he still needed help staying focused, there was a major improvement in his behavior. He continued writing assignments in his daily planner, and he kept his binder organized. And there were no more rumblings from Jason and his friends. Nancy told me on the q.t. that Don threatened to have anyone who harassed Michael thrown off the football team.

Best of all, Michael seemed so much happier. His grades had improved in every subject. He'd even become something of a celebrity after the first issue of the *Morrison High Courier* was published. His article about the locker problem ("Locker Lockout") caused such a stir that some students circulated petitions to have the situation addressed. Since many of the kids made their parents sign, Superintendent Dimmit got rattled and promised to bring the matter before the school board.

The end of the quarter brought—*drum roll*—the dreaded "Report Card Day." The tense silence blanketing homeroom was broken by an occasional groan, cheer, or sigh of relief as I placed report cards face down on each desk. When I got to Michael, I gave his shoulder a congratulatory pat. He turned the paper over and scanned the page, his eyes growing wide: C minus in science; C in math; B minus in social studies; B in Spanish; A minus in English. In addition, there was only one negative comment. "Inattentive" was printed next to the science grade. *And can anyone guess whose fault that might be?*

Michael's face registered surprise, skepticism, and finally, pride. He looked up at me with a broad, disbelieving grin.

When homeroom ended, Jessica ran over to him. "Let me see," she said.

"I don't believe it." Michael handed her the report card and shook his head. "This is the best report card I've ever gotten. I can't wait to show my parents." Then he added, with a trace of bitterness, "Maybe this'll get my dad off my back."

Maybe off mine, too.

Brutus was noisier than usual when I arrived home, so I took him out and settled him down for a head scratch. A minute later, my cell phone chirped. Brutus chirped back.

"Hey, girlfriend," Nancy said. "I just wanted to check in since I didn't talk to you all day. Any news to report?"

"Actually, there is. Did you happen to see Michael Tayler's report card?"

Dead silence on Nancy's end. Then, "How bad was it?"

"Bad? Who said anything about bad?"

"BAD. BAD, BAD." Brutus chimed in.

I burst out laughing. "It's amazing, Nance. His grades went up in every subject. His English average was ninety-one. The only problem was science, and given Jack's attitude, a C minus is pretty damn good. Now you have to admit that Project June Bug's working."

"Let's hold off," Nancy said. "It's still early in the year. We have to give it some time to see if the improvement continues."

"Don't be such a balloon-pricker. You told me a journey begins with a single step, and this is a giant step in the right direction."

"Speaking of steps in the right direction, how are things with Chris? Anything developing there?"

"Yes, I'm developing a major weight problem. Why are you so determined to see us hook up?"

"Because I know what's best for you. Have I ever steered you wrong?"

"That's a discussion for another day. I have to hang up now. Brutus is chewing a hole in my sleeve."

The next morning, I was greeted by one of Don's *See Me* notes. An icy knot formed in my stomach as I pictured Bennett Tayler's hateful face, little curved horns protruding from his forehead. Pushing the vision away, I knocked on Don's door.

"You wanted to see me?"

Don nodded and gestured at the chair.

I sat down, steeling myself for more bad news. "Okay, Mr. Clayton, what have I done now?" I was only half joking.

"The secretary got a call this morning from Claudia Tayler, Michael's mother. She wants to set up a conference with you regarding Michael's report card."

I felt as if I'd been zapped with a Taser. "But—but Michael told me it was the best report card he's ever gotten. Are those people deranged?" I tried some deep breathing. *Inhale—hold for three seconds—exhale slowly.*

While I was concentrating on my exhale, Don said, "Mrs. Tayler didn't give Shannon any specifics. She just said it was important that she meet with you ASAP. Are you free to see her after school today?"

"This is unbelievable. They're like damn piranhas. They just keep coming at me. And all because I'm trying to help their son."

Don smiled. "Reminds me of the saying, 'No good deed goes unpunished.' It happens to a lot of teachers. I'll bet you never learned that in college."

"Yeah. Silly me. I never suspected that my worst problems would come from outside the classroom. I thought my biggest challenge would be explaining the difference between an adjective and an adverb."

"Ah, Jenna. Another wide-eyed innocent gets whacked with the reality stick."

"Okay, okay," I sighed. "Tell Mrs. Piranha I'd be thrilled to meet with her."

"I'll do that. Omitting the sarcasm, however. Now try to relax." He reached over and patted my hand. I didn't realize it had curled into an angry fist.

Since I was late getting to my classroom, most of the students were already inside. Michael and Jessica were standing by the door, surrounded by a noisy knot of kids. I stopped to see what the commotion was about.

"Ms. Bianchi, guess what happened to me yesterday." Michael folded his arms across his chest and grinned.

"From the expression on your face, I'd say you won the lottery." *And the grand prize was a new set of parents.*

"Even better. When my dad saw my report card, he took me downtown and bought me this." He handed me a snapshot of a bright red motorbike. "It's a Hawk Mini-Chopper. I've been begging for one since last summer. A friend of mine from Elgin had a bike just like it, and he let me ride it once in a while. These babies can really move."

"That's great." I tried to sound enthusiastic, but a warning light had flashed on somewhere in the recesses of my brain. *What had I read in one of those ADHD articles? Something about speed?* I shook the fragment of thought away, telling myself I was just jumpy about the upcoming conference with Mrs. Tayler. What possible connection could there be between ADHD and motorbikes?

I realized Michael was still talking to me. "I know I'm always saying this, but thanks. I could never have gotten those grades without all your help."

"You're the one who deserves the credit," I said. "I just gave you a few pointers. You made them work." *Too bad your screwy parents don't share your enthusiasm for my methods.* I handed him the snapshot. "Now don't let this distract you from your homework."

"Yeah, I know. You sound just like my mom."

Bite your tongue. Now I was more confused than ever. If Michael's father was so pleased with the report card, why was his mother coming in to hassle me? The twinges of a tension headache poked at my left temple as I took attendance. I vowed to forget about the conference and concentrate on doing my job.

I kept that vow until lunchtime when I ran straight to the guidance office. Nancy was at her desk, sipping a root beer and holding an open box of animal crackers.

"Come on in. I was expecting you."

"You must be psychic." I grabbed a handful of crackers and plopped into a chair.

"Not really. I heard about your meeting with Mrs. Tayler, so I knew you'd come running for these." She pushed the box across the desk to me. "Here, take as many as you want. God knows, you'll need all the help you can get if the Missis is anything like the Mister."

I bit the head off an elephant. "What on earth could this psycho bitch want to gripe about?"

Nancy leaned toward me. "Did it ever occur to you that maybe—just maybe—she's not coming in to complain?"

I considered this for a moment. Then I shook my head. "No. It's a nice idea, but since she's married to Hannibal Lector, she probably wants my head on a plate with fava beans and a nice Chianti."

Nancy shrugged. "Just a thought. But you shouldn't prejudge the wife because of the husband. She might be a very nice lady."

"With absolutely vile taste in men," I added through a mouthful of cracker crumbs. "I don't get it. Michael was thrilled about his report card. Batty Daddy even bought him a motorbike."

"A motorbike? If Michael has ADHD, a motorbike is the last thing he needs."

"Funny. That's what I thought. Something about that motorbike bothered me."

Nancy opened the top drawer of the filing cabinet. She pulled out an article and handed it to me. "Remember reading this?"

The article was entitled "High Risk Behavior and ADHD." I had just skimmed it because, at the time, it didn't seem to apply to Michael. I read the section Nancy had highlighted.

"Individuals with ADHD often crave high stimulus situations and are likely to engage in risk-taking activities. They are often fascinated by speed, and this, coupled with their impulsiveness, puts them at high risk for accidents and substance abuse."

Yikes! "Can I keep this? I know I have a copy somewhere, but I don't remember where I put it."

Nancy smirked. "Somehow that doesn't come as a shock. Sure, take it. I have others. It's part of the information packet I give to parents of ADHD kids."

The pounding in my head was working its way into my eyes so I massaged them with my thumbs. "Do you happen to have a diet soda?" *Or maybe a fifth of scotch?*

Nancy reached into a bag under her desk and pulled out a can of diet Dr. Pepper. "Here," she said, popping the top. "You really need a course in nutrition. Diet soda and animal crackers aren't part of a balanced diet."

"This is my version of comfort food." I washed down two Extra-Strength Tylenols with a long pull of Dr. Pepper. "And right now, I need all the comfort I can get."

"I can think of better ways to get comforted. Chris Holloway, for example."

"I'll stick with the animal crackers for now. I like to save Chris for emergencies. I don't want him to think I'm the needy type."

Nancy exploded with laughter, spraying root beer onto her desk. "Sorry, but I have a really hard time seeing you as needy. Stubborn, opinionated, hotheaded maybe—but never needy."

Who, me? "You're just saying that because it's true."

She took a tissue from the box on her bookshelf and wiped her desktop. "I always tell you the truth. That's what friends are for."

After dismissal, Damien, Paul, Jessica and Chelsea joined Michael at his locker. Snatches of their conversation drifted in from the hall.

"I saw an ad for that bike on TV."

"Bet that thing can really fly."

"Dude, when can I ride it?"

"I'm taking Jessie for a ride when I finish my lab report."

I thought about warning Michael to be careful, but by the time I poked my head into the hall, he was gone. Anyway, I had a bigger problem to deal with at the moment. It was time to meet the dreaded Mrs. Tayler. And I could almost hear the crying of the lambs.

Chapter Sixteen

When I opened the conference room door, I knew how Dorothy felt when her house touched down in Oz. I was expecting the Wicked Witch of the West but found Glinda instead.

Well, lookee here. Old man Tayler's bagged himself a trophy wife. Claudia Tayler was a strikingly beautiful woman. Her soft, coppery hair curled around her slim face. Her skin was creamy, with a light dusting of freckles across the bridge of her tiny, aristocratic nose. She wore a designer dress of cornflower linen that probably cost more than I'd make in a month. On second thought, forget the dress—her shoes cost that much. I hoped she wouldn't notice my scuffed Birkenstock clogs.

"Hello," she said, disarming me with a smile that revealed two rows of perfect teeth. *Probably caps.* I sat down, half expecting her to ask me if I was a good witch or a bad witch.

"So you're the Ms. Bianchi that Michael has told me so much about. It's wonderful to finally meet you in person."

Huh? I wouldn't have been more surprised if a bunch of singing munchkins had popped through the floor. I faked a cough, stalling for time to come up with a witty response.

"It's—uh—nice to meet you, too." So much for the witty response.

Her smile wavered as she sensed my confusion. "I wanted you to know how pleasantly surprised I was when my son showed me his report card. I don't think I need to tell you that report card days haven't been the happiest in our house. I dread them even more than Michael does. So you can imagine my delight when he came home yesterday, just glowing, waving his report card. At first, I thought he was playing some kind of adolescent prank. But when I saw his grades, well"—she shrugged—"I'm at a loss for words."

By this time, I'd found some of my own. "I'm so pleased that you're happy with Michael's progress here at Morrison. He's shown a lot of growth since the beginning of the year, and he's been working very hard." *Hooray! Got my teacher-mojo back.*

"Those weekly progress reports were a godsend," she said. "It was wonderful to have the constant feedback. They helped me to keep on top of things. In fact"—she reached into her purse—"I'd be so grateful if you'd give these thank-you notes to each of Michael's teachers." She handed me five square envelopes. "I want you all to know how much I appreciate your efforts. I'm sure it entailed a lot of extra work."

I took the envelopes and stacked them on the table. There were going to be four very surprised teachers come tomorrow morning. Five, counting me.

"This is so thoughtful of you," I said. "But we were happy to do it." *Well, maybe not exactly happy.* "We're always pleased when our teamwork helps a student succeed."

Her blue eyes sparkled. "From what Michael tells me, he owes it all to you. You're the first teacher he's expressed any positive feelings about. It's such a welcome change from his constant griping."

"We got off to a rocky start," I said, "but that's behind us now. He's certainly an interesting young man."

She wilted a little. "Michael's never been an easy child. He's such a mystery. I think he's bright enough, but you'd never conclude that from his school records. His entire school experience has been a nightmare." She paused, then added, "For both of us."

I pictured Michael on the first day of school and tried to imagine how difficult it must have been for this mother to watch her child grow into such a hostile young man. I wanted to broach the subject of ADHD, to explain that none of this was her fault or Michael's. But I had to wait for the perfect moment.

"Mrs. Tayler, you're correct about Michael's capability. His IQ is well above average, and from what I've seen of his work, he has real writing talent. He's been a big asset to our newspaper staff."

Her face lit up. "Oh, yes. The school paper. I was thrilled to see Michael interested in an extracurricular activity. He's never wanted to get involved in anything that kept him in school for a minute longer than necessary. I can't believe how much he looks forward to those meetings."

"I think he has a future in investigative journalism," I said. "His locker article caused quite a stir."

"He was so proud to see his article in print that he hung it on our refrigerator." She smiled at the recollection. "Having something to hang on the refrigerator is a new experience for Michael. And he seems to be making some nice friends. A few of them even came by to visit after he'd gotten hurt at the dance."

She stopped, her face flooding with color as she looked away. I assumed the dance was a touchy subject. When she began talking again, her sentences spilled out as if a stream of words would wash away her embarrassment. "Michael's especially fond of a girl named Jessica. She's been to our house a few times, and she seems quite sweet. I think she's made a big impression on him."

"Jessica Corcoran would be a good influence on anyone. She and Michael have become quite an item."

Mrs. Tayler gave an uneasy chuckle. "I thought as much, judging from the amount of time he's spending in front of the mirror. I definitely approve of his new look."

I laughed with her, hoping to put her at ease.

She sighed. "If someone had told me a year ago that Michael would have a girlfriend by now, I'd never have believed it. I guess my little boy is growing up."

"Kids have a way of doing that," I said.

There was an awkward silence as she fidgeted with her exquisite wedding band. Her engagement diamond was so big, I was afraid the sparkle would sear my retinas. When she spoke, her voice was so hushed I had to strain to hear.

"You know, it feels strange to be sitting here talking to you like this. My conversations with Michael's teachers have always been so unpleasant. Everything they said about him was negative. You can't imagine how difficult it is for a parent to hear a teacher criticize her child, even if the criticism is meant to be constructive."

"It's not my favorite part of the job either," I told her.

She brushed a wisp of hair out of her eyes. "Each time I left a parent-teacher conference, I'd cry all the way home—partly because I was angry and hurt—but partly because, deep down in my heart, I knew that everything those teachers said was true."

She looked up at me, her eyes brimming with tears. "It made me feel so helpless. Like such a failure as a mother."

I thought of the spiteful things I'd said about her, and guilt stuck in my throat like a dry aspirin.

She blinked the tears away. "Ms. Bianchi, I'm not a stupid woman. Nor am I blind. I know my son is in trouble. I spend every day watching him struggle with his schoolwork, dealing with his outbursts and frustration. I've seen how difficult it is for him to make friends. I've watched his self-esteem dwindle away. When he was a little boy, I could gather him in my arms and make it all better. But as he got older—well, things weren't that easy to fix. Michael became so belligerent. We seemed to be fighting all the time."

I thought of the cinquain. "Did Michael ever try to explain why he was having so much trouble in school?"

She shook her head. "He's so sullen and secretive. He spends most of his time in his room with the door locked. And sometimes, God help me, I'm relieved that he's in there. At least then I don't have to deal with him." Her eyes filled again, but this time she let the tears spill.

I swallowed hard and handed her a tissue. There was always a box on the conference room table. You never knew when a parent—or a teacher—might need one.

She blotted her eyes. "I apologize for behaving this way. I can't imagine what you must think of me." She gave her nose a dainty little blow.

"No apology needed," I said. "That's why we keep the tissues handy."

She took a deep breath and slowly released it. "Michael is my only child, and I love him with all my heart. There's nothing I wouldn't do to help him, but I feel so overwhelmed. I don't know what to do or where to turn."

Hello? Moments don't get more perfect than this. "When I met Michael, I was just as puzzled by his behavior as you are," I said. "He certainly didn't make a good first impression."

Mrs. Tayler gave a rueful smile and dabbed her cheeks with the tissue. "I can imagine. First impressions were never his strong point."

I smiled back at her. "After I read through his file, I was even more perplexed. With his IQ, there was no logical reason for him to be having problems in school."

She wadded the tissue into a ball and placed it on her lap. "You know," she said, "I feel the same way. I never could understand why Michael wasn't a better student. As a child, he was so curious. Always busy, always getting into things. There weren't enough hours in the day for him. And he never wasted much time sleeping. He was the most active child I'd ever seen."

This conversation was definitely on the right track. "To tell you the truth," I said, "Michael had me so baffled, I conferred with Mrs. Miller. She's our guidance counselor, someone who knows what makes kids tick. She gave me some information that I found extremely interesting." I waited to see if Mrs. Tayler would rise to the bait.

"What information is that?"

Time to set the hook. "Have you ever heard of Attention Deficit Disorder?" My muscles tensed as I waited for her reaction.

She leaned forward, propping her chin on her hand. "ADD. Yes, I've read magazine articles about it and heard it discussed on talk shows. A few of Michael's elementary school teachers mentioned it, but Bennett and I didn't think it applied to him. Isn't it some kind of learning disability?"

Now it was time to draw on all the information I'd gleaned from my research. I told her how ADD made it difficult for the brain to maintain focus, and that hyperactivity plus ADD equaled ADHD. I explained how the condition impacted school performance and interpersonal relationships. She paled visibly when I mentioned that the root of the problem lay somewhere in the brain, so I assured her that ADHD wasn't some kind of brain disease.

"It's a syndrome, a collection of symptoms. And it occurs in seven to ten percent of children, most of them boys. I'm not a doctor, but I can tell you that Michael fits the profile. He has many of the symptoms—hyperactivity, inattentiveness, impulsiveness. I think it's worth looking into."

"But Michael's doing better now. You said so yourself. Does this disorder go away on its own?"

"It doesn't disappear, but as some people grow older, they become better at coping with it. I've been using strategies with Michael that have been known to help people with ADHD, and they seem to be working."

"What could have happened to make Michael this way? I was so careful when I was pregnant. I didn't even take an aspirin."

"Mrs. Tayler, if Michael has ADHD—and that's a big if—it's nobody's fault. From what I've read, no one knows for sure what causes it, but it seems to run in families."

For a few moments, Mrs. Tayler was lost in thought. When she started talking again, she seemed to be thinking out loud. "You know, this is beginning to make sense. Bennett is like Michael in many ways. He gets bored easily, and he's constantly on the go. I've always been amazed by his ability to juggle so many things at once. He's a champion multitasker. That's one of the reasons he's such a successful businessman."

I was hoping to avoid the subject of Hannibal Tayler, but I could see it was going to be impossible.

She looked up at me. "Actually, I'm the third Mrs. Tayler. My husband divorced his first two wives before they had any children. He was so proud the day Michael was born. Now he had a son to follow in his footsteps, to share the business he'd spent his life building. He has such high expectations for Michael. He can't accept that Michael might not be able to live up to them."

I'll bet he can't. With his ego, it figures he'd want a mini-me for a son. I nodded, hoping my expression didn't give me away.

Mrs. Tayler stared straight into my eyes. "My husband is a very determined man. He's willing to do whatever it takes to reach his goals, and he's used to getting what he wants. His forceful nature has helped him succeed, but it's been hard on Michael."

I can imagine, judging from my own experiences with Mr. Forceful. I kept nodding, beginning to feel like one of those bobble-head dolls.

"My son has always felt like such a disappointment to his father. When Michael was a little boy, his desire to please motivated him to try harder. Now it just makes him resentful and rebellious. Bennett thinks he's being lazy or stubborn. He's convinced that he can bully Michael into performing. It's been a constant battle between those two." Her voice dropped to a whisper. "And I'm the one caught in the middle."

Nod, nod, nod.

Mrs. Tayler folded her trembling hands. "Ms. Bianchi, I'm aware of the discord between you and my husband. I've tried to reason with him and so has

Michael. But as I said before, it's difficult to get him to change his views once he's made up his mind about something—or someone."

She waited for me to respond, but I was using all my energy to keep my face in neutral. I could hear the quiet snuffle of her nose as she breathed. Finally, she cleared her throat.

"I love my husband," she said, "but I don't always agree with his sentiments or his methods. That's the main reason I asked for this meeting. It's important that you understand. I do not share my husband's opinion of you, and I hope you won't hold his behavior against me—or Michael."

I was feeling kind of icky for having been so wrong about her. This woman had bared her soul, so she deserved a truthful response.

"To be honest," I said, "this meeting was not at all what I expected. I prejudged you based on my experiences with your husband, and for that, I apologize. You're a caring mother who wants what's best for her son. And as far as my relationship with Michael is concerned, my feelings about your husband were never an issue. It would be unprofessional to have my opinion of a parent influence my behavior toward a student."

Her shoulders relaxed. I could almost see the tension draining from her body. "I can't tell you how relieved I am," she said. "I was so nervous about coming here today. More than anything, I want us to be able to work as a team." She rubbed her hands together. They were no longer trembling. "Where do we go from here?"

I thought of the articles Nancy had given me. "I have some material you might find informative. It will give you some background on ADHD."

"This disorder—is there any cure for it?"

"Not exactly, but it can be treated. Anyway, we're jumping way ahead of ourselves. The first step is to find out if Michael has ADHD, and the only way to do that is to have him examined by a neurologist."

"I'll call for an appointment first thing tomorrow morning."

"And I'll go up to my classroom to get the articles. The secretary can make copies for you. I'll meet you in the office." I got up to leave, but Mrs. Tayler held out her flawlessly manicured hand.

"I don't know how to thank you. This is the first time I've felt hopeful about Michael's situation."

I shook her hand. "Don't thank me yet. We've got a long way to go before the last piece of the puzzle is in place."

"That may be true," she said, holding onto my hand, "but it's always easier to put a puzzle together when you have someone to help you."

I almost ran Chris down at the top of the stairs.

"Whoa! Where's the fire?" he asked.

"Can't talk now. I'm in a rush. I'll call you when I get home. You won't believe my news." I dashed into my classroom, leaving a dumbfounded Chris alone in the hall.

Now where the hell did I put that file? I started tossing papers from my desk onto the floor.

"Dammit," I half-whispered. Then I caught sight of the folder peeking out of my tote. I grabbed it and raced back to the office where Mrs. Tayler was waiting.

"I had a little trouble locating the file," I said, as the copy machine whirred in the background. "I'm not the most organized person in the world."

Before handing her the pile of papers, still warm from the copier, I put the article about high-risk behavior on top where she'd be certain to see it. She promised to call me after she read everything. I walked her out to the parking lot and watched as she slid into her silver Mercedes and drove away. Feeling a little shabby, I opened the door to my dented Dodge and tossed my tote onto the worn back seat. On the drive home, I decided to earmark part of my next paycheck for some new clothes.

Chapter Seventeen

My mood matched the bright autumn sunshine as I drove to school the next morning, singing along with Bruce. Chrysanthemums were blooming, the foliage was blazing, the frost was on the pumpkin, and I was happy to be alive and born in the USA. I even had the guilty pleasure of seeing Yin-Yang get treed by the Rottweiler from down the street.

I'd spent most of last evening on the phone telling Chris and Nancy about my meeting with Mrs. Tayler. Chris was astonished, but Nancy didn't seem quite as surprised.

"I told you not to jump to conclusions," she said.

Encouraged by Mrs. Tayler's reaction, I decided to try a new strategy with Michael. Tomorrow I'd be giving a major test, and I planned to spend today's class reviewing. I was worried that the sheer volume of information might over-whelm Michael. I'd read in my research that people with ADHD can often process large amounts of material more easily if they use a method known as "chunking."

At the end of class, I took Michael aside and asked him if he felt ready for the test. I reminded him that a good part of his report card grade would depend on it. He scratched his head and gave me the generic response about planning to study hard and do his best, la, la, la. I asked to see his class notes. They were barely legible, jotted down on loose pieces of notebook paper in no particular order.

I showed Michael how to make an outline of his notes, breaking up the information into smaller "chunks" of related topics. I told him that if he studied each topic until he understood it, the material might make more sense.

He frowned in concentration, furrowing his forehead in the universal symbol of I-don't-get-it. He shifted from foot to foot and scratched his head. Figuring that my initial lesson needed some clarification, I showed him how the topics were connected. Then I explained that sometimes it's easier to retain information if you learn it a little at a time. He admitted that he had trouble studying anything for a long stretch. He continued staring at the outline until the cartoon lightbulb over his head lit up. It was the "Eureka!" moment that teachers live for.

Just then, Jessica poked her head through the doorway, urging Michael to hurry so they wouldn't miss the bus.

"I'm taking the bus to Jessie's," Michael said. "We're going to study together." Judging from the way Jessica blushed, they planned to do a lot more than study English. Michael joined her in the hall, slinging his arm over her shoulders. She slipped her hand around his waist, hooking her thumb in one of his belt loops as they walked hip to hip. If Mrs. Tayler could only see her baby boy now!

The next morning, Anna and Don were waiting for me in the office. They had the look of people who just found out that a giant asteroid was headed for earth. Anna clutched the jar of chocolates like a life preserver.

I looked from one to the other, feeling a twinge of alarm. "Is something wrong?"

Anna glanced at Don before answering. "Tayler called. Wants to see you after school. Don and I'll sit in. You okay with that?"

My face relaxed. "Sure, I'd be happy to meet with him."

They looked at each other. Then they stared at me as if I'd sprouted a third boob.

"I don't think there'll be any trouble," I said. The way I figured it, Mrs. Tayler had shared the ADHD articles with her husband, and he was coming in to apologize for misjudging me. With all of us on the same page, we could finally get Michael some help. "I'll come down to the conference room right after my last class."

I walked out, leaving Anna and Don too flabbergasted to say a word.

At lunch, I told Chris about Mr. Tayler's impending visit. He didn't share my optimistic outlook.

"Now, please don't think I'm telling you what to do," he said, "but try to follow my logic. Don't you find it a little odd that this man, the same one who's threatened to sue us and who's been harassing you since September, would do a complete one-eighty overnight?"

"You feel that way because you didn't talk to Mrs. Tayler. The woman loves me. She made it sound like I'm her new best friend."

"But she's not the one coming in for a conference today."

He had a point. I took a spoonful of my lowfat, sugarless, taste-free yogurt and thought for a moment. "Well, maybe Mr. Tayler wants to see me privately because he's embarrassed about how he's been behaving. Or maybe he's uncomfortable apologizing in front of his wife. You know, the macho thing."

Chris slapped his forehead. "Jen, we're not talking male chauvinist here. We're talking power junkie. Do you really believe this guy is capable of admitting he's wrong? Or of being embarrassed about anything?"

"Who knows? The way I see it, we may have misjudged him. You want logic? Then let's review what's happened." I held up my fingers to count. "First, his son gets suspended for something he thinks is unfair, so he tries to defend him. It's not unusual for a father to take his kid's side. In fact, it's the norm. Next, his son is injured, and he tries to hold someone accountable. Granted, he overreacted. But you can understand why he'd be upset. And can he really be a complete ogre if he has such a nice wife and son? He must have some redeeming qualities."

"Are you trying to convince me or yourself?" Chris asked.

"I'm not trying to convince anybody. I'm only trying to keep an open mind. I went into the conference with Mrs. Tayler expecting the worst, and I was dead wrong. Maybe this time, I'll be pleasantly surprised."

"Not nearly as surprised as I'll be. This whole thing doesn't smell right. Did Anna give you any clue as to why Tayler's coming in?"

"No. But she and Don are going to be there."

"And doesn't that seem kind of strange? Why would they have to run interference if the man only wants to make nice?"

I hadn't thought of that. But I wasn't ready to take off my Little Mary Sunshine hat just yet.

"Maybe they're assuming the worst, just like you." I could hear the edgy tone creeping into my voice. Apparently, so could Chris.

"Hey, calm down," he said. "I don't want to argue. I just don't want you to be blindsided. Maybe you should ask Marita to sit in."

My eyes narrowed. "Oh, sure. It'll look real nice if I walk in with a union rep. Not too confrontational or anything. And how stupid will we all feel if I'm right, and he only wanted to thank me for helping Michael?"

Chris held up his hands as if to ward off my anger. "Okay, I give up. I guess you know more about this guy than I do."

Yeah. Right.

As Michael worked through his test, he kept staring at the clock and gnawing on his eraser. Was it my imagination, or did he seem more distracted than usual? I strolled by and tapped his desk. He went back to work without glancing up at me.

He was still working on the last item when the bell rang. When he finished, he slipped his paper onto my desk and disappeared before I could ask him how his study session had gone. His behavior seemed odd, but in Michael's case, odd was a relative term. Anyway, he could have been stressed about the test or in a hurry to meet Jessica. I gathered my things and headed down to the conference room, full of confidence and high expectations.

The instant I opened the door, I knew something was wrong. Anna and Don were seated across the table from Bennett Tayler and Stanton Hawthorne. At the head of the table was Superintendent Dimmit.

Now I get it. I'm dead, and this is hell!

Don stood up and pulled out the chair next to his. My heart knocked against my ribs. I could tell from the expression on Bennett Tayler's face that he wasn't here to make amends. My knees buckled as I sank into the chair.

Superintendent Dimmit sat back and folded his hands over his paunchy stomach. "Ms. Bianchi, Mr. Tayler has come to me with some serious concerns about you and your behavior toward his son. It seems he has tried to address this on two previous occasions, but the matter hasn't been resolved to his satisfaction. That's why he found it necessary to involve me."

"I don't understand," I said. My voice sounded high and far away.

"Then let me explain in a way even you can comprehend." Mr. Tayler practically spat the words. "From our first encounter, I was dissatisfied with your attitude toward my son. You immediately labeled him a problem student and went about treating him like one. Now you have the audacity to tell my wife that Michael has some kind of mental disorder." His voice thundered in the small room.

I could feel myself shrinking, like Alice after she ate the magic mushroom.

"As far as I'm concerned," he continued, "you have been grossly unprofessional. Your negligence at the dance resulted in physical harm to my son, and now you are trying to harm him emotionally with your amateur attempts at psychoanalysis. How dare you suggest that there is something wrong with my son's brain! Tell me, Ms. Bianchi—when did you get your degree in psychiatry?"

"Hold on," Anna said. "Explain yourself. She's never behaved improperly."

"If that's what you think, then perhaps you should be more diligent in monitoring your teachers." He held out his hand to Stanton Hawthorne, who gave him the articles I'd given to Mrs. Tayler. "This is the rubbish your 'star teacher' gave my wife in a flagrant attempt to slander my son." He threw the papers onto the table. "Now my wife is convinced that Michael needs to see a neurologist. I'll have you know there's nothing wrong with Michael that some discipline—and a more competent teacher—won't cure."

I stared at the papers fanned across the table top, and my eyes locked on something that flash-froze my bones. A promotional flier for Adderall, an ADHD medication.

The shocked little teacher says what? "Wh—what?" I stammered.

While my brain tried to wrap itself around this latest bit of bad news, Mr. Tayler snatched the flier and waved it in my face. "And you push drugs, too? Quite an enterprising little thing, aren't you?"

The flier from the package Marian sent must have gotten mixed up with the articles I gave to Mrs. Tayler. I opened my mouth to explain, but Mr. Tayler didn't even come up for air.

"I demand that my son be taken out of this woman's class immediately. She is to have no further contact with him." He turned to Superintendent Dimmit. "I also want the school board to investigate Ms. Bianchi's questionable teaching methods. I feel it is my duty as a concerned parent to protect other children from such educational malpractice."

Here I was, trapped in the middle of a real-life horror movie. I tried to speak again, but the words were gridlocked in my throat.

Anna's eyes flitted around the table, and she wet her lips. "We'll transfer Michael. No need to involve the board."

"I've already called the board president and scheduled a meeting for next Thursday." Bennett Tayler turned to me, his eyes smoldering with fury. "In the meantime, I'm warning you—stay away from my son."

I watched in disbelief as he stood and gestured to Stanton Hawthorne. Still glaring at me, he followed his lawyer out of the room, slamming the door behind him.

The concussion of the slammed door gave way to a stupefied silence. For a moment, I thought I was suffocating. Then I realized I'd been holding my breath, and I let it out in a single, explosive burst. Anna and Don turned as one to look at me. Little sparks danced along the edges of my vision, and my head felt as if it had come untethered from my neck. I tried to stand, but a wave of dizziness knocked me back into the chair.

Don grabbed my arm to steady me. "Jenna, would you like some water?" He nodded to Anna who disappeared into the hall, returning seconds later with a dripping paper cup. She put it to my lips, and I sipped, wincing as the coolness hit my knotted stomach.

Superintendent Dimmit stood up and nailed me with a reproachful glare. "You're in deep trouble, young lady," he said. Then he turned to Anna. "I have to get back to my office. I've wasted too much time on this already." He strode out the door without looking back.

Anna pressed her palm against my forehead. "You okay?"

I managed a nod.

She sat down next to me. "What's going on?"

Don was leafing through the articles that Mr. Tayler had left on the table. "I think you should take a look at these," he said, pushing the papers toward Anna.

I took another sip of water and described my conference with Mrs. Tayler. Anna and Don listened in silence.

When I finished, Anna said, "You meant well. Just went a little overboard."

Don rested his chin on his steepled fingers. "Educators aren't in a position to determine that a student suffers from ADHD. Only a medical doctor is qualified to make the diagnosis. We have to walk a fine line in these matters, and Mr. Tayler feels you've crossed that line."

I couldn't believe what I was hearing. "I explained all that to Mrs. Tayler. In fact, I was the one who suggested she have Michael checked by a neurologist. All I did was share some information. I never for a moment led her to think I was making a diagnosis."

"And this?" Anna held up the Adderall flier.

"I never meant to give that to Mrs. Tayler. It was part of some research I was doing."

"We believe you," Anna said. "The board might not. Lawyers make them jumpy."

My insides were churning. The tears I'd been trying so hard to hold back forced their way down my cheeks. I buried my face in my hands as questions swirled through my head. *Why did I have to be so damn stubborn? What the hell was I thinking? Me, a second-year teacher, going up against the most influential man in town. Was I insane? Everyone tried to warn me. Why didn't I listen? All I had to do was mind my own business, and none of this would have happened.* Then I remembered the look on Michael's face when he got his report card, and my pity party came to an end.

An eerie sense of calm settled over me as I took a tissue and wiped my eyes. "There's nothing more I can say. I really believed I was helping Michael. His improvement reinforced my belief. Mr. Tayler doesn't see it that way, so we have a standoff. I guess we'll have to leave it to the school board to decide who's right." I shrugged as a blast of exhaustion hit me like a wrecking ball. "I just want to go home."

The ride home was a blur. When I was safely inside my house, I locked the door and took the phone off the hook. Then I turned off my cell and tossed it onto the sofa. Brutus watched without making a sound as I stumbled to my room, kicked off my shoes, and crumpled onto the bed. I pulled the covers over my head and closed my eyes, trying to empty my mind of everything but the comforting darkness.

I lay there for a while, aware of nothing but the rise and fall of my breathing, until a deep silence enveloped me. Suddenly, I felt a feathery touch on my cheek.

"Nana? How did you get here?"

Nana never looked so beautiful. She was sitting on the bed, wearing a floral print housedress, her white hair tied back with a pink ribbon. She was smiling, and her face was inexpressibly serene.

"Is it really you?" I asked. There was something unusual about her being here, but I couldn't put my finger on what it was.

I nestled my head in her lap. "Nana, I've made such a mess of things. I had to be hard-headed and do everything my way. Now I'm in so much trouble." I reached up and touched her cheek. "I wish I was more like you."

She shook her head and pressed her index finger against my lips. Then she stroked my hair, and I caught a faint whiff of her rosewater cologne. That's when I remembered she was dead.

I clutched her skirt. "Nana, please stay here with me. I really need you." She brushed her lips across my forehead, her touch light as an angel's wing. Then she smiled at me again. Her eyes were so full of love they seemed to glow. And, just like that, she was gone.

"No, Nana. Come back!" I squeezed my eyes shut and pounded the head-board with my fists.

Klunk, klunk, klunk.

"WAAK.

When I forced my eyes open, I fully expected to see my grandmother sitting beside me. My head was throbbing, and my face was soaked with tears, but I felt oddly refreshed. I could still feel Nana's arms around me, and, for an instant, I thought I detected the delicate scent of roses.

Klunk, klunk, klunk.

"WAAAAAAAK."

I looked around, momentarily disoriented. Then I tottered into the living room, tripping over the shoes I'd left on the floor. The screech was coming from Brutus the Watchbird. I scrubbed the last remnants of sleep from my eyes and peered through the peephole. Chris was pounding the door like it was his mortal enemy.

I jerked the door open and came face to face with a startled Chris. His fist hung in mid-air for a beat. Then he grabbed me by the shoulders and smothered me in a hug.

"Jesus! I've been worried sick about you. Don called and told me about the meeting. He couldn't get through to you by phone, so he thought you might be with me. When I tried to call, I kept getting a busy signal. And your cell went right through to voice mail. Do you know how long I've been knocking on this door?"

I pushed him away. "I was asleep. I didn't hear anything until Brutus started up."

"What's with your phones?"

"I took the phone off the hook and turned off my cell. I wanted a little peace and quiet, but I guess that was asking too much."

"Well, excuse me for wanting to make sure you were all right."

"Oh, don't be so dramatic. What did you think I was going to do—throw myself into the Delaware and drown?"

"Hey, Cranky McSnarly. What've you done with Jenna?" He tucked a wayward curl behind my ear and kissed my forehead. "I'm glad you're okay."

"I'm far from okay," I said, feeling the tears well up. "Come on in."

Chris put his arm around me as we walked into the living room. Brutus uttered a quiet growl, but Chris shushed him. I curled up next to Chris on the sofa and sobbed out all the gruesome details of the conference. When I ran out of tears, he tilted my chin up and kissed my wet cheeks. "You could use a little less salt," he said.

I rested my head against his chest, listening to the steady rhythm of his heart as he stroked my hair. I wanted to stay that way forever, but Chris broke the spell.

"I need to call Don and Nancy. They'll want to know you're all right." He wrapped me in Nana's afghan. "Stay here and rest."

I closed my eyes, feeling snug and safe in my little cocoon. Much as I hated to admit it, I enjoyed being pampered like Damsel-in-Distress Barbie.

After Chris hung up, he started rooting around in the kitchen.

I yawned and stretched. "What're you up to?"

"Thought I'd fix us some dinner. Don't you keep any food around here?"

"There should be eggs and cheese in the fridge. And I have some veggies, but those belong to Brutus."

"I'm sure he won't mind sharing. I'll make a little extra for him." Chris craned his neck to look over at Brutus. "What do you say, Cujo?"

Brutus flapped his wings and hissed.

By the time I found the energy to haul myself off the sofa, Chris was stirring a fragrant mixture in a frying pan.

"It's a frittata," he said. "Think giant omelet. I made it with the peppers and zucchini you had in the refrigerator." He finished it off with a generous handful of grated cheddar. "Do you feel up to buttering toast while we wait for the cheese to melt?"

Brutus smelled the food and whistled, so Chris spooned some of the frittata into his dish and topped it with a small triangle of toast. The three of us ate in companionable silence as I fantasized about life with a full-time personal chef.

Before Chris left, I promised to call if I needed to talk. The nap and dinner had energized me enough to grade some tests. But when I took the top paper from the stack, tears threatened to return. It belonged to Michael. I had a sudden urge to shred the paper into confetti and toss it out the window. After all, Michael was no longer my problem. But he'd made the effort to prepare for the test. The least I could do was correct it.

There were only two errors on his paper. He'd scored a ninety-eight. I imagined how elated he'd be, so unlike the angry boy who stomped into my class in September. And I knew that, in spite of everything, I helped make the difference. I put a big, red "A" at the top of his paper. Under it, I wrote, "I'm proud of you!" Then I let the tears come.

Chapter Eighteen

With the board meeting hanging over me like a plume of toxic waste, it was difficult to concentrate on much else. I couldn't get my head around the idea that my future hinged on the decision of nine strangers. I moved through my morning classes like a robot. What was the point? A week from now there might be someone else in my place.

I was on my way to the teacher's room to have lunch with Chris when Anna called me into the office. She was sucking on a chocolate kiss, and she didn't look happy.

"Just wanted you to know. We transferred the Tayler kid. Sent him to Terri."

T-Rex? You've got to be freaking kidding! I tried to keep the shock from registering on my face. "Well, you did what you had to do. I'm sorry things turned out this way." My chest was so tight I could hardly breathe.

Anna put her hand on my shoulder. "Don't feel bad. No reflection on you."

Yeah. I'm sure. I nodded.

"Touch base with Terri. Brief her on Michael. She'll need his records. You know the drill."

"Sure. I'll try to catch up with her before the end of the day."

"Thanks." Anna reached into her pocket and pulled out four chocolate kisses. "Have some. Good for what ails you."

Only if they're laced with Prozac. I took one just to be polite, but my stomach was churning. Could this situation actually get any worse? The answer was waiting for me in the faculty room.

Chris was sitting at our usual table. Next to him was Terri the Slut. In my seat. Leaning so close to Chris that their shoulders touched. Before I could rip off her arm and beat her with it, Chris saw me and waved me over. The relief in his face was so unmistakable that my rage cooled to a simmer.

"Jenna! Terri was looking for you." He pulled out the chair on the other side of his.

I sat down and gave T-Rex my brightest smile. "And now she's found me. Must be her lucky day." I turned to Chris. "I was in the office talking to Anna."

T-Rex regarded me with a smarmy grin. "Then I guess she told you about my new student."

I resisted the urge to pull out her brassy hair by its dark roots. "Yes, she did. She asked me to meet with you to give you an update on him."

"Lovely. Can we do it now?"

Chris was silently following the conversation as if it were a tennis match, his head whipping from T-Rex to me. "I'd really prefer to meet after school," I said, fondling Chris's arm. "Chris and I planned to have lunch together this period." I'm usually not so overtly territorial, but she brought out the bitch in me. *See? You like playing smartass? Me, too.*

Her smile faltered for a second. She made a quick recovery, but I knew I'd scored a direct hit. She pulled down on her clingy sweater and stood to go.

"Then I'll see you later. My room?" She accidentally-on-purpose bumped Chris with her hip.

"Sure." I wiggled my fingers at her. "Bye, now." *And don't let the door hit you in the ass.*

She turned to Chris. "It was nice talking with you. I'll see you around."

He gave her a sheepish wave and said nothing. A wise man, Chris.

After she'd gone, Chris looked at me and exhaled audibly. "So Michael's been placed in Terri's class. I know you're upset, but look on the bright side. Now she gets to deal with his nutty father."

"I really don't want to talk about this anymore," I told him. "Every time I think things have gotten as bad as they can get, something worse happens."

Chris lowered his eyes. "You may be right about that."

"Why? What aren't you telling me?"

He looked up and took hold of my hands. "I talked to Marita last period. She contacted the union about this Bennett Tayler mess."

"And?" I knew the news was bad when Chris's grip tightened.

"And since you're non-tenured, there isn't much they can do. If the board wants to dismiss you, they don't have to justify their decision to the union. As long as they follow due process, which they have, they can pretty much do whatever they want."

I pulled my hands away and rested my forehead on my palms. "God, I can't seem to catch a break. I thought for sure the association could help me. Now, they're throwing me under the bus."

"Nobody's throwing you under anything. Marita said she's going to make sure your rights aren't violated. If the board does anything that's not strictly kosher, Marita will address it. It's just that there's very little protection for teachers until they're granted tenure."

"And from the looks of things, that'll never happen. I'd better dust off my resume. Maybe I can get a job flipping burgers." I set the chocolate kiss on the table.

"That's your lunch?" Chris asked.

"You can have it. My stomach's bothering me."

Chris put his hands on my shoulders and squeezed. "Probably tension. You're all knotted up." He pushed his thumbs into my neck muscles and made small, slow circles.

I closed my eyes and rolled my head. "Mmmm. That feels good."

"I can make you feel even better," he whispered, "but you'll have to wait until we're alone."

After I'd returned the tests to my eighth period class, I had one paper left over. It was Michael's. Since I was no longer allowed to have any contact with him, I decided to ask Jessica to give him his test. She hadn't been her usual perky self for the past two days. Her hand no longer shot into the air when I asked questions, and she avoided my eyes. I figured she was upset about the Michael situation. Maybe this would break the ice. When the dismissal bell rang, I called her up to my desk.

"Jessica, could I ask you a favor?"

"Sure." She kept her eyes focused on the floor.

"I have a test I need to return to Michael. Could you do it for me?"

Jessica took the paper and read my comment. When she looked up, a tear slid down her cheek. "This is so unfair. Everything was going great, and now ..."

I didn't know how to respond, so I didn't.

"Michael feels really awful," Jessica continued, "and it isn't even his fault. He told me how much he likes you, how you were the only teacher that didn't treat him like a freak. You made him believe he was good at something. He was so happy about working on the paper. He was even talking about going to college and maybe becoming a writer." She gave a little sniffle. "Michael thinks his father's ruined everything. He's so angry, Ms. B. I'm worried about what he might do."

I patted her hand. "I'm sure things will work out for the best." It was weird to hear my mother's words coming out of my mouth. "Michael's improving in all his classes. There's no reason he shouldn't continue to do well. And even though he won't be at the meetings, he can still submit pieces for the newspaper."

"But what about you? Some of the kids are saying Mr. Tayler's going to make the school board fire you. Is that true?"

News travels fast. I considered consoling her with a little white lie, but chose to go with the truth, as unpleasant as it was.

"To be honest, there is a chance I might have to leave Morrison. But there's also a chance the board will let me stay. Either way, it's out of our hands. Worrying won't change anything." I gave her a tight smile. "In the meantime, please give Michael his test. And tell him I knew he could do it."

Jessica wiped her cheek with her sweater sleeve. Then she slipped out the door, and I listened to her footsteps fade down the empty hall.

"Jenna. Come in." T-Rex was sitting at her desk, arms folded under her silicone boobs. I handed her Michael's permanent record folder and a printout of his first marking period grades. Then I waited for her to offer me a chair. When she didn't, I sat down in one of the student desks.

"This is everything I have on Michael," I said, trying not to grit my teeth.

She picked up the printout and scanned his scores. "Not too bad. I expected a lot worse, considering all the horror stories I've been hearing."

"English is his best subject. And I think he's a pretty neat kid."

"You're in the minority there. Most of the people I've talked to can't stand him."

"Maybe you're talking to the wrong people."

She looked down at me and sniffed. "Sure. Everybody's out of step but Jenna."

And maybe you'd like to step on over here and let me knock that snooty nose onto the other side of your face. "Oh, you know how it is," I said, mustering restraint I never knew I had. Probably some recessive gene I inherited from my mother. "Kids usually respond better to a teacher who cares about them."

T-Rex arched one of her penciled eyebrows. "Unfortunately, that doesn't always apply to their parents. I hear you've been having a little problem with Michael's father. Too bad."

Yeah, I'll bet it just breaks your heart. "Well, parents can be difficult. I'm sure you've had your share."

"Never one who threatened to sue, or tried to get the school board to fire me." She chuckled and shook her head. "And this is only your second year. Pretty impressive."

Want to see how impressive my foot would look buried in your fat ass? I had to wrap this up fast, before I did something that might get me arrested.

"Listen, T—I mean Terri. I came here to talk about Michael, not about me. He's got a lot of potential, as you can see from his test scores and his IQ. And I think you'll be impressed by his writing ability. But he has attentiveness issues, so cut him some slack. I've made several accommodations for him that seem to be helping." I pointed to the folder. "There's a list in his file. You might want to check it out. If you continue using those strategies, you shouldn't have any problems with Michael."

"I have absolutely no intention of having any problems with Michael." She flipped open the folder and took out the list. After a cursory read-through, she looked at me, still wearing that snotty little smirk. "I don't need to do anything special for this kid. I can assure you, he's going to do just fine in my class."

Maybe it was my current fragile mental state that made me a little slow on the uptake. Or maybe it was my overwhelming desire to slam her against the wall. But it took me a moment to understand what she was implying. "Are you saying you're going to just push him through? Do you honestly think that will help him? He's bright and talented. He doesn't need a free pass. He needs someone to challenge him. Someone who will make him earn his grades."

"Yes, and I can see how well that worked for you." She sneered at me like I was some dimwitted chump. "Jenna, I know who this kid's father is. And, yes, I may be blonde. But unlike you, I'm not that dumb."

I was so angry that I didn't hear Nancy calling from across the parking lot. I looked up to see her hurrying toward me, waving her hand. When she reached my car, she took a moment to catch her breath.

"Anna told me about Michael being transferred to Terri's class. Talk about Murphy's Law. How're you doing?"

I leaned against the front fender. "Let's put it this way. I just left that bitch's classroom, and she's still breathing."

"Well," Nancy said, "I see you've gotten much better at anger management."

I took a deep breath and blew it out. "I don't know how much more of this I can take." I hated the pathetic hitch in my voice. "No matter where I turn, I keep getting kicked to the curb."

"I know things look pretty bleak, but don't give up hope. You've got more going for you than you think."

"Then you know something I don't. According to Chris, even the union considers this is a lost cause."

"There's no such thing as a lost cause. Misplaced, maybe. But not lost."

I studied Nancy's face. There was something she wasn't telling me, but I was too demoralized to pursue it.

"Whatever," I said, fishing in my pockets for my keys. "I'm too tired to fight anymore. I just want this whole thing to be over."

Nancy's expression didn't change, but I noticed a little twinkle in her eye. "Nothing's over until the fat lady sings," she said. "And I'm the fat lady."

It seemed as if that long week would never end. I felt like I was having a non-stop, out-of-body experience as I went through the motions of my life. Fortunately, I had a great support system. Chris sent me a big white teddy bear holding a dozen yellow roses. My mom brought me an enormous pan of baked ziti, and Dad put in calls to every lawyer in the tri-state area. Nancy tried to cheer me up with her sense of humor and her animal crackers. Anna left a one-pound bag of chocolate kisses in my mailbox. Don pledged his complete support. My students were extra attentive, in spite of the fact that my classroom performance was less than stellar. Many smiled or waved when they saw me in the halls. A few of them left apples or candy bars on my desk when I wasn't looking. Even Brutus was abnormally well-behaved.

By Thursday, I was numb to the core, and the core was numb. I somehow made it to the end of eighth period. When the dismissal bell rang, no one made a move to leave. Then Jessica came up to my desk and handed me a large white envelope. Inside was a beautiful card.

"I made it myself," she said. "Everybody in our class signed it." On the front was a watercolor of a beautiful sunrise with "Keep the Faith!" written across the top in big, colorful balloon letters. Inside were messages of support, some misspelled, but all overflowing with sincerity and affection. My eyes were drawn to a familiar, scrawling script in the lower right hand corner. It read, "You were there for me—I'll be there for you." It was signed "Mike T."

My numbness began to disintegrate, burned away by the Bianchi fire. Time to restore balance to the universe. What about karma? Being right had to count for something. Bennett Tayler wanted a piece of me? Well, he wouldn't get it without a fight. No more wimpy victim stuff for Jenna Bianchi. Bring on Tayler, his toady lawyer, Superintendent "Dimwit," the whole school board. I'd show them what this teacher was made of!

Jessica must have sensed the change because she gave a tentative smile. I returned the smile and hugged her, and the rest of the class broke into applause.

"You can't know how much this means to me," I said. "Thank you all. And I promise you—I will keep the faith."

"Way to go, Ms. B. You rock," Damien shouted. The other kids joined in a chorus of cheers.

Jessica hiked her backpack onto her shoulder. "Good luck tonight, Ms. B. We'll see you tomorrow."

"Yes," I replied, "you will."

Chapter Nineteen

I hurried home to give myself plenty of time to prepare for my appearance before the board. I showered, washed my hair, and changed into my no-nonsense navy blue power suit. Then I slipped on a pair of three-inch heels, hoping the extra height would make me more imposing. I pulled my unruly curls into a tight bun and surveyed myself in the mirror. The overall effect was don't-screw-with-me. Just the look I was going for. When I walked into the living room, Brutus gave a loud wolf whistle.

"Thanks for the vote of confidence," I said.

I riffled through the papers on my desk, taking out anything that might be helpful—the articles on ADHD (minus the drug info), my grade book, a copy of Michael's report card, the school paper with Michael's article. I looked longingly at the six-pack of Miller Lite in the refrigerator, but I poured a tall glass of herbal iced tea instead. It wouldn't be good form to show up at a board meeting smelling like a brewery. Before I could take a sip, the phone rang.

"Hi, honey. Dad and I wanted to wish you luck."

"Thanks, Mom." It was so good to hear her voice.

"I'm sure everything will work out," she said. That pretty much summed up my mother's philosophy of life. "Just tell them what's in your heart, and keep that temper under control. You'll be fine. Here, Dad wants to talk to you."

I held the phone away from my ear.

"Hi, Daddy," I said.

"Hey there, Mighty Mite. You okay?"

"Yes, Daddy, I'm fine."

"Now listen to me. Don't take any crap from that son-of-a-bitch! You stand up to him and tell him where to go."

Ah, the fiery Bianchi gene in all its glory. "I don't know, Daddy. Somehow I don't think that will sit too well with the school board."

"Screw 'em. Nobody pushes my little girl around. They should be down on their knees, thanking you for all the hard work you do. ON THEIR FREAKIN' KNEES."

"Unfortunately, that's not the way it works."

"Well, don't you worry. I've made some calls. Those bums think they're the only ones who know lawyers? I'll show them lawyers. If they try to fire my daughter, I'll sue their asses so bad they'll have to crap through their ears!"

Before I could respond, I heard muffled voices on my father's end of the line.

"Honey?" Apparently, Mom had commandeered the phone. "Remember what I said. Try not to worry, and call me when you get home." Her voice dropped to a whisper. "And whatever Dad told you, do the opposite."

That made me smile. "Thanks, Mom. I will."

I hung up the phone and sat down to gather my thoughts. I wanted to make my case so compelling, the board would have to decide in my favor. After tacking Jessica's card over my desk for inspiration, I took out a pad of notebook paper and started writing.

The sky outside had grown ominously dark by the time I set my pen down and swallowed the last of the tea. Bursts of lightning illuminated the undersides of storm clouds that roiled above the treetops. Thunder grumbled in the distance. Little eddies of dust swirled in the gutters. A sudden gust of wind set the tree branches dancing, tousling their leaves. The perfect atmospheric touch for the never-ending horror movie that had become my life. All that was missing was the grotesque monster clawing itself out of the open grave. Oh, wait—that would be Bennett Tayler.

I stared at the slate-colored horizon as random scenes drifted through my mind. *My last day of student teaching. Shaking hands with the dean as I received my college diploma. The day I found out I'd gotten the job at Morrison. My first day in my very own classroom.*

I was jarred back to reality by my chirping cell phone.

"HELLO," Brutus crowed, as I flipped it open.

"Hi, babe." Chris sounded artificially cheerful. "Just called to see how you were holding up."

"I've finished my statement, and I think it's pretty convincing."

"Do you have all your documentation? How about that notebook you were keeping?"

Goofy! I'd almost forgotten. "Thanks for reminding me. That might come in handy."

"I saw Nancy after school. She didn't want to bother you before the meeting, but she said to call her the minute you get home, no matter how late. She's keeping all her fingers crossed. Her toes too."

I had a sudden image of Nancy all tied up in knots. Then I looked at the clock. According to Felix, it was almost seven-thirty. The meeting was scheduled to begin at eight.

"Listen, Chris, I've got to get going. It won't make a good impression if I come strolling in late."

"No problem. I'm on my way over to pick you up. I figured you could use some moral support, and you shouldn't be driving when your mind is on other things. Your driving is scary enough when you're concentrating."

I huffed an exaggerated sigh. "I know what you're trying to do, and I don't know whether to be grateful or insulted. I'm okay, really. You don't have to baby-sit me. I'm sure I can find the board office all by myself."

"I know you can, but I thought it would help to have a bodyguard along. And you know how much I love guarding your hot little body. Anyway, I'm pulling into your driveway as we speak. And you can't leave because I'm parked behind your car."

I looked out the window and, sure enough, there was Chris, waving his cell phone from the front seat of his red Toyota.

"Okay, I give up," I said. "I'll be right out."

On the way to the hearing, I practiced reading my statement. Chris listened, interrupting here and there to offer suggestions. By the time I finished, we were turning into the parking lot of the boxy, beige stucco building with "MORRI-SONVILLE BOARD OF EDUCATION" painted in black letters over the entrance. The windows glowed like malevolent eyes. More than a dozen cars were parked side by side, like a regiment of soldiers prepared for battle. Wind chased dead leaves across the parking lot.

I straightened my spine and rolled my shoulders. As I reached to unlock the car door, Chris grabbed my hand and pulled me toward him. Then he kissed me firmly on the mouth.

"For luck," he said.

A chilly drizzle slicked the blacktop as I walked across the parking lot, trying not to slip in my high-heels. Chris held my arm as I wobbled up to the brightly-lit entrance.

"You really don't have to stay here," I told him. "There's nothing you can do once the meeting starts, so why don't you go on home? I can hitch a ride with Anna, and I'll call you when it's over."

"Are you kidding? I wouldn't miss this for the world. I've seen you in action when you're really angry. Bennett Tayler might need some protection."

We walked hand-in-hand to the meeting room. Before I could open the door, Chris kissed the center of my palm and curled my fingers around it.

"Hold onto that while you're in there. Now give 'em hell, Tiger."

That's right. I'm a tiger! A savage fighter for truth and justice. I tucked a stray curl into my bun, smoothed my skirt, drew myself up to my full five feet two inches (five-five with the heels), and marched courageously toward the firing line.

My confidence wavered as I walked down the aisle. The nine board members and Superintendent Dimmit were sitting side by side at a long conference table facing rows of chairs that filled the room like a movie theater from hell. I took a seat between Don and Anna on the right side of the aisle. Bennett Tayler and Stanton Hawthorne were immersed in conversation on the left. I searched the room for Mrs. Tayler, but she was nowhere to be found.

Freaking terrific. I was hoping she'd be here to corroborate my story, but Hubby Hannibal must have tied up that little loose end. Or maybe he'd tied up Mrs. Tayler. I visualized Claudia Tayler, her wrists and ankles bound with heavy rope, a wide strip of duct tape sealing her mouth shut.

Chris had taken a seat in the last row. Next to him was Marita Lopez. She raised her hand in a wave and smiled at me. Her presence was reassuring, even though she didn't have much official clout.

I turned to Don. He patted my arm and winked. Then Anna slipped something into my hand. A chocolate kiss. I felt my courage return. With a kiss in each hand, I could face anything.

Superintendent Dimmit oozed solemnity as he opened the meeting. "We've come here tonight at the request of Mr. Bennett Tayler. He has some serious concerns regarding the actions of one of our high school teachers, Ms. Jenna Bianchi. Mr. Tayler has met with the teacher in question, her building administrators, and me, personally. Since the difficulties have not been satisfactorily resolved, he has brought them to the board."

Ellen Sieben, the board president, asked Mr. Tayler to present his concerns. He stood, buttoning his meticulously tailored jacket.

"First off, I would like to introduce my attorney, Mr. Stanton Hawthorne, Esquire, of Hawthorne, Hawthorne and Bates."

He shoots … he scores! A murmur shot through the board. Nothing can turn a school board into a quivering mass of Jell-o faster than a high-powered lawyer.

"When my wife and I were researching schools for our son, Michael," he continued, "we were quite impressed with the reputation of Morrison. Even though it is a public school, we felt it would offer Michael an education equal to that of the private institutions he has attended. So we enrolled him here. Unfortunately, I have come to regret that decision." He turned to glower directly at me. I glowered right back.

"The trouble began almost immediately. My son engaged in some harmless horseplay with another boy, and Ms. Bianchi here"—he made a dismissive gesture in my direction—"blew the entire incident out of proportion. This resulted in my son being suspended, causing him extreme embarrassment. According to Michael, Ms. Bianchi took an instant dislike to him. She has taken every opportunity to ridicule him and single him out for censure."

That lying son-of-a-bitch! A geyser of anger bubbled inside me. I tightened my grip on the arms of my chair, but Don put his hand over mine. "Steady, girl," he muttered from the corner of his mouth. I relaxed my hands, discovering that I'd smashed the chocolate kiss. *Dammit.*

"The next incident was far more serious." Mr. Tayler rearranged his features into a wounded expression as he gave his version of the fight at the Halloween dance, casting me in the role of an incompetent airhead who stood by and allowed his poor son to be assaulted.

"As a parent, I trusted the so-called 'professionals' with the safety of my child," he said. "It turns out that, in this instance, my trust was completely misplaced."

"He wasn't even there." I whispered to Don. He shushed me.

Mr. Tayler strode over to the superintendent and stood beside his chair. "To add insult to injury, because of Ms. Bianchi's biased version of the events, my injured son was once again threatened with suspension. It was only due to Mr. Hawthorne's intervention and Superintendent Dimmit's fair-mindedness that Michael was allowed to return to school."

The superintendent smiled up at Mr. Tayler. *Your lips. His ass. Have they met?* I resisted the impulse to roll my eyes.

Mr. Tayler continued without missing a beat. "And that wasn't the worst of it. At a meeting with my wife, Ms. Bianchi had the audacity to claim that my son has a mental disorder. She insinuated that Michael was in imminent danger of becoming a drug addict or worse, to the point of suggesting he take amphetamines. This resulted in great emotional trauma for Mrs. Tayler, all because of an overconfident young girl with absolutely no background in medicine or psychology."

There was some whispering among the board members. A few of them glared at me with open disapproval.

"Therefore," Mr. Tayler concluded, "I feel it is necessary for the board to take action against Ms. Bianchi. Although this will not undo the harm that has been done to my son, I will at least have the satisfaction of knowing that no other child will become a victim of this woman's malpractice. Thank you so much for hearing my concerns. I'm sure your decision will be in the best interests of our children." With that, he sauntered back to his seat, looking over at me with a humorless smirk.

I was so outraged I could barely hear Stanton Hawthorne, "Esquire" through the roaring in my ears. He was explaining, in legal jargon, how his client's rights were violated and how my actions constituted grounds for dismissal, yada yada yada. When he finished, Anna whispered, "Our turn."

Anna began by reviewing my record. She gave the board members copies of my evaluations, as well as letters from parents praising my work. She went on to defend my actions at the dance and dispute Mr. Tayler's claim that I had a personal grudge against his son. But the final part of her rebuttal took me completely by surprise.

"Lastly," she said, "here's a petition. It's signed by two hundred seventeen students. All want Ms. Bianchi to stay. Check the first name on the list."

Don slipped me a copy of the petition and winked again. I stared at the paper and tensed my jaw to keep it from dropping. The first signature, in big, bold letters, was Michael Tayler's.

Anna returned to her seat, looking like a cat that had just rid itself of an annoying hairball. Superintendent Dimmit wiped his upper lip and handed the petition to Mr. Tayler, who flushed a satisfying shade of crimson when he saw Michael's name. I fought off the desire to laugh out loud. This had Nancy written all over it.

After a few minutes of whispered consultation with the other board members, Ellen Sieben turned to me. "Ms. Bianchi, it seems we've heard from everyone but you. Is there anything you'd like to add?"

The next words I spoke would determine my future. My heart was fluttering high in my throat. But I was a Bianchi. And I was ready.

I stood, squared my shoulders, and faced the board and Timothy Dimmit.

"From the time I was a little girl," I began, "I wanted to be a teacher. When I was growing up, my heroes weren't athletes or rock singers or movie stars. My heroes were the people who made learning come alive for me. 'How wonderful it must be,' I thought, 'to share the gift of knowledge with others. To make a real difference in the life of a child.' The proudest moment of my life was when I first opened the door to my own classroom."

I swallowed a lump that had unexpectedly formed in my throat. "From that day to this, I have tried with every ounce of energy to make a difference in the lives of students who come through that door. When I see a student in trouble, I feel honor-bound to do everything in my power to help. This is what I did with Michael Tayler. When I first met him, he was an angry, troubled young man." I shot a glance at Mr. Tayler, who was leaning back in his chair, whispering to his lawyer.

"But under that veneer," I continued, "was a gifted student. I was determined to discover what prevented him from succeeding. When I first read about Attention Deficit Hyperactivity Disorder, I was skeptical. But the more I learned about it, the more it seemed to explain the things I found so puzzling about Michael. It was never my intention to diagnose him. I told Mrs. Tayler only a neurologist could do that. All I did was share some information with her. And I tried some strategies I thought might help her son."

I went on to explain each of the strategies and how Michael had responded. I showed them Michael's article and his report card.

"What I hope this will prove," I said, "is that everything I did was intended to help Michael. If the day ever comes when my actions harm a student, I will leave this profession voluntarily and—"

The sound of a door banging open stopped me in mid-sentence.

"Am I too late? I rode as fast as I could."

A rain-soaked Michael Tayler came rushing down the aisle. He was carrying a motorcycle helmet that dripped a trail of water. He set it on a chair as he approached the board members.

"My name is Michael Tayler, and I have something to say."

"Michael, what's the meaning of this?" Mr. Tayler hissed. "This is none of your concern. I want you to turn around and go back home. Leave this matter to Mr. Hawthorne and me."

Michael turned and faced his father. "I'm sorry, Dad. I can't. This is about me. If it wasn't for me, Ms. Bianchi wouldn't be in all this trouble."

"Now, son—" Mr. Tayler put a fatherly hand on Michael's shoulder in a cheesy imitation of a rational human being. "None of this is your fault. I know you only want to help, but—"

Michael shook his hand away. "These people need to know what a great teacher Ms. Bianchi is. She's the only one who ever tried to help me. It's because of her that my grades went up." He turned in desperation to the astonished board members. "Don't listen to my dad. You're lucky to have a teacher like her."

"That's quite enough," Mr. Tayler shouted. "I want you to leave at once. We'll finish discussing this at home."

Michael held his ground. "I've tried to discuss it with you, and so has Mom. She even told you she doesn't want any part of this. But you won't listen. I thought you'd change your mind when you saw my report card, but even that wasn't enough. You know something, Dad? I don't think this is about me anymore. It's just about you wanting to win."

Mr. Tayler exploded like an astronaut with an alien in his chest. "Young man, I will not tolerate any more of your disrespect. I'm sick of you making me look like a fool. All you've ever done is cause trouble. Well, not anymore. You have embarrassed me for the last time. Get out of my sight!"

Michael froze as if he'd been sucker-punched. Then he turned from his enraged father, ran up the aisle, and slammed out the door. The stunned silence in the room was broken by the revving motor of his bike as it screeched out of the driveway. That's when I noticed he'd left his helmet behind.

Chapter Twenty

I ran out into the night, clutching Michael's wet helmet. The drizzle had become a downpour, and all that remained of Michael was the diminishing glow of his bike's taillight. I stood in the rain, staring at that red pinpoint of light until it winked out in the distance.

Chris and Anna followed me outside. Chris held his jacket over my head. "Please, Jen, let's go back in. It's no use standing here getting rained on."

"He's right," Anna said. "Tayler's blown his case."

"But what about Michael?" I asked. "He was so upset. And he's driving that damn bike without a helmet in this weather."

"Don't let your imagination run away with you." Chris pulled me toward the building. "I'm sure he'll cool off and get himself home. Anyway, staying out here getting soaked won't help him."

Chris and Anna led me back inside. The meeting room was in turmoil. Board members were conferring in small, frenetic groups. Superintendent Dimmit was pacing like a caged weasel. Bennett Tayler was slumped in a chair, staring at the floor. His skin had gone a sickly gray. Stanton Hawthorne was trying to engage him in a conversation but was getting nowhere.

Finally, Ellen Sieben gaveled the meeting back to order.

"After considering everything we've heard this evening," she said, "it is the decision of this board that Ms. Bianchi has done nothing that would warrant her dismissal."

Don's dark face split into a brilliant grin. Anna grabbed me in a hug that forced all the air out of my lungs. Chris flashed me a victory sign from the back of the room. Marita was applauding.

So it's really over at last. It surprised me that I was more relieved than elated. If only Michael could have been there.

While Mrs. Sieben explained the board's decision, Bennett Tayler's eyes remained fixed on the floor. His lower lip trembled. A sudden tug of pity caught me off-guard, but I quickly pushed it away. How could he have embarrassed Michael like that? The poor kid came to my aid like a knight in shining armor, riding a red motorbike instead of a white horse, only to be humiliated in front of everyone by his own father. What kind of man would do that to his only child? A white-hot flame of anger licked at my insides. After freeing myself from Anna's bear hug, I crossed the aisle and planted myself right in front of Mr. Tayler. His eyes didn't move. No matter. If he didn't want to see me, he'd still have to hear me.

"I just want you to know," I said, straining to keep my voice steady, "that what you did to your son was inexcusable. Michael had the courage to stand up for what he thought was right, and you had no cause to degrade him the way you did. You may see yourself as an influential and powerful man"—my voice quivered—"but your son is twice the man you are. You don't deserve him."

I placed the helmet between his feet. "Please see that Michael gets this. And tell him how much I appreciate what he did for me. He's a true hero." With that, I turned on my three-inch heels and left the great and powerful Bennett Tayler staring blankly at his shoes. Karma's a bitch.

Chris was barely able to contain himself as we sloshed out to the car. My toes were throbbing, and I couldn't wait to kick off my shoes. After we locked the car doors, he kissed me so hard, the soles of my aching feet tingled. When we came up for air, he started laughing.

"What's so funny?" I lobbed my shoes into the back seat.

"I wish you could've seen yourself facing off against Bennett Tayler. Little Jenna Bianchi in her elevator shoes. A classic David and Goliath moment. I kept expecting you to whip out your trusty slingshot and pop him between the eyes."

"No need for that. The man wouldn't even look at me. Actually, I was a little worried that he might have blown an artery."

"Guess he's not used to losing. And don't start getting soft, not when I'm in the middle of complimenting you on your fighting spirit. You won. Enjoy the thrill of victory."

"You're right. It'll be such a pleasure to wake up in the morning without the Bennett Tayler cloud hanging over me. I just wish I had a chance to thank Michael before he left."

"Yeah. I can't help admiring the kid. It took real guts to stand up for you like he did. Too bad his old man didn't have the sense to realize that."

I leaned my head back against the seat. "I'll talk to Michael first thing in the morning and tell him how grateful I am. If it weren't for him, the decision might not have gone my way."

Chris started the car and handed me his cell phone. "You'd better call Nancy. I'm sure her fingers and toes are cramping by now."

Nancy gave such a loud whoop that I almost dropped the phone. I gave her all the details, and she invited me to her office for a celebration lunch. "I'll make one of my animal cracker cakes," she said.

"By the way, did you have anything to do with that little petition stunt?' I asked.

Nancy sniggered. "I just put some bugs in a few ears."

"Well, it was a brilliant maneuver. Really nailed Tayler's coffin shut."

"The fat lady has left the stage," she said.

I gave Chris his cell phone and took mine out of my purse. I hit my parents' speed-dial number, and my mother answered on the first ring.

"See?" she said. "I told you everything would turn out all right. Tell your father the good news."

While my father launched into a series of colorful expletives about Bennett Tayler, Chris turned on the heater. The warmth, along with the rhythmic *slap-slap* of the windshield wipers, made me drowsy. I said goodbye to my dad and closed my eyes. The next thing I knew, Chris was shaking me awake.

"Come on, Sleeping Beauty. You're home."

I stretched and rubbed my eyes. Chris had retrieved my shoes from the back seat.

"You might want to put these on. The rain's let up, but the ground is saturated. Try not to break your neck on those heels."

He walked me to the door and waited until I was safely inside. Then he kissed the tip of my nose and said goodnight.

I was so exhausted I barely had the energy to peel off my damp suit. I climbed into bed and was asleep before my head hit the pillow.

The phone jolted me awake. I squinted at the clock. The numbers 2:18 floated like green specters in the darkness. My heart began a panicked thumping.

"Jenna? Sorry to wake you. I've got bad news."

"Anna? What is it?" My whole body seized up.

"Just got a call from Dimmit. There's been an accident. It's Michael Tayler."

Oh God, no! Please! My heart tried to break through my ribcage.

"He was on his way home. Took a turn too fast. Lost control. He was thrown off his bike. Must've hit his head. A passing motorist called 9-1-1."

I gripped the phone so tightly my knuckles ached, too terrified to ask the next question. "Is he—" I couldn't squeeze out the word.

"Oh, no. He's alive, but critical. He's in Morrison General. Last I heard, he was still unconscious. Dimmit said he'd call if there's news."

Suddenly the phone felt too heavy to hold. I stared into the darkness, not knowing what to say next.

"Jenna?" Anna's voice was fading into the distance. "Still there?"

I shook my head, hoping to clear it. "Thanks for the call. Let me know if there's any change."

"Will do." She paused. "You okay?"

"Just promise you'll call the minute you hear anything."

"Definitely."

I clicked off the phone and dropped it back into its cradle.

I don't know how long I sat in the darkness, staring at the phone. The events of the board meeting kept running through my mind like a DVD stuck on replay. If only I'd stopped Michael before he went speeding off. If only I'd noticed his helmet sooner. If only I'd followed him. If only … If only …

I dropped back onto my pillow, willing the tears to come. But they stuck stubbornly behind my eyes, making my head throb. I went into the bathroom, shook two Tylenols into my sweaty palm, and tried to dry-swallow them. They lodged in my throat and made me cough. I choked them down with a glass of water. Then I went back to bed and covered my eyes with my arm. But I couldn't erase the vision of Michael lying crumpled in the rain on that dark road. All because of me.

When I opened my eyes, the room was draped in gauzy, gray light. I buried my face in the pillow, hoping the dull ache in my head would go away. Finally, I gave up and flicked on the television. The accident was the lead story on the Five AM News. A solemn-faced anchorwoman was reporting from the roadside as a police cruiser's lights strobed in the background. Her perky voice was like a spike in my ear.

"The victim, sixteen-year-old Michael Tayler, is listed as critical. A hospital spokesman reports that he is suffering from head trauma, broken bones, and possible internal injuries. Michael is the son of Bennett Tayler, head of TechTron Industries."

A brief clip showed Michael's parents pushing through a throng of reporters outside the hospital. An ashen Bennett Tayler kept repeating, "No comment." Mrs. Tayler said nothing, her hands covering her face.

I clicked off the TV. The ache in my head had worsened, so I dragged myself into the shower. I let the steaming water run over my body and turned my face toward the stinging spray. Maybe I could wash away some of the guilt.

When I walked into the office, Chris was standing by the sign-in desk. He looked atypically disheveled.

"How're you holding up?" His voice echoed the exhaustion in his face.

It was hard for me to meet his eyes. "This whole thing seems so surreal. If only Michael hadn't come to that meeting—"

"I was afraid you'd react this way." He took my arm and guided me out into the hall. "All night I kept picturing you lying there, blaming yourself. I wanted to come over, but I was afraid you'd think I was being pushy. And I couldn't think of a way to convince you that you aren't the cause of any of this. It was an accident, Jenna. If anyone should be feeling guilty, it should be Bennett Tayler, not you."

I pulled my arm away. "I can't talk about this now. I've got to go upstairs and get my act together before the kids come in. Please, let's drop it."

"Okay, okay," He held up his hands in a surrender gesture. "But promise you'll meet me after school to talk this out."

"We'll see." It was hard for me to breathe. I had to get away from him before I lost what little composure I had left.

I felt better when I reached my silent classroom. Was it only yesterday that I left here wondering if I'd ever be allowed to return? I sat down at my desk and stared out the window at the leaden sky. My brain felt bruised. Soon the bell rang, and students began filing in. Many had just heard about the accident, and it took a long time for their shocked whispers to settle into an uneasy silence. Jessica's desk was empty.

I went through the morning on autopilot. I even managed to smile at the students who told me they were glad I'd be staying on as their teacher. Keeping up the pretense of normalcy was exhausting, and it was a relief when my lunch period began. I collapsed into my chair and closed my eyes, concentrating on the faraway drone of a passing plane.

A gentle tapping on the door jarred me back. Nancy was peering in at me.

"When you didn't come down for lunch, I got worried. It isn't like you to forget my animal cracker cake."

Cake? What the hell is she talking about? Then I remembered the celebration we'd planned. "Actually, I did forget. But I'm not hungry. Any news on Michael?"

"Nothing yet. Anna's keeping close tabs on things. The doctors are running some tests this afternoon, so she plans to call back after dismissal." She gave me a hard stare. "Pardon my bluntness, but you look like hell."

"Thanks. I can always count on you to make me feel better."

"You can always count on me to tell you the truth. And the truth is, you have no right to mope around feeling guilty." Her voice rang with uncharacteristic sharpness. "You acted as a professional doing what you felt was best for your student. Anything that happened as a result was out of your hands. So snap out of it. Your attitude isn't helping anyone—not yourself, not your other students, and certainly not Michael. Things happen in this job that we can't foresee or control. Grow up and get used to it, or find another line of work."

I stared, slack-jawed, until her expression softened.

"A little tough love, sweetie. Now close your mouth before you catch a fly."

Something inside me let go and released the tears. Nancy hugged me until my sobs quieted into hiccups. Then she pulled out a small packet of tissues.

"Here. Blow."

I did. Then I took another tissue and wiped my eyes. "Thanks. I needed that."

Nancy smoothed my hair. "That's more like the Jenna Bianchi I know and love. Feeling better?"

"Much better, actually." I blew my nose again.

"Well, you looked like hell before, but you look like the very devil now. Go to the little girl's room and fix yourself up. If you hurry, you'll have enough time for a piece of cake."

At the end of the day, Chris was waiting for me in the office. He'd combed his hair and looked more like his well-groomed self. He dispelled my funky mood with the promise of an upper-body massage and a romantic dinner.

We found a quiet booth at Los Amigos, a great little Mexican place, and chatted over margaritas, a basket of crunchy tortilla chips and a killer pineapple salsa. By the time the waiter brought our dinners, I was feeling more normal than I had in days. But I couldn't silence the persistent little voice in my head that kept whispering Michael's name.

On the way home, Chris called Anna for an update. I could tell by the way his mouth twitched that the news was not good. He clicked off his cell phone and put his arm around my shoulders.

"He's still in ICU, and he hasn't regained consciousness. He has a broken arm, a skull fracture, and a possible concussion. There are also some internal injuries, so the Taylers are flying in two specialists from Johns Hopkins. They're doing exploratory surgery tomorrow."

I felt as if someone had doused me with ice water. "What kind of internal injuries?"

"He broke some ribs. And he may have ruptured his spleen."

"Oh, Jesus." My dinner rose into my throat.

Chris squeezed the back of my neck. "Now don't go off the deep end. Your muscles will get all knotted up again." His fingers kneaded their way down to my shoulder. "Michael's holding his own. He's young and strong. And with his father's connections, he'll have the best doctors around."

I knew he was right. And, as Nancy was so fond of saying, it wouldn't do any good to worry. So I did some yoga breathing and tried to think happy thoughts. Maybe the positive energy would make its way to Michael's bedside.

"Can we visit him as soon as he's out of Intensive Care? I still want to thank him for defending me."

"Sure, as long as we can avoid Bennett Tayler."

"If I never see that vicious bastard again, I'll die happy." Okay, given the circumstances, maybe "die" was a poor word choice.

I invited Chris back to my place for an after-dinner drink. The news about Michael had killed my margarita buzz. I took two beers out of the fridge and handed one to Chris. We settled down on the sofa and channel surfed until we found a rerun of *The Shining*. Then Chris switched off the lights, and before long, I lost all interest in Jack Nicholson.

Chapter Twenty-One

The next morning dawned picture perfect. It was one of those mild November days that make you forget the holidays are right around the corner. I was giving Brutus a shower when the phone rang.

"Good morning, Sunshine." Chris sounded pretty fired up for a guy who didn't get home until after three. "This weather's given me a major case of cabin fever. How'd you like to go for a drive to the shore? We could go to Margate. Maybe stop at the White House for lunch."

White House cheesesteaks? Yum. "Sounds like a plan." I knew this was his way of keeping my mind off Michael's surgery.

"Only one condition: no cell phones. I don't want anyone to intrude on our day."

"Oh, Chris—I don't know. What if there's some news about Michael?"

"Any news, good or bad, can wait until we get home. Can you be ready in an hour?"

"I think I can make myself presentable by then."

"You could walk out the door stark naked and still be presentable."

The White Horse Pike was awash in sunlight. Traffic was surprisingly light. The foliage was past its peak, but there was enough color left in the trees to cast a golden glow over the landscape. Farmers markets were strung along the road like colorful beads. Multicolored cushions of chrysanthemums surrounded heaps of brilliant orange pumpkins. Bins of ruby and green apples and baskets of dusty yams sat in the shade of faded canvas awnings. We stopped at The Farmer's Daughter in Hammonton and bought a bag of Granny Smiths and a half-gallon of apple cider. I picked out a scary painted pumpkin to put by my front door. Maybe it would keep Yin-Yang away.

As we continued driving through the sandy stretch of Pine Barrens outside Egg Harbor, I thought about the Jersey Devil stories that haunted so many of my childhood nights. But Mother Leeds's thirteenth child was nowhere to be found among the scrub pines and pin oaks that whizzed by.

The tang of iodine and salt hung in the air as we approached the wetlands on the outskirts of Atlantic City. The horizon was broken by the boxy silhouettes of casinos that towered along the shoreline. Chris crossed the bridge onto the island

and took a right on Atlantic Avenue. I sniffed out the White House before I saw it.

The White House is an area icon. It's been serving up the best subs and cheesesteaks on the planet since the forties. I was amazed that the perpetual line by the front door was so short. We squeezed into one of the vinyl booths and gave the waitress our orders. I had my usual—a mushroom cheesesteak with provolone and fried peppers, and a can of Diet Pepsi. I know it's ridiculous, but I'd rather eat my calories than drink them. Chris ordered an Italian sub. We decided to split a bag of potato chips since you can't get fries at the White House. While we waited for the food, we examined the framed photos of celebrities that covered the walls. This was probably the only place at the Jersey shore that hadn't changed in over sixty years.

We polished off our cheesesteaks in record time. Then Chris stood up and let his belt out a notch, and I undid the top button of my jeans.

"Now for a nice long walk to burn off all that food," Chris said, as we waddled back to the car. He drove down Atlantic Avenue toward Margate, and when we passed the medical center, I thought of Michael. I wriggled in the seat. Chris looked over at me.

"What's wrong?" he asked. "Eat too much?"

I turned my face to the window. "I was just wondering how Michael's doing."

"Uh-uh," Chris said. "We agreed. No worrying today. Try to relax and enjoy the moment."

He pulled the car into a space across the street from Lucy the Elephant, another Jersey shore landmark. The sixty-five foot wooden pachyderm had been gazing out at the Atlantic Ocean since the1880's. I had played in its shadow during countless childhood days at the beach.

The ocean sparkled as if it had been sprinkled with diamonds, and it was easy to believe that nothing bad could happen on such a glorious day. The beach was nearly deserted. We took off our shoes and walked along the shoreline, letting the frigid water numb our feet. A chilly breeze blew puffs of foam along the sand, and gulls circled and laughed overhead. Chris found a large scallop shell. He dusted off the sand and handed it to me.

"A souvenir of our day," he said.

We walked until we could button our jeans. Then we returned to the car, and Chris pulled a blanket and a picnic basket out of the trunk.

"What's all this?" I asked. "More food?"

"It's a celebration." He opened the basket and showed me a bottle of Moet Chandon, two plastic champagne glasses, a small wheel of brie and a box of water crackers. Then he tossed in two of the Granny Smiths from the farmer's market.

We wrapped ourselves in the blanket and sat on a dune. Chris peeled the foil from the champagne bottle and popped the cork. He sucked away the foam that flowed over the bottle's neck and filled each of the glasses with champagne.

"A toast." He held out his glass. "To your recent victory over the forces of darkness."

I sipped the champagne, enjoying the way the bubbles tickled my nose. Chris cut a small wedge of brie and a thin slice of apple with the Swiss army knife he carried on his keychain. He placed them in the center of a cracker, and handed it to me.

"Dessert is served," he said.

We huddled in the blanket until the champagne was gone and the first evening star appeared. Chris pointed at the purpling sky and said, "Make a wish."

I looked up at the star and wished with all my might that Michael would recover.

When I got home, I ran straight to the answering machine. An urgent blinking "5" indicated that there were messages waiting, so I punched the PLAY button.

BEEP. *"Jenna? Anna. Surgery's over. He's not out of the woods, but getting there. I'll call with any news."*

BEEP. *"Hi, it's Nancy. Don't know if you've heard, but Michael's been upgraded from critical to serious. They were able to repair his spleen and the prognosis is good. I guess all that positive thinking worked. By the way, I hope you enjoyed your day. Chris told me he had a romantic afternoon planned. Sounds heavenly."* I could feel Chris grinning.

BEEP. *"This is your phone company calling. How would you like to save money on your long distance bill?"* I hit DELETE.

BEEP. Silence, followed by a click. Probably a wrong number.

BEEP. Silence again. I was about to hit DELETE when I heard a whispery voice. *"Ms. Bianchi? I hope I have the right number. This is Claudia Tayler."*

I felt as if all the air had been sucked out of the room.

"Um—I just thought you should know that Michael has had surgery and is resting comfortably." Her voice was shaking. *"I had to call you because Michael would have wanted me to. I know what happened at the board meeting, and I know how special you are to him. I only hope that if—I mean when Michael is well enough, the four of us can sit down together and make things right."*

The message clicked off. Chris's touch on my shoulder made me jump. He was standing behind me, holding the painted pumpkin under his arm like a decapitated head.

"The four of us? What do you think she means by that?" I asked.

"Sounds like there's been a change of heart at the Tayler house. Maybe the old goat's come to his senses."

"Stranger things have happened, I guess." I just couldn't think of any.

By Wednesday, Michael's condition had gone from serious to stable, and the hospital reports were tinged with cautious optimism. He'd had two brief periods of consciousness, but he was still being sedated for the pain. On Thursday, he was moved from intensive care to a private room with two full-time nurses. The big news on Friday was that he had responded to his mother's presence with a weak but definite squeeze of her hand.

By Monday afternoon, Jessica was allowed a short visit to his bedside.

"He was asleep the whole time, but I think he knew I was there. His eyelids kept fluttering. Do you think he was trying to wake up?" She looked so hopeful that I tried to keep my answer upbeat.

"It's very possible. I'm certain he'll be back to his old self before you know it." *From my lips to God's ears.*

"Mr. Tayler hasn't left the hospital since the accident," Jessica said. "He's staying in the room next to Michael's, and he said he won't go home until Michael comes with him." She shook her head. "It's funny because Michael never got along with his dad. He thought his dad hated him. I told him he was being silly, that parents don't hate their own children. I wish he could see Mr. Tayler now."

I flashed on the image of a despondent Bennett Tayler at the board meeting. That same stab of pity jabbed at me again, only harder.

"You know, Jessica, sometimes parents get so caught up in controlling their kids, they forget how much they love them. I think that may have happened to Mr. Tayler." Hearing my own words softened the hard edge of my anger. "I'm sure that when Michael gets well, things will be different between him and his father."

"Do you really think so?"

"Yes, I really, truly do."

The big breakthrough came on the Wednesday before Thanksgiving. I was headed for the cafeteria when I heard the rapid tap-tap-tap of footsteps. I turned, ready to reprimand a student for running in the hall, and saw Nancy hurrying toward me.

"Jenna, wait up. I have great news!"

"It must be pretty important to have you moving like Wilma Rudolph."

"Give me a second to catch my breath." She bent at the waist, resting her hands on her knees. "I've been all over this building looking for you. Anna just got a call from Mrs. Tayler. Michael's awake, and as far as the doctors can tell, he's going to have a complete recovery."

I threw my arms around Nancy's neck, and we did a little victory dance. There were a few raised eyebrows from students on their way to lunch, but I didn't care.

"When can I go to see him?"

"Mrs. Tayler promised to call as soon as he's feeling well enough for visitors."

"Has anyone told Jessica?"

"I thought you should do the honors. She's in the computer lab this period."

"I'm on my way." It was all I could do to keep from skipping down the hall.

Thanksgiving dawned blustery and cold. Brutus and I were watching the Macy's parade on TV when Chris called.

"What time are your parents expecting us?" he asked. My parents had invited Chris to dinner, and since his family lives in Florida, he was happy to accept. "I need to know when I should pick you up."

"Mom said we'd be eating around three," I told him, "but I'd like to go over a little earlier to help her out."

"Does this mean you're going to try your hand at cooking?" There was a not-very-subtle note of hope in his voice. Time to shatter that illusion.

"Actually, I meant you could help her out. You want an edible dinner, don't you? The best way to ensure that is to keep me far away from the kitchen."

When the parade ended and Santa was safely delivered to his throne in the toy department, I turned off the TV and returned Brutus to his cage. Yin-Yang was crouched by the painted pumpkin on my doorstep. When Brutus screeched at her, she arched her back and hissed.

I opened the door and shooed her away. She scooted off the step and flopped down on a pile of leaves. My neighbor, Yin-Yang's elderly owner, waved at me from her doorway, and I cringed.

"Happy Thanksgiving," she called.

"Same to you," I said, hoping she hadn't seen me harassing her cat.

She waved again and closed the door. Yin-Yang looked up from the leaves and meowed. Although I don't speak Siamese, I was pretty sure it was some kind of feline profanity.

I'd just stepped out of the shower when Chris arrived. I answered the door wrapped in a large beach towel. Chris leered at me and started to unbuckle his belt. "My Thanksgiving wish has come true," he said.

I pulled him by the arm. "Get inside. You're letting the heat out. I'll be ready in a minute."

He stepped in and grabbed the end of my towel. "If you let go of this, I'll show you how thankful I can be." He gave the towel a quick tug.

I tightened my grip. "No time for that now. Go say hi to Brutus while I finish getting dressed."

I closed the bedroom door and threw on a pair JCrew cords and a forest green cardigan. Then I ran a brush through my hair, dabbed on some lipstick, and dashed into the living room. Chris was staring out the window.

"I just saw an old lady run across your lawn. She was chasing a cat."

"My neighbor. Let's get going."

I buttoned my coat as we walked to the car. Two pies wrapped in foil and a small cooler sat on the back seat. The car's interior smelled like a bakery.

"I didn't want to come empty-handed," Chris said, "so I brought dessert."

"Which would be?"

"A pumpkin cheesecake with toasted pecans on top, and an apple-cranberry cobbler. I used the apples we bought in Hammonton. I even made cinnamon ice cream. From scratch. It's in the cooler."

I reeled my tongue back into my mouth and kissed Chris's neck. "You're getting me all excited," I whispered.

My brother and my dad were tossing a football in the driveway when we pulled up to the curb. I got out of the car, and Anthony loped over and punched me on the arm.

"Happy Thanksgiving, Sis," he said.

"Thanks. Same to you." I rubbed my arm. "When did you get home?"

"Yesterday afternoon. I cut my last class. Western Civ. A real waste. Hey, Chris."

Chris shook his hand. "Happy Thanksgiving, Big T. How about giving me a hand with these desserts."

Anthony hooked his arm through the cooler's handle and grabbed one of the pies. Then he followed Chris to the house. My father waited by the front door, his cheeks rosy from the cold. He clapped Chris on the back. Then he turned to me and ruffled my hair.

"Happy Turkey Day, Mighty Mite," he boomed. "Give your ol' Pa a kiss."

I nuzzled his cold, scratchy cheek, and he bundled me up in his arms. "So how's my favorite daughter?"

We walked into the rich aroma of roasting turkey and simmering tomato sauce. My stomach grumbled. "Yo, Frannie," Dad called. "They're here!"

As usual, Mom was in the kitchen. She dried her hands on her apron and came out to greet us. She gave me a big hug, but she really lit up when she saw Chris.

"We're so glad you could spend Thanksgiving with us," she said, giving him the Italian double-cheek kiss.

Chris and Anthony followed her into the kitchen while I hung up the coats in the hall closet. I could hear Mom oohing and aahing as Chris described the desserts, and I knew I'd pretty much lost him for the duration.

I went into the family room where the Eagles game was blaring from a wide-screen TV. My dad was reclining in his La-Z-Boy, remote in hand.

"Check this out," he said. "The Eagles in hi-def. You can see the hairs in their noses."

And you'd want to do that, why? "That's neat, Daddy," I kicked off my shoes and stretched out on the sofa.

He put the remote down and patted me on the head. "So how're things going at school? Everything all right? Anybody giving you a hard time?"

I filled him in on all that had happened since I last talked to him. Which was two days ago.

"I'm glad the kid's okay," he said, turning his attention back to the game. "But I still think you deserve an apology from the old man. He shouldn't be able to give you all that aggravation and then just walk away like nothing happened. That's bullshit! You should haul his ass into court for pain and suffering."

I reached over and stroked his forearm. "It's all over now. I just want to put it behind me and get on with my life. Bennett Tayler isn't worth another minute of my time."

Dad suddenly jumped up and held his arms high in the air. "TOUCH-DOWN. Yo, Tony, check this out!" My brother materialized, gnawing on a turkey wing. He pointed it at the kitchen.

"Mom wants you," he mumbled through a mouthful of turkey.

Me? Around food? No good can come of this. I pushed myself to my feet and padded into the kitchen. My mother was waiting for me by the sink, dishtowel in hand. Chris was busy stirring something on the stove with a big wooden spoon.

"Honey, could you please dry these dishes and set the table? Dinner's almost ready."

"Sure, Mom." I couldn't help noticing that this job didn't involve food preparation.

At halftime, Anthony and Dad pried themselves away from the TV, and Chris and my mom uncoupled themselves from the stove. I surveyed the perfectly-set dining room table, which was so weighed down with food I could almost hear it groaning. Here was Thanksgiving dinner, Bianchi-style. Meaning, there would be enough food to feed a third-world nation. Our meal was an amalgam of Italian and American traditions. The turkey was stuffed with Italian sausage and fresh fennel. The soup was chicken broth with cheese tortellini. In addition to the mashed potatoes and buttered peas, there was a mound of breaded veal cutlets, a pan of lasagna, and a pile of meatballs. A gigantic salad tossed with olive oil and balsamic vinegar would be served at the end of the meal. Before the huge bowl of fruit. And the roasted chestnuts.

My father stood to say the blessing. We joined hands and bowed our heads.

"We thank you, Lord, for all the ways you have blessed our lives. For this loving family, this bountiful feast, and our good friends. And now we give thanks for all the special ways you have shown your love for each one of us." Chris squeezed my hand. In the silence that followed, I made a mental list of all the things I was thankful for. Michael's recovery made the top three.

After dinner, I was too full to move, so my mother brought out Chris's desserts. The cheesecake was rich and spicy, and Mom had heated the cobbler just enough to soften the ice cream scooped on top. Chris made everyone a foamy cappuccino, and Dad broke out the assorted liqueurs. I was embarrassed at how much more food I crammed into my already bursting stomach. I'd be doing penance for this meal well into next year.

When it was finally time to leave, I thought I'd have to be wheeled out on a gurney. I wedged myself into the front seat of Chris's car, picturing the undercarriage hitting the ground. By nine o'clock, we were turning into my driveway. Brutus was shrieking before my key hit the lock.

"Poor baby, you've been alone all day. And on Thanksgiving, too." I headed straight to the cage, armed with a handful of toasted pecans I'd salvaged from the cheesecake. "Here, sweetie, these are for you. Happy Thanksgiving."

"Don't forget to tell him where they came from," Chris called from the doorway. "I think I deserve some of the credit." Brutus looked up and hissed.

I was about to hang up my coat when I noticed the answering machine's insistent blinking. One message. I hit PLAY.

BEEP. "Ms. Bianchi, this is Claudia Tayler again. There's someone here who has something to say to you." There was a pause. Then, a breathy voice whispered, "Habby Tankshgiving, Msh. Bianchi."

I hit the REPLAY button and listened again. The words were slurred, but the voice was unmistakable. It was Michael.

Chapter Twenty-Two

As the Christmas holidays approached, Michael continued a slow but steady recovery. Life at school settled into its predictable pre-holiday mode, the kids growing antsier by the day, and the faculty wishing for aerial spraying of Valium. By the second Monday in December, forecasters were warning of an impending snowstorm. Anna made an announcement before dismissal reminding everyone to listen to the radio for school closing information. The kids left in high spirits, already discussing how they'd spend their first snow day.

After dinner, I turned on the TV for a weather update. The predictions called for snow through the night and into mid-afternoon with accumulations of five inches or more—an almost ironclad guarantee that classes would be canceled. *Yippee!* When it comes to snow days, the only ones happier than the students are their teachers.

I was grading papers with Brutus roosting on my shoulder when the first feathers of snow drifted from the sky. I experienced an irresistible urge for hot cocoa, a genetic imprint I call "The Snowflake Phenomenon." Brutus seemed impressed as he watched me stir chocolate syrup into the steaming milk.

Outside, the glittering snow was transforming my street into a Christmas card. Lights on neighboring houses glowed like colored necklaces against the velvety darkness, and gray ghosts of smoke floated from chimneys. Yin-Yang tiptoed across the lawn, leaving dark little circles in the white powder. Brutus saw her and screeched right into my ear.

I dropped a marshmallow into my "Teachers Rock!" mug and returned to the sofa, picturing frantic crowds of shoppers ransacking supermarket shelves for bread and milk. I blew on the cocoa and moved the mug out of the range of Brutus's curious beak.

"Sorry, buddy, you can't have this. Chocolate will make you sick."

"DAMMIT," Brutus shrieked, making my eardrum vibrate in a decidedly unhealthy manner.

"Okay, that's it for you. Anyway, it's past your bedtime."

I returned a disgruntled Brutus to his cage and covered him for the night. After draining the last drop of cocoa, I scooped out the little lump of gooey marshmallow with my finger and popped it into my mouth. Then I curled up on the sofa, wrapped myself in Nana's afghan, and watched the falling snow work its magic.

It was still snowing when the alarm woke me in the morning. I switched on the radio to listen for school closings and, sure enough, Morrison High was among the first to be announced. Then I turned off the radio and tucked the covers under my chin, hoping Brutus was still asleep. My hopes were soon dashed by a loud, "Helloooooo, baby." I groaned and pulled on my robe and slippers.

Everything outside was cloaked in white. Crystals of snow ticked against the windows, and snowflakes whirled like dust-devils in the wind. When I uncovered Brutus, he hunkered down on his perch, warily eyeing the window. He wouldn't budge when I put my arm in his cage.

"It's only snow, silly," I told him. "It can't hurt you."

He looked at me and croaked.

"Come on. Don't you want breakfast?"

He lifted one foot and stepped gingerly onto my arm.

"Good boy. How'd you like some Cheerios?"

Brutus flapped his wings.

"I'll take that as a yes." I poured some Cheerios into his bowl, and he started flipping them into the air with his beak.

"You're supposed to eat them, not play ring toss," I said.

The teapot whistled, and Brutus gave a surprised squawk.

"I think you need a birdie tranquilizer this morning." I handed him a walnut.

When the boiling water hit the teabag in my "Super Teacher" mug, the spicy fragrance of cloves and cinnamon perfumed the air. I inhaled the steam, cradling the warm mug in my hands. Then I set it on the kitchen table and microwaved a bowl of oatmeal. Before I sat down to eat, I turned on the news to get the latest weather report. The announcer was still reading the list of school closings. It seemed like the whole state of New Jersey had shut down for the day.

The forecast called for the snow to end by early afternoon. That would give me enough time to check in with my parents and get some papers graded before I started digging out. Shoveling snow is tied for first place with scrubbing mildew from the shower door track on my "Things I Hate to Do" list. I looked out at the monster snowdrift in my driveway and had a sudden brainstorm.

My father answered the phone.

"Hi, Daddy. Aren't you going to work today?"

"Nope. The office is closed. They haven't finished clearing the parking lot, and I hear the side streets are a mess."

"So what are you and Mom up to?"

"Your mother's baking something, and I'm going to crank up the old snow blower and clear the sidewalk." My father's snowblower is his favorite toy. Once he gets started, he never wants to stop. This has made him extremely popular with the neighbors.

"Sounds like fun." *Not.* "I'll be doing some shoveling later myself." I heaved a loud sigh, hoping it came across sufficiently pathetic over the phone.

"Don't be crazy. I'll bring the blower over there when I finish. I've got four-wheel drive on the van."

Hooray! "Are you sure? I don't want you to overdo."

"Overdo what? It'll keep me out of your mother's hair. You stash that shovel, and leave the rest to me."

"Thanks, Daddy. You're the best."

I hung up, feeling like I'd just been given an early Christmas present.

After breakfast, I wiped the kitchen table and sat down to work. "Let It Snow" was playing on the radio, Brutus was dancing on his perch, and I was humming along with the music when the phone rang. As soon as I picked it up, Brutus shrieked, "HELLOOOO." There was dead silence on the other end. I figured an explanation was in order.

"Hello, this is Jenna Bianchi, and that was my parrot."

"Oh, hello, Ms. Bianchi. This is Claudia Tayler. I thought I had the wrong number."

"Don't worry, that happens a lot. It's an occupational hazard for parrot owners. How are you? And how's Michael?"

"I'm fine, and Michael's the reason I'm calling. I heard that school's closed today. If you don't have other plans, could you stop by the hospital for a visit? It would be such a nice surprise for him."

"I'd love to. I've been waiting to hear he was ready for company. When are visiting hours?"

"They start at two o'clock. But if it's not inconvenient, would you mind coming a little earlier? There are some things I'd like to discuss before you see Michael."

"No problem. I could get there by one-thirty. Is anything wrong?"

"Oh, no, it's nothing like that. I just don't want to get into it over the phone. I'll see you this afternoon."

The call left me a little unsettled. What could Mrs. Tayler possibly want to discuss? But if I planned to spend the afternoon at the hospital, I had to get my papers graded. So I picked up my red pen and went back to work.

The snow had tapered to flurries by the time I pulled into the hospital parking lot. Snowplows had been busy through the night, so the main roads weren't too slippery. In addition, Dom Bianchi's Snow Removal Service had blown every last flake from my driveway. And my neighbor's. I hoped that would make up for my run-in with Yin-Yang. Dad had even brushed all the snow off my car and scraped the ice from the windows. There were definite percs to being Daddy's little girl.

I waited for The Boss to finish his dynamite rendition of "Santa Claus is Comin' to Town" before killing the motor. Then I checked my watch. It was a little after one. For possibly the first time in my life, I was too early. I wound my long woolen scarf around my neck and trudged toward the hospital entrance. My boots kicked up puffs of snow, and a blast of arctic air made my eyes water. I picked up the pace.

The hospital lobby was practically deserted. I pulled off my mittens and loosened my scarf. The thermostat must have been turned up to eighty. An elderly lady with big, round eyeglasses and a badge that said *Volunteer* was sitting behind the information desk. She smiled at me.

"Can I help you, dear?" she asked. Her eyes, magnified behind the thick lenses, goggled at me.

"Can you tell me what room Michael Tayler is in?"

"Is that 'Tailor' with an A-I, or 'Taylor' with an A-Y?"

I spelled out the name, and she hunted through her list until she found it. "He's in Room 413. Take the elevator to the fourth floor, and follow the corridor to the waiting area. Room 413 is the first one on the left. And you'll need one of these." She handed me a plastic-coated visitor's pass.

I thanked her and checked the time again. I still had ten minutes to kill. On a whim, I stopped in the gift shop to pick up something for Michael. I browsed the shelves, passing over the stuffed animals and boxes of candy until my eyes settled on a book with a blue leather cover. Inside were blank lined pages. A journal. Perfect! I handed the cashier my credit card, praying that it wasn't maxed out. Then I crossed the hall to the elevator and pressed the button for the fourth floor.

When the elevator door slid open, I was face to face with Bennett Tayler. My first impulse was to punch "CLOSE DOOR" and plunge back down to the lobby, but something in his face stopped me. He looked as if he'd aged ten years.

"Ms. Bianchi, thank you for coming." His voice had lost its arrogance. "It was gracious of you to agree to this visit, especially considering the circumstances of our last meeting."

I resisted the urge to tell him that my visit had nothing to do with him or our last meeting. The man was trying to declare a truce, and I wouldn't be the one to break it.

"As I told your wife," I said, sounding frostier than the air outside, "I've been looking forward to visiting Michael." At that moment, Mrs. Tayler rounded the corner. Her face was tired and pinched, but she perked up when she saw me.

"Ms. Bianchi, how nice to see you again. Come, sit down." She led me to the waiting area, where overstuffed chairs circled a coffee table covered with dog-eared magazines.

"Would you like something warm to drink?" she asked. "There's a vending machine down the hall."

"A cup of cocoa would be nice," I said, sinking into the nearest chair.

"Of course. Bennett, would you please get us some cocoa?"

He disappeared without a word. When he was gone, Mrs. Tayler turned to me. "I hope I haven't been presumptuous by arranging this meeting without giving you an explanation. I know this can't be very comfortable for you."

I couldn't disagree with that.

"You see," she said, "things have changed considerably since Michael's accident. My husband is so ashamed of his behavior at the board meeting. When it looked as if we might lose Michael, Bennett blamed himself." Her eyes misted over, and she sniffled. "He promised that if Michael survived, he would do everything in his power to make things right. The first step is for him to make peace with you."

She broke off suddenly. Bennett Tayler was walking toward us, juggling three Styrofoam cups.

"Here's the cocoa. It's not the best I've ever tasted, but at least it's hot." As he handed me a cup, his fingers brushed against mine. He gave me a sheepish smile. "You might want to let it cool a bit before taking a sip."

I thanked him as he took a seat beside his wife. He placed the remaining two cups on the table, along with a stack of napkins and some little wooden stirrers. Then he looked at me with those green eyes, so like Michael's. It was more than just the color. They now had the same vulnerability. I found myself warming to him, even though part of me was trying like hell to resist.

"I saw Michael's doctor down by the vending machine," he said. "He told me Michael can come home for Christmas." He leaned over and kissed his wife's cheek.

I felt as if I were intruding on a private moment, so I pretended to concentrate on stirring my cocoa.

"Perhaps we can ask Ms. Bianchi to arrange for the school to send us Michael's textbooks," Mrs. Tayler said. "I'd like him to keep up with his studies."

I looked at her and smiled. "I'd be happy to. I'll take care of it first thing tomorrow morning."

"That's very kind of you," Bennett Tayler said. He picked up his cocoa. Then he put it down and ran his hand through his hair. "Ms. Bianchi, I have some explaining to do. And I'm not making excuses, because there is no excuse for the way I behaved."

Ya think? I took a napkin from the stack and folded it in half.

"I only hope that, after you've heard me out, you'll find it in your heart to forgive me."

I wouldn't hold my breath there, Gonzo.

He cleared his throat. "I have always been difficult to get along with. I'm sure my wife can attest to that." Mrs. Tayler put her hand on his knee. "Even my mother blamed me for her gray hair. Things never came easily for me, and I was often frustrated. But I persevered."

Boo-hoo. Sucks to be you.

He picked up one of the stirrers, put it in his cup, and swirled it round and round. "I built a successful company and made a name for myself. I did it through hard work and sacrifice, and I've always demanded the same from those around me."

Some of the cocoa sloshed over the side of his cup and dripped onto the napkin. "My people skills aren't the best. My wife has been trying to help me with them, but I often act without considering how my actions will affect others."

Don't wait for me to disagree with you. I smoothed the napkin I'd been fiddling with and set my cup on it.

Bennett Tayler stopped stirring and looked down at his shoes in an uncanny replay of the board meeting. "That's what I did with Michael. And that's what I did with you."

The uncomfortable silence hurt my ears. I considered saying something to break the tension, but he started speaking again before I had the chance.

"When Michael was born, I was thrilled. I had almost given up hope of ever having a child. Now I had a son, an heir who would benefit from all my hard work. I was determined that he would become the person I'd always wanted to be—intelligent, personable, popular. But as time went by, I began to see in Michael many of the demons that plagued me. I became obsessed with exorcising those demons. I made unrealistic demands on my son, hoping he'd work harder to meet my goals. I became defensive when anyone even hinted that Michael was less than perfect. Now I realize that I made things worse."

Ladies and gentlemen—we have a breakthrough! I tried to keep my expression impassive.

He searched my face. "Please understand that, through it all, I was acting out of deep love for my son. As a result, I almost lost him."

Mrs. Tayler dabbed her eyes and took his hand.

"When I read the articles you gave my wife," he said, "I recognized myself on every page. The more I read, the guiltier I felt." His eyes strayed toward Michael's room. "All the things I'd been blaming Michael for were my fault. Part of some defect I had passed on to him. The only way I could deal with the guilt was through denial."

I swallowed hard. "I can understand that," I said. "Guilt can be a tough thing to work through." *Take it from someone who's been there.*

"I suppose that's the reason for my savage attack on you," he explained. "You were trying to tell me something I desperately didn't want to hear." He released his wife's hand and leaned toward me. "You were right, of course, and that made me even angrier. I guess I thought that by silencing you, I could make the whole thing disappear. But I think I always knew the truth would eventually come out."

"And the truth will set you free," I murmured.

"Yes," he said. "I hope it will."

It was finally time to visit Michael. Mrs. Tayler peeked in to see if he was awake. "There's someone here to see you," she told him.

When I walked into the room with his father, Michael's eyes almost popped out of his bandaged head. There were still shadows of bruises on his face, and he'd lost a lot of weight. His left arm was encased in a white plaster cast, and his chest was wrapped with bandages. He grimaced as he tried to yank the blanket over his pajamas with his good arm.

"Here, son, let me help you with that." Bennett Tayler took the blanket and tucked it around Michael's legs. "You've got to be careful not to disturb your cast."

Michael's head turned from his father to me. He had the same look Brutus gets when he's confused. Then Bennett Tayler came over and stood beside me, and Michael's face relaxed into a smile. "Ms. Bianchi, how'd you get here in all this snow?" he asked.

"It would take more than a little blizzard to keep me away once I heard you were ready for visitors. Your dad and mom and I thought we'd surprise you."

He looked at his father and settled back on his pillow. "Yeah, well—you sure did that."

I pulled a chair up to his bed and filled him in on the latest news from Morrison High. By the time I finished, his eyelids were at half-mast, but he was still smiling.

"I'll leave now so you can get some rest. But before I go, I want to give you something." I handed him the journal. "It's for you to write down your thoughts, your feelings—anything that comes to mind. It's what all good writers do. Maybe you can put something together for the newspaper."

Michael beamed. "Thanks. It'll give me something to do. Daytime TV's pretty lame."

"I'm the one who should be thanking you, Michael. What you did the night of the board meeting was one of the bravest things anyone's ever done for me. I'll never forget it."

He lowered his eyes, and his face glowed red against the white bandages.

"Now don't be embarrassed," I said. "The compliment is well-deserved. Take care of yourself, and I'll see you again soon."

Mr. and Mrs. Tayler were waiting in the hall. Mrs. Tayler turned to her husband.

"Bennett, why don't you go in to Michael? I'll walk Ms. Bianchi to the elevator."

Mr. Tayler thanked me for coming and disappeared into Michael's room.

When he was gone, Mrs. Tayler reached into her purse and removed a large envelope. "I wanted you to know that we had a neurologist examine Michael. She's fairly certain that Michael does have ADHD. She asked that his teachers fill out these questionnaires. The information will help with the diagnosis."

I took the envelope from her. "I'll bring these to school tomorrow, and I'll get them back to you as soon as possible."

"Thank you," she said. "And you might be interested to know that the neurologist believes Bennett has ADHD as well. She told us that there are medicines to help adults with ADHD, and Bennett has agreed to give them a try."

The final piece of the puzzle snapped into place. I could now picture Michael happy and whole.

"My family owes you a debt of gratitude we can never repay," she said. She gave me a quick, tight hug as the elevator door slid open. Even though I was going down, I felt like I was on top of the world.

Chapter Twenty-Three

By the morning of Christmas Eve, the weatherman was predicting more snow. It looked like we'd be having a white Christmas. Michael had been released from the hospital earlier in the week, and the Taylers arranged for him to be tutored over the holiday break to help him catch up with his work. I agreed to be his English tutor. Our sessions would start the day after Christmas. I figured it would be fun to work with Michael, and the extra money would help pay for all the Christmas gifts I'd charged.

The radio was tuned to an all-holiday music station, and I was putting the finishing touches on my little Charlie Brown tree when Chris phoned.

"I wanted to stop by on my way to the airport and give you your gift." Chris was spending the holiday with his parents. "Will you be home this afternoon?"

"I'm not going anywhere. Brutus and I are decorating. I'm trimming the tree, and he's throwing bird food all over the floor."

"Sounds lovely. I'll see you later."

I had to hurry and wrap Chris's gift so it would be under the tree when he arrived. I couldn't wait to see his reaction. It was a cookbook he'd been lusting after—a huge first edition, signed by the author, with hundreds of recipes and pictures that made you want to chew on the page. I started saving for it in September, and I even had enough left over to buy him an apron that said "Kiss the Cook." It's hokey, I know, but a little encouragement never hurt.

When the gifts were wrapped, I removed a tired-looking angel from an old cardboard box. She had belonged to my grandparents and had watched over them from the top of their Christmas tree for as long as I could remember. The years had worn away some of the paint from her ceramic face, leaving her with one eye that seemed to be winking and a funny half-smile. Her yellow hair was flat and matted. The tips of her prayerful fingers were chipped, but there were still some hot pink remnants of the manicure I'd given her when I was seven. Most of the tiny pearls that trimmed her sleeves were gone, victims of time and dried-out glue. Her feathered wings had molted, and bare spots revealed the cardboard underneath. I fingered the fabric of her once-white gown, conjuring the Ghost of Christmas Past. I could almost hear Nana laughing as Grandpop Bianchi swung me high in the air to place the angel atop the tree. This honor was reserved for me. I accepted my responsibility with the utmost gravity, making certain the angel was perfectly straight before I'd let Grandpop set me down again.

I gently centered the old girl on top of my little tree, adjusting her so that the slim upright branch didn't sag under her weight. Then I looked up at the ceiling and closed my eyes.

"Merry Christmas, Grandpop. Merry Christmas, Nana."

When I opened my eyes, the angel was looking down at me, and, for an instant, I thought she had my Nana's smile.

At just after eleven, there was a knock on the door. I opened it, expecting to see Chris. Instead I found Nancy. She was holding a huge jar of animal crackers with a red and green plaid bow on the lid.

"I'm on my way to my daughter's, but I wanted to drop this off first. Think it'll last you until we're back in school?"

"It just might. Come on in."

Nancy followed me into the living room, trying to navigate around the scattered bird food. "Aunt Nancy has something for Brutus, too." She hung a shiny brass bell from the top of his cage. He grabbed it with his beak and banged it against the bars.

"Look how you love Aunt Nancy's present," she cooed. "Now you can wake Mommy up every morning."

"You're a real sweetheart. Does a bottle of Tylenol come with that?" I reached under the tree and picked up a flat box wrapped in red and green striped paper. "I have something for you, too."

"Hope it isn't something you cooked."

"I wouldn't do that to you. You're my friend, remember?"

Nancy opened her gift—an etched crystal picture frame holding a snapshot of Brutus and me.

"I love it. What a great picture—of Brutus, that is."

"Now you'll always have something to remember us by."

Brutus clanged his bell again.

"Yes, and you'll have something to remember me by. Have a merry Christmas."

Brutus was still clanging when Chris arrived.

"You bought that bird a bell? Are you insane?"

"It's not from me. It's from Nancy."

"I thought you two were friends." He reached into his pocket, pulled out a sprig of mistletoe, and held it over my head. "Now close your eyes and hold out your hands." When I did, he kissed me and handed me a box. "Merry Christmas."

I ripped off the colorful paper and tossed the lid aside. There, nestled on a bed of white tissue, in all their day-glo orange glory, were ...

"Oven mitts. How romantic."

"They're just like mine." Chris's proud grin made me want to shake him. "Now you won't have to use your sleeves. Try them on."

This was starting to remind me of my mother's story about her first Christmas with Dad. From the look of things, Chris was going to need some serious work. I tried to appear at least mildly enthusiastic. "I'm sure they'll fit. They're huge."

"That's so you'll always be able to find them. Come on, let's see how they look on you."

I slipped my hands into the mitts, and my fingertips touched something cold and hard.

"Hey, something's in here." I turned the mitts inside out and shook them. An earring fell from each one. I picked them up and examined them. They were braided gold hoops set with sparkling diamonds.

Diamonds? This relationship is definitely heading in the right direction. "Oh, they're gorgeous!" I put them on and turned my head. "How do they look?"

He fingered my earlobes. "A lot more attractive than the oven mitts."

"Now it's your turn. Here." I reached under the tree and handed him the gift-wrapped cookbook.

"What do we have here?" Chris held the package to his ear and shook it. "It's not ticking, and it's too small to be a Porsche." He untied the ribbon, rolled it up, and placed it on the coffee table. Then he examined the wrapping, looking for the place where the paper overlapped.

The suspense was driving me crazy. "Just open it already," I said. Chris was one of those methodical unwrappers. He slid his thumb under the tape, carefully lifting it away from the paper. Then he unfolded the flap and pulled the book through the open end. The expression on his face when he saw that book was worth twice its price.

"I can't believe this." He opened the front cover and ran his finger over the signature on the title page. "A signed first edition." He leafed through the pages until I ran out of patience.

"Now open this one," I said. "And please don't make a big production of it. Just rip off the paper. Live dangerously."

"Two presents. I must have been a very good boy." He tore one end of the packet and removed the apron. Then he smoothed the wrapping paper and set it aside.

I shook my head. "Could you be any more anal?"

"Are you talking dirty again?"

He modeled the apron for me, insisting that I "Kiss the Cook." I was happy to oblige.

When it was time for him to go, he linked his hands around the back of my neck and rested his forearms on my shoulders. "Will you miss me while I'm gone?" he asked.

"You know I will." I circled his waist with my arms and nuzzled my face against his chest. "Call me as soon as you land in Tampa."

"Absolutely. And every day until I get back."

I held onto him, hating that he had to leave. "Don't forget. We have a date to ring in the New Year."

"How could I forget? I've heard that the first person you kiss in the New Year is the one you're destined to spend the rest of the year with. And I want to make sure that person is you."

The sun had just set when the snow started. I made my cocoa and sat by the window, letting my thoughts roam over the past year. So much had happened, some of it still painful to think about. But all in all, I was really lucky. My life had gotten back on track. My relationship with Chris seemed to be entering serious territory. And Project June Bug was an unqualified success. My fondest wish, that someday I would make a difference in the life of a student, had come true. I knew Michael would be okay now. Mr. and Mrs. Tayler too.

A warm sense of serenity enveloped me as I watched the snowflakes dance in the pewter sky. I was blessed with good health, a wonderful family, a job I loved, and a man who could cook circles around those Food Network celebrities. What more could a person ask? Brutus clanged his bell as if he could read my thoughts.

"I didn't forget you, buddy. Who else has such a musically talented parrot?"

I was refilling my mug when I heard another knock at the door. *Who on earth could this be?* I peeked outside. There on my doorstep, wearing matching Santa hats, were Jessica and Michael. They greeted me with a rousing chorus of "We Wish You a Merry Christmas."

I clapped my hands. "What a great surprise! Come in out of the snow."

After brushing the snow from their jackets and stomping their boots on the welcome mat, they followed me into the living room.

"I was about to have some cocoa. Want to join me?"

"That'd be terrific." Jessica rubbed her hands together. "It's freezing out there."

"Yeah." Michael craned his neck to look out the window. "You'd better bring your cat inside. She was sitting on the step when we came up. I guess our singing scared her away."

"She's my neighbor's cat," I said. "And she doesn't scare that easily."

As I poured the cocoa, Jessica helped Michael out of his jacket, taking care to avoid his cast. Then Michael pulled off his Santa hat and ran his hand over the coppery stubble that covered his head.

"How do you like the new look, Ms. Bianchi?"

"I like it a lot better than the bandages. Are you supposed to be out and about so soon?"

"The doctor said I could take short trips to help build my stamina. I was visiting Jessie, and we decided to come by and see you."

"I'm glad you did. I can't think of two people I'd rather share my cocoa with."

Jessica unzipped her jacket. "Look at my Christmas present from Michael." She reached under her collar and pulled out a heart-shaped locket. It was made of rose gold, with a delicate scrollwork "J" engraved in its center. It hung from a chain of tiny rose gold links.

"Oh, Jessica, it's lovely. Michael has very good taste."

"And this is what Jess gave me." Michael extended his good arm, and Jessica pushed back his cuff to reveal a new sports watch. "It has a bunch of alarms and settings to help me keep track of the time. Perfect for somebody with ADHD."

I was glad Michael seemed comfortable talking about this. "Since you brought up the ADHD, would you mind me asking when you'll be starting the medication?"

"Doctor Graziano wants me to wait until I'm back in school. She doesn't think I'll need it while I'm home."

"Are you all set for your tutoring sessions? I'll be there bright and early the day after tomorrow."

"To tell the truth, I'm kinda looking forward to hitting the books again. It was fun being out of school for a while, but then it got pretty boring."

"Michael," Jessica whispered, "tell her about the article."

"Oh, yeah. I'm working on an article for the *Courier* about what it's like to have ADHD. I got the idea from that journal. I started writing down my feelings, like you said, and before I knew it, I filled eight pages. I thought maybe it could help other kids."

"That's a great idea." I said. "I'll bet there are lots of students who'd benefit from reading about your experience. I'm proud of you."

Jessica hugged him. "Me, too."

After we finished the cocoa, Michael and Jessica got up to leave. Jessica helped Michael into his jacket, and he reached in the side pocket.

"Ms. Bianchi, I have something for you, to thank you for everything you did for me. Not just the school stuff, but the family stuff too. I used to feel like a total loser. I hated my life. I made my dad mad, and I upset my mother. Now I'm doing better in school. I have Jessie. My dad and I are getting along, and my mom smiles a lot more. None of this would've happened if it wasn't for you."

He looked at Jessica, and she gave him a tiny nod. Then he handed me a small box wrapped in silver foil, topped with a gold bow and a sprig of fresh holly.

"Oh, Michael, this wasn't necessary. I'm just happy that everything worked out so well."

Jessica's eyes sparkled. "Open it, Ms. B. We asked Mrs. Miller what you'd like, and she gave us the idea."

"My dad had his jeweler make this especially for you." Michael's gaze was fixed on me as I opened the box.

There, hanging from a shimmering chain, was an exquisite gold June bug with two tiny emerald eyes.

"Mrs. Miller told me this would mean a lot to you," Michael said. "That it would always remind you of me."

I looked into his face and saw the promise of a bright future, a future I had touched.

"Michael," I said, holding the glittering June bug to the light so its green eyes twinkled, "of all the gifts I've ever received, this is the most wonderful gift of all."

Epilogue

Reprinted from the <u>Morrison High Courier</u>

ADHD AND ME
By Michael Tayler

Have you ever tried to watch TV when somebody else has the remote and keeps flicking the channels? You get bits and pieces of a lot of different shows, but you never get the complete story of any of them. This is what life is like for me and millions of other people like me. We have a condition known as ADHD: Attention Deficit Hyperactivity Disorder.

For as long as I can remember, I've always felt different. I can picture myself in kindergarten, wiggling and squirming while the other kids sat quietly and listened to the teacher. In elementary school, I was the kid who was always getting into trouble. It was like I had a motor inside me that was revved up too high. I really wanted to pay attention, but when my teachers were talking I'd get bored after a few minutes. Their words would get all jumbled up, and my mind would wander. No matter how hard I tried, I couldn't stay focused. When I asked questions, the other kids laughed at me because I was usually asking about something the teacher had just explained. After a while, I stopped asking questions because I felt so stupid.

It was hard for me to make friends. I had a reputation as a troublemaker. I had to be the first one in line, the first one out the door, the first one the teacher called on. I was always saying and doing things without thinking. Since I got bored so easily, I couldn't stick with any activity long enough to see it through. I'd lose my temper over the smallest things, usually because I'd misunderstood somebody's words or actions. When I got angry or frustrated, I'd lash out at anybody. The other kids didn't want me around. I figured it was because there was something wrong with me.

Doing assignments was always a major problem. I'd start off fine, but before I could finish one thing, I'd get sidetracked by something else. Then I'd focus on that until another idea jumped into my head. I felt like I was being pulled in a hundred different directions. If I managed to finish an assignment, it would be full of mistakes because I never took the time to check it over. Or I'd put off doing an assignment until the last minute, and then do a rush job that was never as good as it should have been. Often, I'd forget to do the assignment at all. My grades were in the cellar. My teachers thought I didn't care. My parents kept telling me I had to try harder. Only I knew how hard I was trying. I started to believe I was a total loser, so I finally stopped trying altogether.

Things got worse as I got older. My teachers said I wasn't motivated. My parents were always arguing about me. My dad said I was being lazy and stubborn. My mom said I just needed to apply myself. My parents tried everything to get me to succeed. They bribed me. They grounded me. They moved me from one school to another. Nothing worked. The thing they didn't understand was that I couldn't control the way I acted. I got so sick of hearing them, I'd go into my room and lock the door. I thought a lot about running away. I really started to hate myself.

This year, something happened that changed my life. I was diagnosed with Attention Deficit Hyperactivity Disorder. When I got the news, everything fell into place. Finally, I saw that there was a reason for the way I was. That reason had a name, and it wasn't "Michael Tayler." It was "ADHD." Best of all, there was something that could be done about it. There are medications that help with the symptoms. There are also lots of things I can do to help myself. I was lucky to find a teacher who understands my condition and works with me. I've learned ways to be more organized. I take lots of notes in class and write <u>everything</u> down. I use a calendar and a notebook to keep track of my assignments. I'm learning how to manage my time. When I have to learn new material, I break it down into chunks so that I can study more effectively. I try to work in places where I won't be distracted. I remind myself to think before I speak and to consider the impact my actions may have on others. It's not always easy, but it's a lot better than feeling like a victim with no control over my life.

I've come a long way, but I still have a long way to go. I'm still impulsive and I'm easily distracted. It's a real effort to stay organized, and waiting in lines still drives me crazy. But I understand now that these things are just part of my condition, not flaws in my character. I know that ADHD won't go away, but now I know it's something I can live with. I often wonder how different my life would have been if I'd been diagnosed when I was younger. But I realize it doesn't help to dwell on the past. Instead, I try to look to the future. Everyone faces different challenges in life. ADHD is mine. Now I see it as a challenge I can rise above. And I know that by doing this, I can finally become the person I've always wanted to be.

Project June Bug Strategies

#1. Don't take Michael's impulsive behavior personally. People with ADHD often say or do things without thinking about the consequences.

#2. Involve Michael in activities that will boost his self-esteem. Dealing with the problems associated with ADHD can cause feelings of guilt, hopelessness, failure, and depression.

#3. Don't embarrass Michael by singling him out. People with ADHD tend to be sensitive about their behavior. Calling attention to them can increase their feelings of frustration, and stress can make the behavior worse.

#4. Use a discreet signal to help Michael refocus his attention. Since people with ADHD are often unaware that their attention is wandering, a gesture such as a tap on the shoulder can serve as a reminder to stay on task.

#5. Help Michael learn to express his feelings more appropriately. People with ADHD are often unaware of how their behavior might affect others. They also have difficulty "reading" people. Activities like conflict resolution or role-playing can help. So can teaching them to use "I" statements (ex. "I get really upset when you stare at me" instead of "Who do you think you're staring at?")

#6. Give Michael preferential seating in a place where distractions are minimized. Sitting at the front of the class or away from windows and doors can make it easier to pay attention.

#7. Give Michael some help getting organized. Suggest that he:

—Write down all assignments, and cross them off when they've been completed;
—Clip finished homework papers together so that they can be located with ease;
—Use a calendar to note important dates (due dates, test dates, etc.);
—Use differently colored folders to separate work into subjects.

#8. Show Michael how to break down large tasks into smaller components. People with ADHD often have trouble managing time and can become overwhelmed if a task is too complex. It's often easier to focus on a single part of the task for a limited period of time, and then take a break before going on to the next. It's also best to tackle more difficult jobs first, and save the easiest ones for last.

978-0-595-45528-7
0-595-45528-X